VAMPS OF '29

VAMPS OF '29

A Novel

Alice Jurow

DEDICATION

For all my dear fellow time-travelers (you know who
you are!)
And especially, always, indelibly, for C.

Now, these old vampire women have really got
this day . . .

    –   *Vamps of '28* by Clifford Hayes

This is a work of fiction. Any historical figures who are named or suggested are treated as fictional characters whose actions are completely invented.

New Year's Eve, 1927

Harry's Bar, Paris

The most beautiful girl in the room was sitting at the sleek, chromium *bar américain*, her endless exquisite legs displayed to perfection on a tall stool. As he watched, she folded back her brief black satin skirt to well above the knee—he gasped—and drew a small silver flask from her garter. She doctored the dark red drink in the cocktail glass before her, replaced the flask and took a long sip. She had been beautiful before, with her angelic, angular features and perfect build, but now she seemed to glow and radiate an unearthly gorgeousness.

Suddenly aware of his gaze—she must have felt the heat of his adoration—she turned his way, with a smile and a most un-angelic wink. He stood up quickly and took the seat next to her.

"I'd like to have what you're having—it makes you utterly radiant."

Sally took another sip and regarded him with amusement, dark eyes wide, fine eyebrows almost disappearing into her fashionable crisp bob.

"It's Fernet and absinthe, mostly. Shall I order you one? It's rather bitter; not many like it."

With an involuntary grimace (girls and their cocktails!) he shook his head. "I'll stick to whisky. But what's your special additive?" He glanced meaningfully down at her skirt. "Seems to me, *that's* what puts the sparkle in your eyes."

"Oh," she smiled, "just my health tonic. An ancient recipe of my grandmother's."

"May I try it?"

"I don't think you'd like it." Somehow she had gestured fluidly and a whisky had appeared. "Let's drink up and take a walk."

"I'd like that." He tried to look deep into her eyes, but felt himself slipping; he couldn't catch hold, couldn't touch bottom. Perversely, he reached for her drink and drained it.

As they stood up, he saw her look over his shoulder and nod to someone. He was momentarily on edge—did she have some lowlife confederate who would follow them? With an effort, he turned his head; no, she was just letting her girlfriends know she was going.

"Are you a tart or just a modern girl?" The blunt question slipped out; he hadn't meant to say it aloud. What the hell was in that drink?

She laughed, not offended. "I'm a mannequin. A *model girl*," she added in English.

"You certainly are. The very model of a modern girl." She was almost as tall as he was. He slipped his arm around her shoulders and they went out.

He could still taste her strange cocktail—bitter, but not only that. Complex, haunting . . . so many notes of flavor and fragrance . . . or was that her scent? She was so close to him, her glossy hair brushing his chin, her lean elegant body leaning into his, the thrilling heft of round dense breasts beneath her sliding satin dress . . .

And that was all he remembered. His head throbbed, he felt bruised in a dozen obscure places—and what was he doing under a bridge, with the *clochards*, rubbing his eyes against the brilliant morning light? Still in evening clothes, he wrapped his white silk scarf around the small wound on his neck and went home.

10ᵗʰ arrondissement

The most beautiful girl in the room had blazing eyes and vivid russet curls escaping her chignon. She was tall and carried herself like the ballerina she had once been. No one in this room, she reflected—passionate balletomanes all, no doubt—could have seen her on the Mariinsky stage. Though she looked not a day over twenty-four, Natalie's memories were hundreds of years deep, and the last time she'd danced had been over a century ago.

Turning her back on the lavish spread of vodka and *zakuskie*, she accepted a glass of champagne from a passing waiter and drifted across the ornate, over-heated room. Clustered on settees, standing in tight groups near the samovar, hovering over the refreshments, Russian emigrés were everywhere, chattering away in the mother tongue as if they might never have another chance. Natalie sighed, wondering why she had come.

"Talia, darling, there you are! Come and say hello to some old friends."

These particular old friends of her hostess (a Moscow society matron whom Natalie genuinely liked) were a countess, a princess and a naval commander. Natalie made polite conversation, keeping her private assessments well-concealed: she had seen the commander working as a hotel doorman, and as for the so-called princess, she'd known both her mother and grandmother and would not have described them as regal in any way.

An hour later, Natalie had had enough—the laments for "our vanished way of life," the complaints about Paris ("Yes, of course it is beautiful, but so crowded, so rude, so expensive!"), the wearying introductions to impossible numbers of self-proclaimed aristocrats.

Heading toward the exit, she almost collided with a tall, well-dressed man, and they each took a step back.

"Aleksei Petrovich!" Natalie exclaimed with pleasure. "If only you'd come earlier; I'm afraid I am terminally bored."

"Natalia Ivanovna! You must not leave yet. Step into the library and we'll catch up." He opened a door to a mercifully empty room.

"Darling, how I've missed you," he murmured into her hair. "No one in Paris has a perfect Russian body like yours."

"And no one in Paris has rich, healthy Russian blood like yours." She raised her mouth from his throat. "Don't worry, I won't take more than you can spare. It's so good to see you, darling."

Natalie left smiling, licking her teeth. There was a reason to have come, after all.

Le Boeuf Sur le Toît

The most beautiful girl in the room, petite and precisely sculpted, was talking in halting Japanese to the artist Tsuguharu Leonard Foujita. He had been curious about her origins; she was explaining that she was born in Indochine and had picked up a very few Japanese phrases in her travels. Gracefully sidestepping an invitation to pose for him, she turned to Picasso and switched briefly to Spanish before they all resumed speaking in French.

"You don't want me to pose for you, Léo," she said again. "That would just keep both of us locked in the stereotypes of orientalism. Better to let Pablo give me three eyes."

Picasso laughed, but studied her seriously for a moment. "Ah non, Lucienne ma petite. Your eyes are in just the right places. But the planes of your face— you *are* cubism."

"Thank you, chéri. And now excuse me; I must go and say hello to Sonia and Robert."

Taking leave, Lucienne gave each of the artists a friendly hug, nuzzling their necks like an enchanting, sleek cat. Her silky bobbed hair fell forward, and no one could possibly notice the dainty fangs that emerged as she took a few sips from the bull-like neck of one and the slender throat of the other.

February, 1928

Rue Cambon
Only a dozen clients filled the gray velvet chairs, but they were among the most valued and influential. Mlle nodded, and her indispensable assistant, La Mèduse, began:
"Introducing . . . Our Spring collection for 1928, worn by three of our loveliest *mannequins de la maison.* On your left, direct from Indochine, in tangerine crêpe de chine, the delicate oriental beauty, Lucienne! On your right, in cream-colored kasha, with embroidery à la russe, the Russian redhead, *la rousse de russie,* Natalie! And in the center, English tweeds, an English-rose complexion and an English name, but she's *parisienne* through and through: Sally!"

While three other mannequins worked the outer

room, the three friends changed: Sally slid into black satin with a diamanté bow at the neckline; Lucienne wore black crepe with a scalloped frill of lace, Natalie a black velvet *taillure* with a creamy charmeuse blouse.

Natalie was having trouble with the tiny hooks at her waistband. "Ugh, I must have put on a quarter-kilo; I feel like *une vache*."

"Well, it's no wonder, the way you were gorging yourself last night," Sally remarked with a twinkling tartness that was reproving yet somehow not unkind.

"I couldn't help it—that Belgian was so delicious; he tasted like chocolate. I've always adored chocolate," Natalie said dreamily.

Sally and Lucienne caught each others' eyes and exploded into gurgles of laughter. "*Chocolat!*" Sally winked. "You should have been backstage with us— we were sampling the whole box of chocolates!"

"It was . . . dandy!" Lucienne purred.

Natalie widened her eyes at them. "No! You mustn't fool around with the Chocolate Dandies!"

"And why not?"

"If you drain the jazzband, we'll have no one to dance to!"

"Nat, darling," Sally came over to her and bent to fasten the skirt hooks. "You just have to learn the discipline—tiny sips. Just a taste here and a taste there—they never even notice it. And I think they played better than ever, afterward. Didn't you love their third set?"

Natalie gasped, either from the realization, or the tiny bite of her skirt hook.

Lucienne, checking her *maquillage*, murmured, "She's right, you know, Talia. You've got to be a modern girl now—no need to settle in deep with your Belgian count, even if he can afford it. You know the gossip's sure to start, sooner or later. Better to keep it light, just sample the goods—no need for a serious purchase. Come on, we're up again!" She slid her jade amulet carefully under her neckline and flounced through the door.

Les Ambassadeurs

The music of the Chocolate Dandies was irresistible; Lucienne and Sally had found their way backstage after the show almost every night during the run of Blackbirds. Sally—always the most jazz-mad of the three of them—was ecstatic to learn that the band was being offered a year's residency at Les Ambassadeurs, one of the larger and more fashionable clubs.

"We are so lucky!" she said, sotto voce, to Natalie. "To think that—born when we were—we can be here now for the age of jazz! What could be more exciting?”

Natalie raised her eyebrows. “Oh, I don’t know—a Tschaikowsky premiere, perhaps? You know I danced in Swan Lake at the Mariinsky. This is fun, but we’ll see how it holds up. However . . .” she added with a smile, “there’s no denying their talent. Look at that embouchure!” She rolled her eyes toward the saxophonist, lip-locked with Lucienne.

“I hope I’m not making a nuisance of myself,” Sally told the pianist, Claude. Unlike the others, he still lingered at his instrument, an aperitif resting on the lamp-stand.

“Oh, *pas du tout*, Mlle Sally.” Claude’s French was notably better than his band-mates’. His accent, though, not exactly American, was unique and non-Parisian. “You’re special, you and your friends—not like the girls we meet who just want sweets from the chocolate box,” he winked. “You really care about what we do, our art. You’re a kind of muse, I’d say. All the boys know that—well, maybe not Li’l Red, the drummer. He just thinks you’re fine fillies.”

Sally laughed, borrowing a sip of Claude’s drink. “Tell me, why is your French so good? I keep wanting to practice English with you, but you’ve got me beat.”

“Well, I’m from N’Awlins, little girl—Nouvelle

Orléans. French was in my mamma's milk. Hey, gimme that!" He slapped her hand playfully away from his drink.

"Ah, I knew there was something especially *sympathetique* about you." Sally slid her flask out of her garter and clinked it against Claude's glass.

He eyed her keenly. "Well, it's not just that I speak your language. I know about your kind, too. There's quite a few of your type where I'm from."

"Really? Fabulously chic, tall, jazz-mad mannequins?"

Claude smiled and closed his eyes. "Oh, you know what I mean." He slid down, leaning against the wall, and pulled his collar away from his neck. "C'mon now, gimme a little of your special mojo."

April, 1928

Rue Cambon

There were usually a handful of men at the showings, often tagging along like wayward pets with their fashion-obsessed wives or mistresses. These two, however, were on their own together, sitting near the back. The slightly older, stockier one lazily twirled his ivory-topped walking stick; the taller younger one—with beautiful eyes and patent leather hair, Sally noted—was smoking a mauve, gold-tipped Russian cigarette. Natalie joined her in peering through the louvered door from the back room where the models were getting ready.

"Pretty men! But, pft, a mauve cigarette—not susceptible to our charms."

"I wouldn't be so sure," Sally said, studying them

intently. "I'll bet Monsieur Mauve (look, his tie too!) will be most happy to take me out for a drink after the show."

"Who do you suppose they are?" Natalie wondered. "Not husbands. They don't look like press; they're far too elegant."

"Definitely. And they couldn't be competitors—La Mèduse (their nickname for Mlle's implacable assistant) knows everyone and she'd never let them in. My guess is they need a diversion from the burden of their leisured wealth—they'll tell themselves they are scouting out gifts for a mistress, but they're really whiling away an idle afternoon, with an eyeful of us."

The show was well underway: Mlle's Summer line of gauzy afternoon frocks, daringly bare evening dresses and even her marvelously shocking beach wear.

"Enjoying yourself?" Gaston asked Edouard with a grin.

"More than I can say." Edouard's eyes were locked on Sally, who was modeling black and celadon striped beach pyjamas cut to her coccyx. "That girl," he gestured with his cigarette holder, "You can see every one of her vertebrae. Do you suppose she eats at all? And yet there's something enchanting about her."

She swept by them just then, and though her face was deeply shadowed by a huge sunhat, she was able to shoot an unmistakeable wink in their direction.

"I would have to agree," Gaston murmured. "Usually I like a bit more to hold onto in a woman, but these girls—they're like a new kind of woman, some incredible pleasure automaton of the future. Maybe not all of them . . ." Nanou was walking by in a beige linen that did little for her washed-out coloring, an artificial simper pasted on her plain face, "but those three are so radiant: your pyjama girl, and the redhead, and the petite chinoise."

"Champagne at the Ritz?" Edouard proposed.

Gaston winked. "If they'll have us."

"Champagne at the Ritz—what did I tell you?" Sally grinned at Natalie. "Loulou, aren't you ready yet? You're already perfect, darling."

Unperturbed, Lucienne remained in communion with the mirror, adding microscopic strokes of mascara to her lush lashes. "Trust me, they don't mind waiting for us."

The Ritz Bar

The gentlemen's eyes, wide with appreciation, confirmed this observation as the models made their entrance. The five of them were soon settled around a prime table, and agreeably frivolous chatter commenced once the bubbly was poured.

"Let's see . . ." Edouard addressed Sally with a

mock-earnest regard. "You must be from Indochine, n'est-çe pas?"

"Mais non, monsieur!" Lucienne interjected. "Surely you can see that *I* am the exotic, doll-like oriental beauty. You are confused because Sally has stolen my hairstyle."

"It's true, I have, but only because Loulou is chic personified. And by the way, if *you* call her exotic or doll-like, she'll break your fingers."

"But in the nicest possible way, I don't doubt," Gaston smiled. "And Mlle Natalie—you are here in Paris because of the unfortunate troubles in your country?"

"No, as it happens, I . . . that is, my family . . ." (Natalie rapidly calculated her apparent age in relation to the 1917 revolution.) "My parents were cosmopolitans and had decided to make their home in Paris quite some time before the recent upheavals. Of course, there is always turbulence somewhere in my homeland . . ."

"But I am hurt, monsieurs—you are overlooking me," Sally cut in quickly to head off a disquisition on Russian history. She batted her eyes prettily at Edouard. "Just because I lack the distinction of being foreign-born like my friends . . ."

"I assure you, lovely ladies," Gaston said gallantly, "your diverse origins are merely the decorative icing sugar on the petits fours of your extraordinary beauty. And the charm of your personalities—the cake within, if you will—whose delicious aroma is evident even in the prosaic setting of a dressmaker's salon."

"I see." Sally looked from Gaston to Edouard. "We are delicious patisserie. Well, I must insist that you do not devour us in a single bite. It should take two, at the very least."

"Oh, I should think it could be an even longer process," Edouard said. "Perhaps the exquisite cakes are spiced and will bite us back."

Natalie had taken out her silver and amber cigarette holder and case of Sobranies. Accepting a light from Gaston, she inhaled thoughtfully. "It's true, we might bite. We are vampires, after all."

Gaston inclined his head courteously. "I appreciate your warning, mademoiselle. Be assured, my nephew and I offer ourselves up willingly to your fangs."

Edouard laughed a bit nervously. "Heavens, the conversation has taken a bloody turn—only a moment ago, it was all pastries and cream."

"You've nothing to worry about, my dear sir. We are the very nicest of vamps," Sally said lightly.

"Bien sur." Lucienne had taken out her own scented cigarettes and a jade and ivory holder. "The modern vamp's technique is all delicacy and consideration. We would never drain a man dry, but only take a little here and a little there, never more than he can easily afford to give. Thank you, monsieur," she added, as Edouard produced his monogrammed gold lighter.

Sally took out her smoking requisites as well, but found her case empty. Placing an elbow on the table, she displayed her empty cigarette holder (a particularly elegant one of guilloche enamel) in a fetching manner, hoping to be offered one of the mauve cigarettes that had first caught her eye. But both gentlemen were now too wrapped up in flirtatious banter to notice her gesture. She turned away with a small sigh.

Oh well, she mused; there's no point being angry with one's food.

Rue Cambon

La Mèduse: She was called this, behind her back, by all the mannequins for three reasons—first, her long and uneuphonious real name, Mlle Medoc-Dubosse; second, her antiquated coiffure of numerous braids piled on her crown; third, her icy glare, which they all lived in fear of. She had been with Mlle for no one knew how long—certainly since the first opening of the atelier, but it was rumored that they went back much further. La Mèduse might have been her teacher or even her nanny, if Mlle had not come from such famously simple origins. In any case, Mèduse was fanatically devoted to Mlle, and no matter how early one arrived or how late one stayed at Rue Cambon, she was always there.

Day after day, season by season, she seemed to wear the same plain black dress—but if one looked closely (and Lucienne always did), it turned out not to be the same. Her black frock varied from crepe to satin to challis to voile, always cut to the same pattern, with clever seams that accentuated her surprisingly perfect figure. A short necklace of very good pearls was her only accessory; her lip rouge was a deep red; and her curious, intricate pile of plaits was the color of tarnished silver. She had never been seen to smile.

"Mlle Leung," she nodded curtly to Lucienne—she seemed to be the only person in Paris who could pronounce her name properly. "A word, please."

Mildly alarmed but intrigued, Lucienne followed the older woman to her tiny office. She remained standing perfectly still, as a mannequin should, while La Mèduse sat down behind a small ebony desk.

"Mlle asked me to speak to you," Mèduse began directly. "Your work is quite satisfactory."

Though she didn't move a muscle, Lucienne felt herself inwardly sag with relief.

"Your poise," La Mèduse went on, "your movements, your exotic elegance—in short, you show the clothes to good advantage, and your work habits have been irreproachable, so far. Just . . ." She narrowed her eyes, as did Lucienne, looking levelly back at her—the word 'exotic' always annoyed her

—"Just be careful. Too many late nights, too much hollow darkness about the eyes . . . a model's career can be ruined. Tell your friend Natalie too."

Lucienne, startled, widened her eyes. "Natalie? What about Sally?" she blurted, to her immediate regret.

La Mèduse lifted one eyebrow ever so slightly. "Ah, Mlle Lafayette can take care of herself; we see no cause for concern. *Alors*, you may go."

Le Grand Duc

Le Grand Duc was open all night and was a favorite of jazz musicians after hours, and other night owls. Sally suggested they stop in, and soon found Claude nursing a cognac in a quiet corner. "So, Claude, would I like this Nouvelle Orléans—and the folks who are 'my type' there?"

"Well, it's a beautiful city—not like Paris, but still, pretty. There's no place like it for music, and if you're from there, of course, it always feels like home. But there's reasons so many of us are *from* there, not there now. And as far as *your* people . . . no, I can't see you there. You couldn't have this kind of life, going out everywhere like you do, mixing. Folks there are more apt to stick to their own kind, as a rule. And, well, if I can be blunt—*les vampyres* there lead a much more . . .shadowy existence. Let me ask you, Sally— how come you can go out in the daytime, to work and such?"

Sally laughed lightly. "It's hard, when we keep jazz musicians' hours—but luckily, we don't have to be at the atelier too early. But I know what you're really asking. It's true that some vamps are completely nocturnal, but we're all a little different. It's possible to make adjustments, as long as we're careful to avoid prolonged exposure to direct sunlight."

"Okay, that makes sense. What about . . ." he thought for a moment, "crossing running water?"

"It would be difficult to live in Paris if that were really a problem; one is constantly crossing the Seine!"

"Having to be invited into someone's home?"

"Well of course! It's only good manners."

"Are you repulsed by garlic?"

"In France? Don't be silly."

"How about that thing with mirrors. Aren't you supposed to not have a reflection?"

"I've heard that—and I've never understood it. Aren't we vamps notorious for our elegance and perfect grooming? How the hell could we fix our hair and do our makeup if we couldn't use mirrors? Look, there's Natalie with her compact out right now."

Claude grinned. "I always thought there was something wrong with that story. Okay, just one more—do you sleep in a coffin?"

Sally drew closer, slipped an arm around Claude's slim shoulders and nibbled his ear gently. "I don't think we know each other well enough for you to be asking about where I sleep. But maybe someday . . ." She leaned in and gave him a long, warm kiss on the lips.

Claude pulled away after a moment and touched her cheek. "Miss Sally," he said softly. "You know I think you are the most gorgeous creature, and I'm as much in love with you as any of the boys here. And maybe I am stupidly misinterpreting what you did just now, but I think you should know that I, uh . . ."

"Oh! You're . . ."

"I like men." Claude held her eyes, making sure she understood.

Sally looked back earnestly, and then smiled. "Well, so do I! I always knew we were kindred spirits. And, we're both used to living with a certain degree of . . . discretion."

"True enough." He took a meditative swallow of cognac. Across the room, several of his band-mates were exclaiming over a late-night pot of gumbo the kitchen had produced. He sniffed the air appreciatively. "Hey, Sally, that's another thing—food. I know vamps don't eat as a rule . . . and you fashion gals hardly would anyway, but I've seen you with a plate now and then. How's that work?"

"You're right, we don't eat much—and luckily, no

one expects us to. Mortal food doesn't nourish us; we have to leave room for blood. But we do enjoy the flavors and textures, and of course, it's often a social necessity to eat a bit. Cocktails, on the other hand . . . I find a well-made cocktail to be the perfect compliment to my *favorite* beverage." Sally tossed off the rest of her Negroni and then leaned over for a last taste at Claude's throat.

He leaned back, gazing at her dreamy-eyed. "So . . . could you really be killed by a stake through the heart?"

She blinked. "Well, yes. Couldn't you?"

At home

"Sally!" Lucienne tried to get her friend's attention, which was always difficult when there was a new jazz record on the Victrola. Sally twirled, eyes closed, in a world of her own. "Sally!!" Lucienne raised her voice, which was unusual enough that Sally opened her eyes to look at her.

"*Quoi?*" she quacked. "I'm Doin' the New Lowdown, darling. Can't it wait?"

With a sigh, Lucienne threw herself into an armchair to await the end of the song. Sally flopped down beside her when it came.

"Sally, I think La Mèduse is onto us." She described the morning's interview.

Sally tapped her oval-nailed forefinger against her front teeth. "Onto us . . . because she's one of us, maybe." She grinned at Lucienne.

Lucienne stared back. "*Vraiment?* But why does she look so old then?"

"Maybe it suits her. Maybe she turned late. Anyway, aside from her gray hair and a few wrinkles, she doesn't actually look that old. Her *embonpoint* is pretty perky, really."

"I've noticed. But . . . it's so hard to imagine. She never seems to leave the atelier at all."

Sally giggled. "It's like what people say about how they can't imagine their parents having sex."

"Or their grandparents. She really is an antique."

"Now now, *ma vielle*. She might very well be younger than us."

"Speak for yourself, Miss Eighteenth Century," Lucienne teased. "Me, I'm a Belle Epoque babe, a mere fifty-something. Mèduse has to be a century, at least."

"Well then, some respect, young upstart! Pray that you're still tits-up when you hit the hundred mark."

Lucienne frowned at Sally's perpetual British slang. "I thought tits-up meant dead. You know . . ." She threw herself onto the couch, stretched out on her back with hands folded together in prayer.

Natalie flung the door open and took in the scene. "Ooh, what are we playing?"

Lucienne swung her feet to the floor. "Oh, just trying to understand Sally's English. We were talking about the Mèduse—is she one of us?"

"One of *us*?" Natalie was rapidly shedding clothes as she spoke—cloche, shoes, scarf, coat, frock. "Let's see: pretty/plain; cheery/dour; mad for thrilling night-life . . . hey, you two, aren't we going dancing at L'Olympia ?"

"Of course, but no need to get there the minute the doors open." Sally smoothed her hair, peering into a mirror. I haven't the faintest idea what to wear."

"What to wear . . . that *is* a problem. I know—what about black satin!" Natalie exclaimed, winking at Lucienne. Obviously, Sally seldom wore anything else.

"Ha ha, very funny," Sally retorted. "At least I don't look like a complete tart." Natalie had shed her step-ins and, wearing nothing but her stockings and garters, slithered into a silk sheath cut ridiculously low both front and back.

Natalie fluffed her curls. "What? I have to do *something* to attract the boys, now that I'm skinny as a stick from your slimming regimen."

L'Olympia

The Chocolate Dandies were tearing up the stage—several of them, anyway, along with a few French sidemen and an extraordinary blonde girl at the piano. Sally got to know her immediately, going up to the piano to lavish praise on her between sets. The pianist called herself Lili, "in hommage to the divine Miss Hardin," Louis Armstrong's wife, whom she'd heard on records. Like Lil Hardin Armstrong, she was a tiny thing, but with immense rhythmic power. She thanked Sally graciously for her compliments and then sat back, regarding her with an amused look.

"I've noticed you and your *amies* on the dancefloor. *Vous etes charmantes.* I will dedicate the first song of the next set to you." Sally thanked her, and they exchanged kisses on each cheek. Lili went off and conferred with her bandmates.

They had each found someone to dance with: Sally had a game old geezer, good-humored, stout and impeccable in his 50-year-old tails, eager to learn all the latest moves. Lucienne had captivated an icily handsome northerner, Swedish perhaps, with a monocle glinting under his blond brows. And Natalie . . . Sally, looking over at her, sighed; how *did* she always find them? Natalie was deep in conversation behind a champagne bucket, with a young, soulful, dark-eyed Slav, who had taken her hands and could barely keep from constantly kissing her wrists.

Sally nudged Lucienne, flicking her eyes at their

friend and her enamored companion. "He looks as if *he's* about to devour *her.*"

Lucienne glanced and shrugged. "Maybe he is. Not our place to worry though. She's older than us, after all. I'm sure she knows what she's doing."

"It's because she's older that I *do* worry—she's from a different world in some ways. Oh well." Sally turned brightly as her old gent approached from the bar. "Is that for me?" She took the cocktail glass from his hand and toasted him. "Ooh, the band's starting again. Come on, I'll show you the shimmy."

"I'm counting on it. Can we do it this slow, though?" The piano was leading off with a haunting, leisurely, bluesy phrase.

"Mm, I know what to do." Sally wrapped her arms around her partner's neck and pulled him close.

The clarinet player put down his reed and began to sing, "These old vampire women have really got this day . . ."

May, 1928

Harry's Bar

"A Blood and Sand, please," someone said to the barman. Sally turned and looked down the bar, startled not just by the unusual and intriguing order, but the voice giving it—young, female and American.

She was even more startled to see a young woman who was practically her mirror image—slender and charming, with dead-black, dead-straight hair cut in a strictly clipped bob. Aware of her scrutiny, the girl turned and looked back at Sally, a direct intelligent gaze below perfectly straight eyebrows.

Sally slid off her chromium-legged stool and moved down to where the stranger sat. "Hello, I'm Sally," she said in English, putting out her hand.

"Louise." The American shook her hand, still holding

her eyes with a level look.

"You're American! And you like Valentino?"

A slight shrug. "Poor dear, he was a sweetheart, really. I didn't care for the film all that much, but it's a tasty drink." Right on cue, the barman placed a chilled cocktail glass before her and filled it with the fragrant, reddish-brown contents of a shaker.

Sally raised her own Gin & It (rosy with Italian vermouth) in salute. "I *do* like red drinks, don't you?" she ventured, "Though they don't always make them strong enough here." With a wink, she retrieved her silver flask from her garter and added a few deep red drops to her glass.

Louise watched her, eyes wide. "How interesting," she said softly.

"Isn't it?" Sally winked.

"You're not English, are you?"

"I'm hurt that you would say that—my English is flawless, *non*? *Alors*, I am a tremendous Anglophile, but you are right, I am pure Parisian French, for generations."

"I thought so. You're one of those European vamps."

Sally sipped her drink carefully. "Yes, you could say that. And you . . .?"

"That's what everyone thinks I am. A vamp, a man-eater. I've had to come here, to make films in Europe —no one understands me back home. They say I'm immoral . . ."

"Immortality, yes, it has its problems . . ." Sally interrupted eagerly.

Louise shrugged. "Maybe I *am* immoral; I don't know. I'm a dancer, really."

Fragments of the American girl's conversation were starting to piece themselves together in Sally's mind. "You're in films! And you actually *know* Valentino? You must be from Hollywood!"

"New York, actually—that's my real home, and originally, the American Midwest—but yes, I suppose I am from Hollywood currently."

"And you're a vamp?"

Louise's silky hair fell into her face as she shook her head. "Type-casting. I suppose it's because I don't really care if my clothes stay on or not." Her satin frock, which was improbably low-cut in front, in back and at the sides, seemed to be slipping from her shoulders even as she spoke. She shrugged it back into place. "So, Sally—what do you do for fun around here?"

Sally's eyes brightened. "Come and meet my friends. I'm sure we can come up with something."

At home

"You *what?*!" Lucienne hissed, through the narrow opening of their apartment door.

"Brought someone to visit. A friend. She's one of us —from America."

"But, *here? Bozhe moi*, the place is a mess," Natalie complained.

"Don't worry. She won't mind," Sally whispered. "Come on, you're embarrassing me."

With a final bit of rustling from within, the door opened and Louise, who had been politely inspecting the corridor wallpaper, came in.

Introductions, smiles all round, and Louise sank comfortably onto the divan. "Ah yes, lovely squalor!" She grinned, taking in the clothes strewn everywhere, open books, black tulips drooping in a vase. "It's how we always live, isn't it?"

Lucienne frowned. "I wouldn't say always . . . If we'd known we were having company . . ."

"Actresses, dancers—Sally said you're models? Working girls, girls who live by our wits . . ." Louise stretched, clearly feeling quite at home.

"So, Louise," Sally went to a corner cupboard. "Can we offer you something to drink?"

"Oh Sally, no," Natalie interposed urgently. "She doesn't want any of that plonk. It's unfit for human consumption." She was frantically trying to catch Sally's oblivious eye. "And there's hardly any left, anyway."

"Yes, but, just a *touch* of the real thing . . ." Sally protested. "Do you know what Louise was drinking in Harry's Bar? A Blood and Sand—that's why I had to meet her. *Tres chic!*"

"Delightful," Natalie said distractedly. "But really, we've got nothing drinkable here. We should go out. Let me just fix my hair."

La Florida

Sally, Lucienne and Natalie were used to making an impressive entrance when they went out together. With the addition of Louise, the effect was hugely magnified—when the four stunning young women in black satin came through the beaded curtain into La Florida, all conversation, noise and movement literally stopped. Louise was shorter than the three mannequins (so many of the leading men in films were small, she explained, that her diminutive size was an advantage), but she seemed to radiate a glow, a glamour in the technical, bewitching sense. People stared quite openly—there was an audible dropping of monocles—until the four of them had been seated at a mezzanine table, when there was a club-wide exhalation of held breath and an extra loud resumption of comment, query and speculation.

It wasn't long before the first suitors (or dance partners, or prey) began to appear. Sally, Lucienne and Natalie sat up a little straighter, gazing with glittering eyes at the young men . . . who all wanted to dance with Louise. Men nodded and chatted politely with the other three; they ordered bottles of champagne and drank them, hardly noticing the lovely young women beside them; and in an entranced, almost worshipful way, they waited their turns to spin round the floor with the visiting movie star.

"*Que suis-je, paté de fois gras?*" Lucienne said to her friends, with a moue of adorable discontent.

"We might as well not be here," Sally observed. "What's her power? Do you think she's much older than us?"

"Listen, *ma chère*," Natalie leaned close, although the only two young men at their table now were both English and very drunk to boot. "Sally, I've been trying to say this since you first showed up at our door with this—charming girl. She is *not* one of us. Her *power*, as you call it, is simple animal magnetism. Sex appeal—you know, 'It.' Simple as that."

"But, she said . . ."

"She's a 'vamp'? It's slang, cherie. Don't you ever look at the illustrated weeklies, the movie magazines? She's in them all the time; I can't believe you didn't recognize her."

Sally stared at her friends in shock and disbelief. "*You* read movie magazines? But you're the two biggest snobs I know."

July, 1928

Le Train Bleu

Martine and Nanou sat side by side in second class on the train to Cannes, mending hems. "Fancy Mlle's little pets being left behind," Martine crowed. "We're on holiday at the beach for a month, and they've got to stay in gray old Paris."

"When Mlle said she'd be opening a resort boutique this summer, I was sure she'd take *them*, the triad." Nanou paused to bite the end of her thread, brushed the front of her blue linen traveling suit and went on. "Perhaps it's because they can't do this," she raised her tiny scissors and snipped the air. "*Les grands mannequins*, so languid, so elegant—they can wear the clothes but they can't make or even mend them."

"Hm, you may be right. Oh, I've got to take off my hat, it's crushing my brains." Martine stood up and carefully placed her flower-trimmed straw cloche on the shelf. "Maybe it's their laziness catching up with them. That one, the indochinoise, told me once, 'I don't *do* mornings.' Do they ever come in before four in the afternoon?"

Nanou snorted. "Did I ever tell you what that boy, René, told me? Mlle sent him to deliver a package to them, at the flat they share—some frocks for a private showing. It was three in the afternoon, he said. He rang the bell—no answer. He knocked and called. He was going to go back, fearing Mlle's wrath of course, but he tried the door and it was open." She leaned in close, glancing at the old couple drowsing across from them. "He said he looked in, and the room was quite dim, all the curtains drawn, and they were each in bed in an alcove, looking quite dead. He just dropped the parcel and ran. And then later that afternoon, there they all were, wearing the new frocks, cool as cucumbers, not a hair out of place."

Martine laughed. "Lazy cows—they're all right gadding about to champagne parties half the night, but they couldn't do an honest day's work for anything. I'm glad they're not coming."

Le Grand Duc

At least once a week, sometimes more, Sally would finish her night by spending an hour or so with Claude at Le Grand Duc. They talked about anything and everything; sometimes, if he was sitting at the piano, he'd teach her to play a few jazzy strains or would make up little songs to amuse her. When it was time to say goodnight, he'd loosen his collar and invite her to have "dessert."

Sally was licking her lips with a sigh of satisfaction when Natalie walked into the club. Her coat was wet, and her thick curls sparkled with rain.

"Sally, cherie, I was passing and I *thought* I saw you. It's started to bucket down out there. Oh, hello," she added as she registered Claude's presence a moment later.

"Natalie, you remember Claude St. Clair? The pianist from the Chocolate Dandies."

"Of course. I've seen you play many times, but I don't think we've actually met." Distractedly, she half-extended her hand.

"Enchanté," Claude murmured, kissing it lightly. Natalie seemed to freeze, and Claude drew back, an odd expression on his face.

"Anyway, darling, I'm hoping you've brought your sensible *parapluie*. We really ought to be getting home."

"I suppose you're right," Sally said reluctantly. "À bientôt, Claude."

"Au revoir, Mlle Sally; I'll see you soon. Mlle Natalie," he added, but she had already turned away.

August, 1928

Rue Cambon

Natalie pushed open the heavy front door, and the other two followed her in. The atelier was cool, with its high-ceilinged, lavender-walled salons, and was astonishingly quiet since Mlle and the bulk of the staff—vendeuses, seamstresses and mannequins— had left for Cannes. They crossed the pale carpet to the semicircular reception desk where La Mèduse was ensconced.

"You're late," she snapped upon seeing them, but as her eyes strayed to the crystal, onyx and enamel Cartier desk clock, her expression softened. "About thirty seconds late. Not bad." One corner of her mouth twitched as if a faint smile of approval was trying to form. "*Alors*, Mlle has given you your instructions?"

"Just that we're to do a private showing, with four changes each from the new collection, for some very special clients," Sally answered. "She said you would give us the address and particulars."

"The showing is for three or four ladies who are among our best and oldest clients. You will not have met them, as they do not choose to mingle with the public here, nor are they in the best of health. The Duchesse de Chevreuse will be hosting them at her *hotel particulier.* The clothes have already been delivered, and a car will call for you in an hour. All you have to do is prepare yourselves." She looked them each up and down and added, almost reluctantly, "You all look quite suitable as you are. Just freshen your powder and have some tea. I'll ring when the car is here. And, I'm sure I don't need to say, remember at all times whom you are representing."

16*th* arrondissement

"It's as big as the Louvre!" Natalie exclaimed as the car pulled up a tree-lined drive to an enormous mansion. "I didn't know there were houses this big in Paris!"

To their gratified surprise, the car brought them to the grand front entrance, not around back. The door swung open at the sound of the car, and an ancient butler greeted them rather kindly, directing an immaculate young maid to show them to their dressing room. This was a luxuriously furnished suite on the second floor, with mirrors, benches and dressing tables for each of them. Their ensembles had been laid out with professional care, each with its proper accessories and shoes. The maid, Floris, showed them a short passage leading to the drawing room where their clients were waiting, and from which they could hear a faint but convivial murmur of voices.

"Right-o, gels, let's get to it," Sally said briskly. She bent forward, rounding her shoulders, and let her traveling dress slide off over her head. She then powdered her chest and shoulders lightly and picked up her first change, a jersey day dress and jacket ensemble, in black with zigzag insets of tangerine.

She finished first, snugging the matching toque over her smooth hair—Sally had a reputation as the ultimate speed-dresser—and buffed her black kid shoes idly while the other two finished: Lucienne, utterly chic in a black and ivory checked suit, with ivory silk gardenias on her cloche and lapel; Natalie in a slim black coatdress with a flattering flounce of apricot organza at the throat.

The three of them clasped hands briefly, then put on their professional attitude—posture perfect, faces radiant, with the small aloof smile of goddesses— and glided through the door.

The ladies applauded at the conclusion of their final change—evening gowns, all in black satin, each with different, daring cuts, and accessorized with large red ostrich-feather fans. The sound was as soft and dry as dead leaves falling, but the audience appeared genuinely appreciative.

"Join us," the Duchesse said, taking Sally's hand as she moved toward the door. "We're having ruby port. Let me pour you some."

"Merci, Mme La Duchesse, you are too kind."

"Not at all; we insist," the older woman said, quite forcefully.

Gracefully, Sally, Lucienne and Natalie accepted glasses and sank into soft seats, enjoying the warm, elegant room. It had all been a bit of a blur before, as they worked intently to get through their changes and display each ensemble effectively to each of their clients. Now, however, Lucienne noted the refined taste shown in the paintings and *objets*. The room was full of priceless things, but there was nothing ostentatious about it; it was designed for comfort and pleasure, with deep velvet armchairs in a cozy semi-circle around the fireplace.

Natalie was staring, discreetly over the rim of her glass, at their hostess and the three other women. They were all definitely "women of a certain age," but she would have found it hard to say what age. What good skin they all had—there were wrinkles, true, but also a soft, almost waxy smoothness. They were all quite pale, not a hint of color anywhere, except in their dresses—all four wore loose tea gowns of blood red velvet, a curious choice for the time of year.

Sally was also noticing that the four women were dressed alike, even to the cut of their gowns, with loose sleeves and cowl necklines falling away from their pale throats. Each of them even wore the same kind of necklace, a heavy choker of four strands of pearls. None of it was the least bit fashionable—chokers were completely out of mode at present—and she wondered what interest they could take in a showing of the current styles. She shivered imperceptibly, just as Mme Albert, next to her, turned.

"I see you are admiring my pearls. Please, take a closer look." She turned in her seat and presented her nape to Sally, indicating that she should unclasp the necklace.

"Oh no, I . . . They're lovely, but you should leave them on. You wear them so well—all of you."

The old lady laughed faintly. "Oh, but I always take them off, before a treatment."

Sally shivered again and glanced at Natalie, whose eyes were wide with sudden alarm. She could practically hear her friend's voice in her head: *Bozhe moi*, they're vamps. They think they're going to feed on us.

The Duchesse, sitting on Sally's other side, took her hand. "Don't be alarmed, my dears. Did Mlle not explain? We have been very special clients of hers for a very long time. In addition to her utterly chic clothes—simply the best, the *dernier cri*—by the way, we've written down all our orders on this notepad here—where was I? Oh yes, Mlle also provides us with her very special beauty treatments. I'm sure you're just as *gifted* as the other young ladies she has sent in the past." She reached behind her neck and began undoing the platinum clasp.

The other three older women, Sally now saw, were all unclasping their pearls, with an unaccountable giggling anticipation. Meanwhile, the three young women were shooting each other looks of baffled alarm. Suddenly, something caught Sally's eye as she looked at the Duchesse's now bare throat—faint but unmistakeable, a double puncture mark. She threw a frantic telegraphic look at each of her friends. Lucienne was close enough to see what she saw.

"Your beauty treatments," Lucienne now said carefully, glancing at her wristwatch, "How long do they normally take?"

Mme Albert replied with a gurgle of laughter—the ladies appeared to be growing giddier by the moment. "I really couldn't say. It's as if we go into a sort of delicious trance the whole time."

"All we know," the Marquise de Rambouillet interrupted, "is that we wake up feeling a little stiff in the neck, but as soon as we put our pearls back on, we're right as rain. And looking in the mirror is so gratifying."

Cafe Deux Magots

They had the driver drop them off on the Boulevard St. Germain, ("I don't care if he reports back to La Mèduse—we need the rest of the day off after that!" Sally hissed) and then they walked to the Cafe Deux Magots and took an inside table. It was four o'clock. Sally ordered *the à l'anglais* to toy with; Lucienne got one of the bitter aperitifs she favored, and Natalie, in a foul humor, ordered bright blue mint Ricclès.

"Ugh." Natalie grimaced, tasting her toothpaste-flavored drink, which the waiter had set down with a dubious look. She sipped some more. "It's vile, but at least it will get the taste of old-lady blood out of my mouth."

Lucienne undid the snaps on her tight silk sleeve and studied her bruised wrist. She put her mouth to the tiny cut there and sucked at it, like an unhappy child. "What the hell!" she said finally. "How long has *that* been going on? How much does Mlle know, and how many other vamps have been in her employ? 'I'm sure you're as gifted as the *other* young ladies,'" she quoted with a snort.

Sally was stirring her tea cup, round and round. "They knew the whole drill. They were only half-conscious the whole time, but they were directing us: 'mouth here; drain me halfway; stop now; now I must have some of yours.' How old *are* those old dears anyway? I mean, Mlle's house has only been open, what, seven or eight years? Somehow, I think they've been on this eternal-youth-and-beauty kick a while longer than that. How did she find these *special* clients —or they her?"

Natalie had actually drained her Ricclès, sucking up the last bit noisily through the straw. "I know," she said to her staring friends, "it's terrible stuff, and I'll no doubt feel sick later on, but I'm sorry, I just *really* did not like that. I mean, I don't mind women— though I prefer lovely young men on the whole—but there was something so dry and dusty and stale about them. It reminded me of . . . well, bad times, in Russia. Famine . . . when the human body begins to devour itself, and those of us who devour . . .disgusting . . ." Her eyes unfocused in reverie, but after a moment she shook herself and returned. "And why did there have to be four of them? I know we all took turns, but I'm sure I got the lion's share of that little marquise, and she was the worst! The whole thing was dreadful. I've got a good mind not to go back to the atelier, ever."

September, 1928

The Ritz

A bright September day, the kind of autumn weather that feels like spring. Natalie was wearing an exquisite afternoon frock, borrowed (with permission) from Mlle's upcoming Spring collection: black lace over a flesh-toned slip, with floating panels at the shoulders, an uneven hemline and a huge, deep-red satin rose at one hip. A horsehair hat trimmed in lace and deep-red satin ribbon concealed most of her auburn hair and dipped low over her left eye. Her right was visibly filled with tears.

Vladimir reached across the table and took her hand. "Don't cry, cherie, please. I beg of you. It is for the best, it will be all right." He had taken her to the Ritz for tea, something he could scarcely afford, and now it was hopelessly spoiled. The entire room seemed to be filled with genteel yet ardent lovers, some murmuring happily, others, like her, pale with anguish.

"How can it be all right, Vladi?" Natalie's voice was choked with tears. "I want to be with you, always."

"I know, my darling, and . . . there's no one I'd rather spend eternity with, believe me. But I cannot do what you ask. It's . . .wrong."

Natalie turned away from him, fumbling in her tiny bag for a handkerchief. "You despise me. You think I'm evil."

Vladimir drew in his breath with genuine shock. "No, never! Never could I think ill of you, chere Natalie, my angel. But, I believe I have a God-given destiny . . ."

Natalie flinched violently at his words. "A God-given destiny—to marry a nice girl, produce children, grow older, grow sick and die. Oh, I can't bear it!" Holding her handkerchief (finest lawn trimmed in black lace) to her eyes, she stood and fled the tearoom.

Vladimir sat stunned for a moment, then hastily flung some francs on the table and hurried after her. She was around the corner, in a narrow alley leading to the kitchens, when he caught up with her.

"Natalie, my darling, stop, please." Vladimir's voice was hoarse with emotion. "I can't live without you." He embraced her from behind, turning her toward him.

Her fangs were out, her eyes wild. She stared at him inscrutably, and her head sank to his neck for a long, long drink.

At home

Natalie lay on her side, shivering slightly, under a fur-trimmed, black velvet throw. She'd been in bed in her alcove for three days straight—they'd made excuses for her at the atelier, but La Mèduse looked increasingly menacing as the major shows approached.

"Natalie, Natalie," Sally stood over her, while Lucienne sat on a hassock pulled up beside the bed, holding blood-dipped fingers to Natalie's unresponsive lips.

"Natalie, damn it, answer me," Sally said again. "You've got to pull yourself together. You could lose your job. Ours too, if we keep trying to cover for you."

Natalie stirred finally, half-opening her eyes. "Vladi," she moaned, almost inaudibly.

"Cherie," Lucienne whispered, "Tell us what's wrong, what happened. Vladimir—is he dead? Is he . . . undead?"

Natalie's eyes suddenly opened wide. "I . . . I don't know!" she cried, "if he's dead or . . . not. He wanted —wants—to leave me. To have a normal life, fulfill his 'destiny.' He refused to . . . stay with me, because it would be wrong. I was shattered, miserable, furious—he came after me and . . . I don't know what I did."

"Wait!" Sally had turned away, pacing the room in agitation. "He refused to 'stay' with you? You—you wanted to keep him? You wanted to turn him! Oh, Natalie, after all the times we've been through this, I can't believe . . ."

"Enough, you infernal, interfering bitch," Natalie snarled, rearing up with a ferocious glare. "Don't you dare tell me how to conduct my affairs. I was a vamp when your great-great-grandparents were sniveling, snot-dripping children. You think you're so clever and modern, you think you've got it all figured out. You think we are soul-less, you think our hearts are cold—you know nothing." She threw herself back onto her pillows.

Lucienne looked up, wide-eyed, at Sally, then turned back, bending over the bed. "Natalie," she implored, "please, speak to me. I want to help. Tell me what happened with Vladi. Where were you? Maybe we can find out something."

There was no answer; the narrow figure under the fur and velvet seemed to draw into itself. Sally sighed in loud disgust. "Let her be. She can figure it out—she's *old* enough. Come on, Loulou, we should get to work."

Lucienne, still leaning over Natalie, didn't stir for a moment, and so heard her murmur, "The alley near the Ritz."

The Ritz

Improbably enough, Lucienne found him. The alley, where she immediately noticed blood on the paving stones, led to the kitchen, and when she slipped in, inconspicuous in her plain black coat, instinct or luck or perhaps a whiff of blood led her directly to Marie-Paule. A sturdy young woman from Provence with close-cropped dark curls, Marie-Paule was a determined, precedent-smashing sous chef, who had noticed the handsome young Russian unconscious and bleeding in the alley as she'd arrived for work three mornings ago.

"Look, I still have his blood on my jacket." Lucienne's nostrils flared as the young woman pointed out a smear among the sauce stains on her chef's whites. "I lifted him—he was so light—into a cheese van that had just come, and we took him to the hospital. Les Petites Soeurs des Pauvres; it's not far." She paused, looking Lucienne over briefly. "It is good that you have come; he should have a friend with him. So handsome! I went to see him once, but he was raving. I do not know if he can recover . . . I'm sorry."

"Don't be sorry," Lucienne said quickly. "I'm grateful

to you for helping him." She opened her purse. "If there's anything I can do to thank you . . ."

Marie-Paule smiled. "No, no, you don't need to thank me—I could not be a human being and leave him lying there. But if you ever lunch here—don't come for dinner, the prices are ridiculous, unless you are with a very rich man—but if you're lunching, and you're in the mood for sole provençale, and if you enjoy it—tell the waiter. It's my *specialité*."

"Thank you. I will remember that."

Les Petites Soeurs des Pauvres

Everything at the hospital was white—the walls, the starched habits of the nursing sisters, the sheets on the narrow beds and the bandages wound around Vladimir's head and throat. His face was utterly pale, the only color his thick dark brows and the faint violet of his closed eyelids.

"Here is your . . .friend." The sister who had led Lucienne to his bedside glanced at her doubtfully, perhaps seeing the figure in black cloche and coat as a blot on the pristine cleanliness of the place. She went on kindly, though, "Try talking to him, softly, even if his eyes do not open. It helps. But don't stay too long. I'll come back for you in a little while." She glided away, silent as snow.

Lucienne pulled up a chair by the bedside, as she so recently had with Natalie, and spoke softly.

"Vladimir. I'm a friend of Natalie's."

At the sound of the name, his forehead creased in a frown, and a moment later his eyes flew open. "Where is she? I must see her."

"She's . . . not well," Lucienne prevaricated. "She asked me to come."

Vladimir groaned and touched the bandages at his neck. "She has to give me more. Drink more of me, and give me more of her. They took her blood away and gave me something else—some human muck."

"A transfusion?"

Vladimir nodded. "When Natalie first told me what she wanted to do, I refused—I thought it would interfere with my destiny, the things I have to do. But she came after me anyway . . . and then I realized what a magnificent gift she had given me. I could accomplish even more than I'd ever dreamed. But she has to come and give me more, and get rid of this . . ." he grimaced, "vin ordinaire. I must get out of here—she has to help me—I must go . . ."

"Go where?"

"Russia, of course. The Soviet Union. I can see now how wrong I was to have allied myself with the Whites. The future is Red. But I feel so weak and sick; they put this muck in my veins . . ."

"Yes, you said that." Lucienne glanced around—no one nearby. She leaned in closer to the bed, folding back her tight cuff and pricking her wrist with a fang. "Listen, I shouldn't do this, and there isn't much time —quickly, drink."

Rue Cambon

"It's not right. It's not fair. It's not natural." Martine was getting more and more worked up by the moment, staring across the dressing room at the mirror, her three-fold nemesis. "Why the hell am I still jealous of them, when *we* got to go to Cannes all summer, and they didn't?"

"Because, my dear idiot friend, we didn't exactly have carefree seaside holidays, did we? Cooped up in the shop all day serving rude *nouveaux riches*, and then sewing all evening in our stuffy little room. How many times did we actually get to the beach—three? Four?"

"Too many, as far as I'm concerned. Look at me, I'm still a lobster." Martine turned, pouting, toward her red-skinned reflection.

"Pauvre cherie," Nanou comforted her. "Did you try that cream?" She regarded her own reflection with equal discontent. "Ugh, I'm all blotchy. I thought we'd turn sleek and brown like Mlle. That reminds me—La Mèduse stopped me on my way in and said that Mlle wants us both to use extra powder until our sunburns fade."

"Not only that. She grabbed me like this--" Martine gave Nanou a pinch just above her left hip-- "and said I'd better drop the extra kilo or I'd be out on my ass." Martine's eyes filled with tears. "It's not fair— ice cream was the only good thing about Cannes! And look at those three—still as slender and neat as line drawings."

"It's because they never eat."

At home

"Lunch at the Ritz? Are you crazy? I never want to see the place again," Natalie groaned. She was up and about again, but just barely.

"Please, cherie. It's our old friend, the Baron—he doesn't ask much, and he's so generous. He only wants to take us to lunch, just the two of us."

"Ugh, lunch. How can I?"

Lucienne sighed. "Haven't you been to see Vladi yet? He's weak but not in danger, and he desperately wants to see you."

"Yes, so he can desert me after I turn him."

"Natalie! If you truly care for him, have some compassion. What do you want for him—a long, slow convalescence into a sort of half-life, just so you can know he's nearby?"

Natalie ran her fingers through her hair in irritation.

"Sally was right. I never should have tried to meddle in his life. And I shouldn't have let myself care."

"Sit, cherie." Gently but firmly, Lucienne pushed her down onto the low chair by the vanity, picked up an ivoroid-backed brush and began to smooth Natalie's thick wavy hair. "Sally doesn't know everything, you know—she just thinks she does. *She* isn't invited to lunch—the Baron thinks she's too hard."

The Ritz

Peonies, tulips, roses, orchids, ranunculus: the Baron had brought luscious hothouse bouquets for each of them, seeming to somehow know that Natalie would be in rose-colored chiffon and Lucienne in saffron cream velvet. Lucienne glanced over at Natalie, sipping champagne with her eyes demurely lowered below the tiny brim of her cloche. She was glad they'd abandoned their habitual black and worn flower colors; she knew how it pleased the old man, and she had to admit, they looked quite credibly fresh, pretty and soft.

"But you are not eating your Dover sole—it is superb, n'est-ce pas?" the Baron said just then, patting her shoulder.

"Pardon, M le Baron." Lucienne began to push her fish about industriously. "I was daydreaming—your country house sounds so lovely. The sole is, as you say, perfect; we should send our compliments to the chef." She took one small bite and then another, before laying down her fish fork and knife. "But alas, you know we mustn't overeat—if we gain even one centimetre, Mlle will be most upset!"

"Ah, yes, Mlle's precious frocks that must hang upon stick figures. How I wish I could adopt you both, take you to my chateau and let you eat my cook's good provincial cuisine to your hearts' content. Long walks, fruit from the orchard, cream from the dairy, the good country wine—you'd be blooming with health in no time."

Natalie laughed, a girlish melodious sound that cheered Lucienne. "Blooming with health and plump as dairymaids—and you'd never give us a second look. You'd be here in Paris taking some other *elegantes* to the Ritz."

The Baron laughed heartily. "Ah, *jolie* Natalie, you see through me as if I were crystal. Come, let us order our next course, even if you will only take two bites." He signaled the waiter and ordered filets mignons, sauce bearnaise, "cooked *à point*."

"Pardon, s'il vous plait, bleu pour moi," Natalie corrected.

"Et moi aussi," added Lucienne.

"Ah, that's right, the young ladies like it bloody—*mes petites vampires,*" the Baron said with a wink and an indulgent chuckle.

October, 1928

Martine regarded her reflection with discontent. Her sunburn had faded, and now her skin looked dull and washed-out. She'd had her hair gold-rinsed and bobbed, and it didn't suit her; the color brought out green tones in her complexion, and the length emphasized the blocky shape of her jawline. Worst of all, nothing she did could rid her of the two-and-a-half kilos she'd put on over the summer. She breakfasted on black coffee, had given up lunch and allowed herself only the tiniest dinner, but the bulge at her hips persisted—the only effect of her regime seemed to be a slight tremor in her hands and a permanent bad mood.

Even Nanou got on her nerves these days. (It didn't help that her erstwhile best friend had shed her extra weight rather easily by taking vigorous swims at the Piscine Municipale. Martine had gone with her once, but she couldn't bear the dank changing rooms or the unfortunate effect of the chlorinated water on her hair-dye.) But, a thousand times more annoying than Nanou was her current *bête noire*, Lucienne. Martine herself could not have said exactly why. *L'indochinoise* had a quiet, modest demeanor and was careful to be polite and agreeable to everyone—compared to her obnoxious friends, Sally and Natalie, she was practically a saint. Yes, Ste. Lucienne the Perfect, with her smooth, pale-golden skin (exactly the result Martine had aimed for with her sunbathing), her fine glossy hair that was never out of place, her delicate build and tiny feet. With a snort of rage, Martine pulled off the shoes that had been pinching her all day and flung them across the room.

Quai Voltaire

It was Thursday, a free afternoon, and Lucienne could not shake the feeling that she was being watched and followed. Sally was at the hairdresser—she had decided to go from black to palest blond, again. Natalie was enjoying an afternoon of reminiscence and Russian conversation with the two impoverished countesses who embroidered for the atelier. Lucienne, savoring her solitude, was taking a long, dreamy walk, revisiting some of the out-of-the-way corners and quirky pleasures she had discovered when she first came to Paris. She strolled along, looking over the paintings in progress on easels lining the quai. Most were quite indifferent, but if she caught a glimpse of real talent, she would stop to watch for a while, perhaps chatting with the artist; she had occasionally purchased a small city-scape. Today though, she saw nothing that did not strike her as banal or crudely done.

The colors are all wrong, she thought with irritation, studying a view of Luxembourg Gardens. With a frown she realized that her sense of wrong colors extended beyond the canvas—at the edge of her vision, up near the end of the row of painters, a familiar figure hovered. Oddly greenish-gold hair fluffed out below a purple cloche, with a matching *taillure*. Though not exactly pleased to see Martine, Lucienne was at least relieved to be able to make sense of her strange unease; she was instantly sure her fellow mannequin had been following her. Lucienne moved forward briskly, fixing Martine with a direct look and a wave—the other girl would not be able to get away without obvious embarrassment, and Lucienne wanted an explanation.

Martine had a slightly wild look, but stood her ground as Lucienne greeted her with a ritualized air-kiss, as was only appropriate between co-workers. Poor dear, she couldn't have picked a worse color to wear, Lucienne thought. Aloud, she said, "So, are you an art lover as well? I haven't seen anything good today, have you?"

Martine hesitated, at a loss for words. Lucienne looked at her closely and said, "Have you been following me today?"

Again, Martine was wordless, opening her mouth and closing it, biting her lip. Finally with a sigh of mingled irritation and pity, Lucienne said, "Come on, let's go have some lunch and you can tell me all about it. I bet you haven't eaten yet."

"Lunch—oh no, I can't!" Martine exclaimed.

"My treat. Oh, come on, I won't bite," Lucienne linked arms with her firmly, though Martine tried to pull away. "We may not be friends, but I'm not your enemy. We work together; we should get to know each other."

They were quite near a small, old restaurant that was one of Lucienne's favorite spots from her first days in Paris. By the time they arrived, Martine had fallen apart—she collapsed into a chair, sobbing and rummaging desperately in her bag, while Lucienne ordered for them both: leek soup, mussels with saffron and salad, with a half-carafe of red wine. "I hope you don't mind red," Lucienne said as she poured, "White doesn't agree with me." Martine shook her head and took a long gulp of wine. "Have some water, too," Lucienne directed.

Moments later the soup arrived, and even Martine seemed heartened by the aromatic bowl. After a few spoonfuls, Lucienne cautiously began, "I can't help noticing, you've seemed unhappy since coming back from Cannes. Oh, please, don't start crying again—pull yourself together, ma chère."

Tremulous at first, but increasingly steady, punctuated by spoonfuls of soup, Martine outlined her litany of complaints about her summer at the seaside. "We thought it was going to be such a treat, but it turned out you and your friends were the lucky ones."

"Oh, I wouldn't say that. Paris is dreadfully dull in August, you know. All we did was technical fittings, and a private showing for some antique countesses."

"There, you see—countesses! I bet it was in a fabulous mansion, with lavish appointments. I bet they gave you champagne, and wrote you into their wills!"

Lucienne laughed. "What an imagination! It was a huge old pile, to be sure, but dark and stuffy. They had a fire going in summer! I suppose they needed it; they really were frightfully old. No champagne, though they gave us little glasses of port—and their wills? I *don't* think." She shuddered a bit at the memory. "Be glad you weren't there. You really are a silly goose."

Martine's eyes flashed, but she kept quiet as the soup bowls were replaced by shallow dishes and a big tureen of saffron-scented mussels. Martine took a deep, appreciative sniff, which turned suddenly, to

Lucienne's dismay, to a grimace of disgust.

"Oh God, I'm going to be sick," Martine moaned.

"Don't you like *les moules?*" Lucienne asked with concern.

"No, it's not that—I adore them, but look at me! I slurped down that whole bowl of soup like a pig, a fat, disgusting pig. And I ate bread!" Staring in horror, she seemed to notice her bread plate for the first time. "I'm going to the lav and make myself puke—it's the only way."

"Martine, stop. Listen to me." Lucienne took the distraught girl's hand firmly. There were floods of tears; Martine's fierce and woeful recriminations over her intractable extra weight; her accusation of Lucienne as one who couldn't possibly understand as she was always petite and perfect, and on top of that, never seemed to eat . . . Lucienne waited patiently, fed her companion and herself first a spoonful of ethereal broth, then a mussel apiece . . . Finally, as Martine's rant ran down, Lucienne began a calm, well-organized disquisition on diet: small, wholesome, regular meals; plenty of mineral water along with one's wine; avoidance of excess while allowing tiny indulgences and so on.

"And you really eat three good meals a day and stay so svelte?" Martine asked, patting her swollen eyes gently with her napkin.

"Of course," Lucienne answered, though neglecting

to note that at least two of them were blood. "It's important to be consistent, so one's body knows it's going to be nourished—then it can go about its business and not bother you with silly cravings." (Where am I getting this? she wondered inwardly; I've never given a thought to diet in my life.) "And, we mustn't forget to nourish our souls as well."

She signaled the waiter, and a moment later he brought two glasses of a fragrant, bitter digestif she was fond of. She raised her glass to touch Martine's. Light glinted from the half-curtained front windows, through the dark liquid, and glittered in Lucienne's eye—she was casting a glamour. A bit of a waste, but she'd always sensed Martine and her friend Nanou were a threat, and this was an easy way to disarm it.

At home

Lucienne, in a yellow silk teddy, sat at the vanity removing her makeup and telling Sally about her day.

"So, the two of them are quite eaten up with jealousy of us, especially Martine—lately she's even jealous of Nanou, her best friend. Nanou apparently says there's something 'not quite right' about the three of us. But I would guess Martine is actually the more dangerous one, because she's so stupid. But now I've made a sort of friend of her and . . . and you're not listening at all, are you?"

"Hm?" Sally seemed to be thrumming with nervous

energy, shifting position constantly in the armchair where she'd thrown herself, her long, silky legs jiggling. She sighed and fluffed the silver lace trimming her short black evening frock. "Do you want to go out again? I feel I could go on dancing for hours. Oh, I *love* my new hair!"

Lucienne turned from the mirror and stared at her friend. "It suits you," she said, approving Sally's platinum head, "but what's gotten into you, darling? It's almost four, I'm dead tired and we have fittings tomorrow. What did you do tonight? And where's Natalie?"

"La Rotonde. Enormous dancefloor," Sally answered briefly. She had stood up and was flipping through the stack of records by the gramophone.

"What are you doing!"

"Putting on 'Potato Head Blues,' silly, what does it look like?"

"Are you insane? The neighbors will go mad! People do sleep, you know."

The door swung open just then; it was Natalie. "Sleep? What's that?" She caught Sally's eye and they both burst into laughter.

"What is going on with you two?" Lucienne exclaimed. "You look altogether too bright for this time of night, even for vamps. What have you been doing?"

"You mean, *who* have we been drinking?" Natalie answered merrily. "Bright Young Things full of cocaine!" She giggled. "When did you figure it out, Sal?"

"Well, I noticed that young man's bitter taste right away, but I just thought he was—I don't know—sardonic. But then his friend had the same flavor . . . and then I got all tingly, and everything was suddenly hilarious. Oh, I don't want it to end—can't we go back?" She flung herself into Natalie's arms; they hugged and then started dancing to their own inner gramophone.

"You dear wild thing," Natalie laughed. "La Rotonde is closed, and our new friends will have gone off to various beds to entwine their limbs . We'd best leave them to it."

"Entwine our limbs!" Sally pronounced, forceful and only semi-cohcrent. Grabbing Lucienne with one hand and Natalie with the other, she whirled them around the limited floor-space until they collapsed on the nearest bed. The thump of a broom against their floor was muffled by their laughter.

Rue Cambon

Mlle had, of course, created her Fall collection—light wools, startling tweeds, jazzy printed velvets—in April, followed by a Winter show in early September. Now that autumn light gilded the trees, and the little bistros and boites drew in, intense and cozy against the chilly nights, Mlle was thinking of Spring. On this October afternoon, ignoring the outer world with its crunch of crisp orange leaves, she had her mannequins lined up (shivering slightly) in fragile underthings of lilac, pale green or sky blue silk. One by one, she'd call the girls forward, slipping over each neat head a new summer frock of white lawn or ecru linen.

"The saints forbid we should wear color in July," Sally muttered, nudging Martine. They both looked utterly wraithlike, with their white dresses, pale skin and bleached hair. In order to not worry about staining the new clothes during the endless fittings, they had foregone their usual blood-red lip rouge. Ever since her lunch with Lucienne, Martine had become not quite a friend, but at least an amiable hanger-on. Sally had taken her to her own clever hairdresser to repair her hideous dye job, and the two of them were now bonded in blondness.

Mlle, however, had sharp ears and was not pleased by their humorous, mutinous murmurs. "Sally, step forward, please." She narrowed her eyes at the tall, pale figure. "You will wear white, white and more white if I decide it." Her head cocked critically to one side, she added pearls, a silk gardenia and a white gauze headscarf to Sally's white dress and jacket ensemble.

"You too," she gestured to Martine, quickly adding

more and more pale accessories, stepping back now and then to scrutinize the effect. Like the proverbial snake hypnotized by the mongoose, Martine stared at herself in the full-length mirror, as Mlle, all in black, darted around her. "Unless you think it needs a slash of color." The couturière snatched up a narrow length of scarlet silk and wrapped it hastily around Martine's neck as a long, trailing scarf.

There was a general gasp—the effect was so startling, so Grand Guignol. "Oh, you stupid, stupid girls," Mlle snorted, "Take these things off and get out."

Outside Le Grand Duc

Four in the morning, Claude was walking Sally home from Le Grand Duc; he suggested it whenever it had gotten particularly late, possibly as much for his protection as hers. Claude seemed a bit unsteady tonight, in fact; Sally had fed more deeply than usual. She took his arm and he looked at her with a faint smile. "Shouldn't have had that last cognac."

As they turned a corner, Sally noticed a familiar figure half a block ahead, on the other side of the street—a tall slim woman in a loose black coat. "Oh, there's Natalie!"

Claude squeezed her arm hard as she was about to call out; she could feel him trembling. "Don't, please."

"Claude, what is it? You don't seem to like her."

He stopped, turned away. "I should go home—you're all right from here, aren't you?"

"Not until you tell me what's going on."

"I'm sorry, Sally. I know she's your friend, but I can't really be around Natalie. She's . . . she's not like you and Loulou. There's a darkness in her—I feel like she could kill me in a heartbeat and not think twice."

"Oh Claude, I don't know how you can say that. You just need to get to know her better."

He stiffened. "Please, Sally, if you care about our friendship, don't ask me to do that. Natalie is . . . I won't use the word evil, that doesn't really apply. She is what she is. But even you should be careful around her. Listen, ma chère, she's stronger than she looks. Good night, Sally; I really have to go now."

At home

Lucienne was dreaming of a small pet tortoise her brother had once had. In the dream, it lived in a beautiful little house of carved teak, and a pangolin had come to visit it. Tap tap tap, went the pangolin's claws on the polished door, tap tap tap.

Jacques, Lucienne called in the dream to her older brother (in actuality long dead, after a prosperous career) Jacques, answer the door for your tortoise; he can't turn the knob.

Her eyes opened then, and she realized the tapping was at the real, life-size door of their flat. Cautiously, on noiseless bare feet, she moved toward the door and took a deep sniff. Martine's scent of cheap cosmetics and generic eau de cologne was unmistakeable. Stifling a groan, she tiptoed to Sally's bedside.

"Wake up, cherie—our little mortal friend Martine is here."

Sally's eyes opened slowly, at first glance holding centuries of darkness. Her face was ageless in that moment, infinitely experienced, weary yet eternally enduring. Then her eyes opened wider, brightened; the lines of her face resolved into her usual perfect expression of fashionable beauty, circa 1928. She grimaced, but it was a modern, pretty grimace. "Martine! We have a hairdresser's appointment today —but I didn't tell her to come here, silly cow. What time is it?"

Lucienne peered a bit myopically at the clock on Sally's bedside table. "Two-thirtyish."

"Merde. Can you tell her I'll be right there?" Sally groaned. "Are you awake enough to talk to her? I'm so sorry."

"It's my fault too—I started things with her. Let me just see to Natalie first—she mustn't get up."

Lucienne padded away, singing out a melodious *"Un moment"* toward the door as she hurried to Natalie's bedside.

More than any of them, Natalie tended to revert to her true age when she slept. Her hair spread about the pillow was still thick and russet, but her face was engraved with a web of fine wrinkles, the skin translucent and almost blue. The effect would be gone within seconds of her waking, of course, once she reasserted her youth and glamour, but the unexpected sight of her could be fatally shocking to a visitor.

"Natalie," Lucienne whispered, crouching by her friend's pillow, "Don't get up. Martine is here—we'll get rid of her quickly." Natalie stirred, a faint frown adding its creases to her forehead, and turned over. Lucienne shut the curtains of her bed alcove firmly and hurried back to the door, which she opened a few inches.

"Martine, cherie! Good morning . . . er, afternoon. You must forgive us—we had a *very* late night." Lucienne rolled her eyes suggestively. "We've been sleeping like *les mortes*. Sally will be ready in just a few minutes," she continued, raising her voice a bit. "What time is your appointment?"

"Oh, it's not til three-thirty, and it's just round the corner, but I thought I'd come round and see you all." Martine held out a small bunch of yellow chrysanthemums. "Something for your household."

"Oh, you're sweet—but I really can't ask you in. The maid . . ." Lucienne stopped herself with a small laugh. "Who am I kidding; we can't afford a maid— we've all been lazy as pigs lately, and the place is absolutely foul. We don't even have so much as a tea leaf to offer you."

Undeterred, Martine was peering through the narrow opening. "I don't care about that, Nanou and I let our digs get pretty grotty too. I just want to see what kind of place you have. Is it a flat, do you have a kitchen? How much do you pay?"

"Sally, are you ready yet?" Lucienne called urgently. "Otherwise I'll take Martine down to the corner for a coffee."

Martine leaned around behind her, craning to look into the room, just as Natalie flung open her bed-curtains and emerged, hair wild, face antique, in her shroud-like, old-fashioned nightgown.

"Merde! Can't a woman get any sleep in here?"

November, 1928

The Ritz

It had been a busy week, and Natalie, Lucienne and Sally were treating themselves to tea at the Ritz, wearing exquisite *tailleurs* of oatmeal tweed, accented with ivory silk and velvet flowers. Mlle encouraged them to wear things from the new collection in high-profile settings, and they were always happy to oblige.

"Don't look now," Lucienne leaned toward her friends, "but I see a certain pair of very elegant gentlemen heading this way."

"It's always just those two, isn't it?" Sally grumbled. "I may as well take a walk; I know I'm *de trop*."

"Oh, come on, Sally, you can hardly expect to see men roving in packs of three, unless they're musketeers," Natalie cajoled. "Anyway, we always have fun together; why not stay?"

"No, I already know Gaston likes you, because your hair suggests an old-fashioned girl . . ."

"Hah, he has no idea *how* old-fashioned!" Natalie laughed. "And Edouard?"

"Oh, he's clearly fallen for Lucienne—because, honestly, who *doesn't* fall for Lucienne? I'm just going to step out for a breath of air; I'll see you in a little while." Sally picked up her appliquéd clutch and walked off before they could say more.

She made a leisurely circuit of the large, quietly luxe salon, taking the long way to the door. One exceptionally chic woman stood out; Sally was intrigued by her very pale round face and air of quiet intelligence, but she did not linger.

Opening the door to the outside, she nearly smashed the noses of Martine and Nanou, who were peering in.

"Hey, watch where you're going, *duchesse!*" Martine said in a hostile tone.

Ever since they'd given her the memory-cleansing tea, to wipe out the ghoulish apparition of Natalie rising from bed, all vestiges of their budding friendship had fallen away. If anything, Martine was colder than she'd ever been before.

"Well, hello darlings—sorry, I didn't mean to smash into you! Are you on your way in?"

Martine glared. "*Some* of us can't afford tea at the

Ritz."

"And how can *you?*" Nanou challenged. "Martine says you live in squalor."

How the hell does she remember that? Sally wondered inwardly. But she laughed and said, "That's just it—with what we save by sharing such a cheap flat, we can splurge occasionally. Besides, we have these gorgeous clothes available, and it's a shame not to show them off. It's part of our job, really." Looking at the other two, who were clearly not wearing couture, she added, "I've been meaning to ask, why don't you ever wear things from the collection to go out? Mlle likes us to represent the house."

"Perhaps she does, but she doesn't own me in my off hours. I prefer to represent myself," said Nanou. "I made this frock, and my hat."

I'm sure you did; it's appalling, Sally thought but did not say.

"Yes, I prefer to look like myself," Martine concurred —which evidently involved a lot of fussy flounces. "Anyway, like we said, we can't afford the high life."

"Oh, for God's sake, it's only a pot of tea," Sally said, growing irritated despite her resolve to remain calm, but as she followed the gaze of the other two, she saw that Lucienne and Natalie were now sharing a bottle of champagne with Edouard and Gaston.

"Unless, of course, some charming gentlemen decide

to treat one!" Sally winked.

"Oh, so that's it." Nanou turned to Martine with a raised eyebrow. "Gentlemen buy them things."

"Ah, I see!" Martine mirrored her friend's exaggerated expression. "But what does that make them, then?"

"I'm sure they don't realize it. We'd better go warn them. Come on, Martine."

It all happened dreadfully quickly—before Sally could block their path, they were through the door, marching determinedly across the room and emptying a pot of (mercifully tepid) tea across Natalie's and Lucienne's laps, while shouting some very insulting words.

Gaston Robineau adjusted his waistcoat and swung his walking stick jauntily as the two gentlemen strolled away from the Ritz. "Who on earth were those angry young women—were they anarchists?"

"I believe their motivations were personal rather than political," his nephew answered, with the *sagesse* of youth.

"Well, really, who would not be jealous of those three charmers?" He patted his waistcoat again, and could not resist drawing forth a visiting card from his pocket, inscribed with the names Natalie, Lucienne and Sally, and an all-important telephone number. "I shall give them a call later tonight—perhaps we will all go dancing? What do you think?"

"It was delightful to see them again, but are you sure? I didn't know you fancied that type, uncle—you don't find them too vampy? They said it themselves, after all."

"Oh, my boy—you do not know what is a *vampire*. Before the War, there were such women . . . Beautiful? Without doubt! Alluring? *Mon dieu*, what ways they had! Exquisite creatures, but they would absolutely suck a man dry, ruin him: jewels, gowns, carriages, country homes . . . not to mention the incessant devotion they required . . . They would practically compete, as to who would have the biggest heap of corpses at her feet—the suicides, the bankruptcies, the shattered husks of men. *Those* were vampires—marvelous vampires . . . I can smell their fragrance still . . . And thank heaven they are gone!

"But these girls—so lively and healthy and good-humored. So sure of themselves and independent—living on their own in Paris, earning their own way in the fashion business. And yet, so perfectly feminine and enchanting! That petite *indochinoise* with her pretty manners; that glorious redhead—you notice, she has not 'bobbed' her hair like the others, but you can still tell she's a modern girl."

"And the tall goddess who ran away, and then came back—Sally . . . Ever since we met, I can't get her out of my mind," Edouard said dreamily.

"Aha, I thought she was the one for you! My heart sank when I saw her leaving the table just as we approached—but it all came right in the end."

"Uncle, you don't think it was presumptuous of me to offer to pay for the damage to their clothes, do you? Or . . . imprudent to give them the blank cheque?"

"Not at all, dear boy—as I have said, these are not the vampires of old. Besides, Mlle is an old friend of mine—I'll have a word with her."

At home

Natalie returned from the concierge's office, where she'd been summoned for a telephone call. "I told him we already had plans to dine, but we'll meet them at Le Select for dancing around eleven."

Lucienne nodded. "Thanks for getting us out of dinner—I don't feel up to another night of pushing things around on my plate."

"Suits me, too." Sally swiveled around in her chair and clinked her stoneware flagon against Lucienne's. "A simple pick-me-up at home—and maybe a bite later."

"Oho!" Lucienne laughed. "You have designs on that young man, don't you? Aren't you glad you came back from your self-imposed exile?"

"Well, yes. I suppose I have to be grateful to Martine

and Nanou. He seems awfully nice. You know, I hadn't noticed til we all stood up to leave—he's taller than me!"

"Be sure you treat him well; he's a real gentleman," Lucienne admonished. "He didn't have to offer to pay the cleaning bill—it's certainly not his fault that our co-workers are idiots." She got up and went over to the clothesline they'd strung up, where her and Natalie's pale, narrow skirts and jackets hung, the tea stains reduced to a faint shadow by a soak in cold water and baking soda.

Le Select

"You dance divinely," Edouard murmured against Sally's cheek. He pulled back a bit and laughed. "Oh God, what a frightful cliché, isn't it? But I can't help it—you do!"

"I don't mind clichéd flattery, from you." Sally pressed closer, relishing the way their long limbs fit together. To the surprise of her friends, she'd departed from her usual evening uniform of stark, scandalously-cut black satin, and wore a floaty gown of cream-colored chiffon. Jet drop earrings and an ebony bangle were her only concessions to "my midnight soul," as she'd said while dressing. They danced past a mirrored column, and she smiled at the elegant reflection of her pallor against Edouard's immaculate evening wear and patent-leather hair.

At home

Sally was already up, wide-awake if a bit dreamy, reading in an armchair with an empty blood-flask beside her when the other two got up the next day.

Natalie raised her eyebrows. "Hungry this morning, are we? You don't usually hit the bottle so early."

"Yes, I thought you would have snacked adequately last night.," Lucienne remarked. "Didn't you slip off with Edouard?"

Sally closed her book and sighed happily. "Yes, but I didn't have a bite. We walked and talked, almost all night. And we kissed . . . just kissed. I think I want to take things slow with him. I think . . . he might be the One."

"The One? Oh my," Natalie commented drily. She was peering at the tea-splashed suits on their clothesline. The stains left by yesterday's contretemps had been reduced to faint shadows, but would doubtless still be visible to Mlle's sharp eyes. "Mm, I'm afraid we'll have to use that cheque for professional cleaning after all—or to pay Mlle back entirely, if the cleaners can't take care of it." She drew a folded paper from her jacket pocket.

"Please don't use Edouard's cheque," Sally said quickly. "I'd really rather you didn't."

"Easy for you to say—you were well out of the way!" Lucienne said ruefully. "Was that the point of your debutante get-up last night—maintaining your *spotless* reputation?" She laughed lightly, but there was still a perceptible bite to her voice.

Sally stood up and snatched the cheque from Natalie's hand, tearing it in half. "I just want to be like a real girl, having a real romance—for a while."

La Rotonde

"It's not that I never eat," Sally said, turning her almost bare back to Edouard—she knew it fascinated him. "But I do tend to spend most nights dancing. It's terrifically slimming."

"Terrifically slimming," he repeated her English phrase with a smile. "Sally, *ma chère, tu es une* . . . 'terrific girl'."

Sliding her manicured hand over his snowy shirtfront, she lifted the monocle that hung on a silver chain (a new affectation of his) and put it to her eye. "Thenk kew, m'deah," she said in her poshest manner.

"The Queen of England! Do I dare dance with such a grand creature? Come here, your majesty." He pulled her to her feet and reached around to finger her vertebrae like saxophone keys, playing along with the band.

Dancing close to "Ev'rybody Loves My Baby," looking over Eduouard's shoulder, Sally found her eyes returning with each circuit of the floor to the oddly familiar, pale face of a woman. Moon-round and moon-pale, the face glowed like a beacon in the dim corner where she sat with a couple of companions. Unreasonably curious, Sally excused herself after the tune ended and drifted closer.

She was quietly dressed, but Sally's trained eye instantly spotted the quality of her pale-gray long-sleeved silk frock, possibly one of Mlle's. Her only jewelry was a large string of superb pearls, but even that seemed superfluous—her huge violet eyes and exquisite hands were clearly her real ornaments. Sally had the impression she was watching the room carefully, with a subtle mischievous alertness, even while she kept up a murmur of conversation that seemed to enchant her friends.

Taking all this in in a few seconds—if she focused, she could just barely scent the woman's violet perfume—Sally made her way to the ladies' lounge. She was checking her mascara when, like moonrise, the unmistakeable face appeared behind her in the mirror.

"I saw you checking up on me, so I thought I'd better find out why." The moon spoke French with an English accent, and a smile.

"Oh! I didn't mean to be so obvious. I wanted a closer look at your dress. Is it one of Mlle's? I'm a *mannequin de maison* there. Sally." She put out her hand for an English-style handshake.

With a lovely ripple of laughter, the moon raised Sally's hand to her lips. *"Enchantée*, Mlle Sally. I'm Dolly." She laughed again, letting Sally's hand go. "I'm an *anglaise* who seems to spend all her time in Paris—and you're an English French girl. *Parfait!*"

"Shall we talk in English?" Sally asked.

"Do, let's. We'll sit on this couch and have a cigarette and a chat. I feel I've seen you before—the Ritz, was it?"

Sally wasn't sure afterward what they'd talked about —just that it seemed the whole world existed simply to provide them with an amusing conversation. Dolly was witty—she *had* to be, she explained; she was Oscar Wilde's niece—and while talking with her, Sally felt that she herself was suddenly endowed with unaccustomed cleverness.

"You're much too intelligent to be a mannequin," Dolly said at one point.

"But you are much too beautiful to be a writer," Sally replied. "What else do you do?"

"Ah well, there's my secret life," Dolly said with a wink. "And you?"

"Yes, of course—doesn't everyone have one?"

Dolly sighed and a faint melancholy seemed to cloud

her brilliant eyes. "No, I don't think everyone does. We should get back to our other friends—that pretty young man you were dancing with will be frantic. But we must meet again." She produced a tiny card, with her name and a telephone number.

"I don't have a card, but you can find me chez Mlle," Sally said.

It was only as she returned to her table where Eduoard, though laughing with Gaston and Lucienne, did actually look a bit frantic, that she realized what Dolly had said: she'd been watching Sally on the dance floor.

Pont Neuf

Sally and Edouard were on another of their twilight-to-midnight walks, something that had acquired the force of long-standing habit in just a couple of weeks. They had a routine, which Sally found entirely surprising, though agreeable: She would wait at her favorite cafe with an aperitif; he would join her just after dark and have a single drink, and then they would set out walking—along the Seine or through parks or quiet streets, until deep into the night. Sally wore something different and enchanting every night, but she almost didn't need to—after their first few meetings, he no longer suggested dinner or dancing in nightclubs, though sometimes, crossing a bridge perhaps, he'd hum a tune and pull her into a close foxtrot or maxixe. It was unusually warm that November, so they didn't need to bundle up in heavy coats; in any case, Sally didn't feel the cold, and Edouard seemed not to either.

"You're sure you're warm enough?" Sally asked as a sharp breeze ruffled her scarf.

"With you, always. Your eyes give me all the fire I need," Edouard murmured, brushing back her silky bangs and tracing the long narrow arch of her eyebrow.

Sally sighed and gave herself up to the pleasure of kissing. "But darling . . ." she said, when they paused for breath. "Can we go on like this? I can't help it, I worry about you. Out with just me, night after night . . . You don't eat dinner or see other people, even your uncle or my friends; I worry you'll get tired of just being with me."

"Dinner's over-rated—I eat a big luncheon. And nightlife, other people—pff, I don't want to be distracted. I want to spend this time just with you."

She caught something in his phrase. "*This* time. It's going to end, isn't it?"

"Sally, come here." Edouard sat down on a bench. "I need to tell you something. I haven't been completely open with you about who, or what, I am."

Sally's head swam as she snuggled in beside him. If it weren't for the sweet, mortal smell of him, the rich blood she could practically hear rushing through his veins, she would think he was going to announce he was a vampire. So many things pointed to it—his preference for darkness and solitude, his indifference to cold or food, and the extraordinary harmony and understanding that seemed to exist between them. But she knew it was impossible. When he began, with an uncharacteristic hoarseness and a bit of a stammer, "I'm m . . .," she almost laughed, "Of course I know you're mortal, you dear man . . ." but she kept quiet and he cleared his throat and said, "I'm married, Sally dear."

"Oh," was all she could think to say. "But you're so young."

"Well, so is she. And our child . . . is a newborn. She's been away in the country, having the baby, but soon she will return and . . . all this must stop."

"Ah." Sally slid away from him, feeling an odd burning in her eyes. "So I've been a diversion."

Edouard closed the space between them and folded her in his arms. "Never, my darling—you cannot think that—not after the nights we've shared. We've talked of everything in the world, we've touched each others' souls. Have I acted like a man looking for a diversion? If that was what I wanted, I'd know better than to look to you. No, you're no diversion—you're wisdom, passion, depth—you're extraordinary, like some kind of ageless immortal. I think you must actually be a vampire."

For a moment, Sally went completely limp, before she pushed him away and stood up, staring at him. "What did you say?"

"You're not offended, are you? I don't use the word the way my uncle does—for glorious, greedy courtesans who drain their lovers dry—of course not. No, I think I know what you are, Sally: an immortal, inhuman creature who lives by . . . by drinking blood. And also a wise, beautiful, utterly enchanting girl, with whom I've shared the most extraordinary time. You could have bitten me at any time, yet you haven't—that tells me you've enjoyed being together as much as I have."

"Yes, I have," Sally said sadly. "I didn't want it to end, but I knew it would have to. When does your wife come home?"

"Tomorrow afternoon."

"Ah. You said 'soon,' but you really meant this is our last night. Perhaps I should bite you now. I could turn you—we could be immortal together."

"Believe me, I've thought of that. In fact, I've thought of little else. But . . . I love my wife. And I *will* love my child. I would hate to abandon them."

"Should I care about that?" Sally whispered, letting her fangs come out. She grabbed Edouard's face with both hands, stroking his cheek, and then leaned in toward his throat.

After a moment, her fangs retracted, and she kissed

him softly. "I guess I do care, because I care about you. You really are a perfect gentleman," she told him, pulling back.

"Thank you, Sally. You know I will never forget you."

"Of course you won't." She straightened her clothes. "Will you walk me home now? Tell me about your wife—what's she like?"

"Oh, Marie . . . we've known each other since childhood. She's sweet and funny, but she hasn't developed her mind much. And she's a tall girl, like you, and pretty, but she doesn't . . ."

"Carry it off? Have a sense of style? Have her come round to Mlle's. You can easily afford it, with all the dinners you haven't been buying me." Sally laughed. "And take her dancing, or out for long walks, when the baby's in bed. You may find she's got more on her mind than you think."

"You mean, if I see that she's dressed in the height of chic and take her out as if she's an enchanting companion, she'll be my very own vamp at home?"

"Something like that."

At home

It was almost dawn when Sally came it; Natalie and Lucienne were at their bedtime toilette. Sally's face had a feral look that meant she'd fed recently, and her hair was newly re-dyed jet black. She held up a hand to forestall the questions Natalie was clearly about to ask.

"Talk about it tomorrow. Tired. All done with Edouard. Found that hairdresser who did such a botched job on Martine; made him dye my hair and then drained him, mostly. Sleep now."

Luxembourg Gardens

Mlle released them early the next day, into an afternoon of golden light. The three of them took their autumnal tweeds and silks for a stroll in the Luxembourg Gardens until teatime. Children were everywhere, running and shrieking in miniature-chic school uniforms, or watching wide-eyed from the nanny-supervised sidelines.

"Oldest story in the world," Sally was saying. "He was amusing himself while his wife was off in the country having a baby. Now he wants to be a good husband and father."

Lucienne made a disdainful, hissing sound. "Hypocrite."

"No, not really . . ." Sally looked away. "At least he was honest about it—eventually. And, he's so sure he's going to love his child—isn't that remarkable?"

"No, not remarkable," Natalie answered. "It's just what people do."

"I never wanted a baby, not for a minute," Lucienne

said. "One of the many things I'm grateful for is never having to give that a moment's thought. Can you imagine . . . ?" She gazed off toward a pair of perambulators not far from them. As if on cue, a whimper came from one, and a squall from the other, causing the starched nurses in attendance to lean in and fuss with their charges.

"What about you, Natalie—did you ever want a child?" Sally asked. As she turned toward her friend, she was astonished to see Natalie dabbing at her eyes, which were moist, and fishing out a pair of dark glasses from her purse.

"I'm sorry," Natalie said, composing herself again. "It hits me sometimes. It's just that . . . I was pregnant when I . . . when I was turned."

Sally and Lucienne stared. "Mon dieu," Lucienne said, "I didn't even know that was possible. What happens? Would the baby . . .?"

"I don't think it *is* possible," Natalie said quietly. "I lost the baby a few days later."

"Oh, Natalie, I'm so sorry," Sally said. "I mean . . . had you wanted it?"

"Oh yes. My fiancé and I were impatient . . ." she laughed briefly, "but our wedding was to be in just a few weeks. No one would have known. But . . ." she sighed deeply, "my great-aunt guessed what was going on, and she knew she had to hurry. I don't think she could have turned me if I'd given birth—

I'm not sure why, but that's what I concluded."

"Your great-aunt turned you? I didn't know it could be a blood relative." Sally was shocked.

"Yes. It's often kept in families—didn't you know that? I'd always known there was something odd about her, and I tried to keep my distance, not be alone with her. But she sent for me, saying she had a special wedding present to give me—I couldn't really refuse."

Lucienne and Sally were silent, absorbing what Natalie had told them. "I suppose she did it out of love," Sally said slowly. "It really *was* a gift she was giving you . . ."

"Not one I wanted, though," Natalie said bitterly. "I knew all about her kind, and I didn't want any part of what she had to offer. I thought I could escape, have a normal life with a husband and family . . . like my mother and grandmother. But it wasn't to be—they'd made a bargain years before I was even born: my grandmother's first granddaughter would carry on Sonya's line."

"Where is she now?" Sally asked.

"Still in the old country." Natalie laughed drily. "The old family farm has probably been collectivized now. I've no idea what she makes of the Bolsheviks, but I expect she likes all that red. Perhaps she's become a Party member."

Lucienne, still lost in thought, shook herself with a

tiny shudder. "That's all just so . . . surprising. I didn't know about families passing it on. I thought—well, it's so different from what happened to me—I thought it was usually more of a . . . well, more of a sexual thing. More like a demon lover."

Natalie smiled. "You had a demon lover?"

"That's how I thought of him at the time. Luc. I was just seventeen; he was a little older—or so I thought —and he'd visit me at night. Not every night—I never knew when he'd come. He'd tap on my window, and we'd go out into the gardens. My family had a big house, with beautiful grounds, full of fragrant, night-blooming flowers. I was so young and naive—I didn't even know what was 'normal,' but I knew he wasn't like any of the boys I saw at school or around town. He was very serious, very gentle and courtly; he'd recite poetry to me, some classic and some his own. I was enthralled. I started to live for the nights; my days seemed to pass in a dream. Girls I knew would talk about their sweethearts, about kissing and making plans, and I'd just smile and hold onto my secret." Lucienne paused, her eyes far away, and sighed.

There was silence, until Sally said, "Well? What happened?"

Lucienne laughed lightly. "What do you think? Here I am." But her eyes again looked off into the past.

December, 1928

Barge party

The American couple was apparently unimaginably wealthy. They'd taken over a quai where a lavish barge was tied up, for a party at which everyone was to wear something referring to water or the sea. Amid a host of *matelots* and women in oceanic aquamarine and Nile green, they knew they stood out: Natalie as a mermaid, with her hair loose and a tail of sparkling paillettes; Lucienne as a fountain in silver-beaded panniers; Sally as a waterfall, her hair dyed pale blue and a Fortuny silk gown of the same shade falling in flashing streaks, pooling at her feet.

The crowd parted for them, with audible sighs of admiration, as they made their way past a lavish buffet of oysters, lobsters and shrimps on ice to accept blue cocktails from a Neptune-bearded, starfish-crowned bartender.

The three of them stood for a time, sipping their drinks and listening to the jazz band which was playing in an enormous clamshell, before a rather dashing swordfish requested the honor of a dance with Natalie. It was a tango, during which she managed her tail in a masterful manner, flinging it this way and that as they changed direction. But the floor became crowded during the next number, a one-step done to the tune of the moment, and Natalie returned, escorted by her solicitous partner.

"Say, that was all right—but I don't want to endanger the appendages more than necessary!" He straightened the large serrated blade affixed to his headpiece. "You okay, honey?"

Natalie smoothed her tail and nodded, then turned to her friends. "Allow me to present Mr. Lewis."

"Wow. You'll forgive me, ladies—it's what we Americans say when we're overcome." He gazed at the three of them with frank appreciation. Just then there was a commotion as someone swung from a rope down to the deck—a dashing pirate, complete with eye-patch, gold earring and long black beard.

"Aha, our host," Lewis remarked. "I wondered what sort of grand entrance he'd make."

"Ahoy, mateys! Bring that chest aboard, double-quick, ye scurvy sea dogs!" the pirate captain called out in a thin but commanding voice. Half a dozen ferocious crewmen heeded his command, wrangling a large, heavy chest into the midst of the crowd.

"Stand back!" Blackbeard commanded, flamboyantly lifting a large key which hung on a chain around his neck. He unlocked the chest, revealing a heap of gilded glitter. "Aha, me pirate gold—doubloons, pieces of eight and . . . argh!"

Rising up out of the gold-heaped chest, a blond woman in a glittering, gold-sequined dress scattered fake-gold coins everywhere, as she stood and flung her arms around his neck.

"Aha! The ultimate treasure—me lady wife!"

"My pirate king!" she answered, with a radiant smile. She bent down to fling handfuls of coins at the crowd.

"Quite the grand gesture—I'd expect nothing less," Mr. Lewis remarked. "Do you know Cerise and Garry well?"

"Oh—no, not at all, really," Sally answered, as he'd addressed the three of them in general. "We're here on behalf of our employer, the House of Mlle."

"I see." He seemed to give them all a brief reassessment. "So, you're here to dress up the proceedings? Professional beauties, you might say?" He grinned affably, but suddenly seemed less wholesome in his appreciation.

Natalie's reply had a touch of ice. "We are here to have a lovely time."

"Well, in that case, let me bring you some more drinks!" the American said obligingly, moving off.

"Natalie, what's up?" Sally asked. "You seem to have taken a sudden dislike to that fellow."

"Hmph. He may be dressed as a swordfish, but he acted more like an octopus on the dancefloor—arms everywhere! I thought perhaps I was mistaken, that perhaps he was just looking out for my tail . . ." She couldn't help giggling. "But did you see the way he looked us over after you said we're mannequins—he thinks that means we're cocottes."

Lucienne laughed, downing the last of her blue drink. "Oh, Nat darling, who cares what he thinks— silly American man. Come on, let's get out of here before he comes back with more of these nasty cocktails."

The band was very good, the party was very gay, and the next few hours were a pleasurable blur. They nibbled seafood, giggled with bubbly bright young things, sniffed up grains of fairy dust laid out on glass plates. Fueled by enough intoxicants to negate the cold, one of the wilder guests flung himself overboard to swim, splashing the laughing audience before being pulled out of the chilly water. Across the festive mob, Sally glimpsed Dolly Wilde, and

Lucienne was sure she saw Louise, but as in a dream, they were gone when one looked again. No matter, though—there was dancing and light, amusing flirtation, sips of champagne and swigs from flasks.

The three of them were taking a quick moment, regrouping by a railing, when Mr. Lewis found them again. He was accompanied by two other men who were, like him, American and very drunk.

"There you are—been looking all over!" he hailed them slurrily. "The It girls. Can't get enough of *it*, right? Well, we've got it for you—all the It you can handle."

His friends rumbled with crude laughter and moved forward.

Natalie looked sea green and sickish, but took charge. "I know what you want," she said, calmly but with a lascivious smile. "Let's find somewhere a bit more private." She led the way to some unoccupied benches in a dim alcove.

Moving as if choreographed, Natalie eased Lewis onto the bench and herself onto his lap; Sally took the taller of the two friends, Lucienne the shorter and did the same. Arms about the men's necks, almost in unison they kissed their partners, clinging to them with passionate moans.

Appreciative cries from the men became apprehensive: "Hey, slow down there, darling!" as the luscious mouths broke lip contact and moved, each to a spot on the neck of her chosen target.

Lewis, the most heavily built, was the last to thud to the deck, and Natalie was still drinking.

"Natalie, come on; we can't drain them completely," Lucienne said quietly.

Natalie raised her head with a snarl and a wild look, but after a moment she smoothed her mermaid gown and pulled out her compact, checking her lipstick and teeth, delicately wiping a smear of blood from her chin. Her friends were completing their own compact checks. "All right, I'm full. Shall we go?"

They were just starting down the gangway when a low, musical woman's voice called to them. It was their hostess, in her golden gown. Out of the spotlit glitter, they could see the enormously long string of pearls she wore.

"Hello?" she said again, with a curious timidity that was at odds with her magnificent appearance. "I've been admiring you all evening, but we never got to talk. I'm so glad you came."

They introduced themselves, returned her compliments and thanked her for the party. The woman in gold seemed reluctant to let them leave.

"Must you go? I was hoping we could spend some time together."

"You are so kind, Madame, but I'm afraid we are quite exhausted—and we must be up early for fittings tomorrow," Lucienne apologized. Natalie was, indeed, swaying with fatigue.

"Then you *must* come and have tea with me. Oh, please say you will—tomorrow at five? You'll be done with your fittings and things then, won't you?"

"Merci, Madame, we will be delighted," Sally said, accepting a card with the address before taking Natalie's arm firmly and hurrying them away.

Maison Massey

"Richer than the Queen of England, from what I've heard," Sally said. "Mlle will be pleased if we can woo her away from Patou." They were dressing carefully for tea, in simple but impeccable afternoon frocks.

Sally insisted they wear creamy, pale colors: "You know what blondes are like—I am, anyway, when I'm bleached. They want the whole world to reflect their coloring."

She was proved correct as they were shown into a beautiful, spacious drawing room of exceptional lightness. Their hostess, insisting "Please, call me Cerise," greeted them in a tea gown of pale rose crepe de chine, accessorized only with her famous pearls. She embraced each of them, in a cloud of subtle scent. As they settled among the pale, puffy furnishings, she pulled a bell for the butler and turned to her guests. "I thought champagne would be nice? Unless you'd like something . . . darker?"

Despite a certain surface glitter of well-known names and avant garde allusions, the conversation was remarkably vague and general during the first bottle. However, after the butler had discreetly popped a second cork, refilled their Lalique saucers and withdrawn, Cerise leaned forward, giving each of them a long, searching look. Her blue eyes seemed wide with pleading or even fear, and her pause before speaking was almost unbearably tense.

"There are reasons I wanted to get to know you," she said finally. "I think we may be able to . . . do certain things . . . to help each other. Oh, I put that badly," she finished with a self-deprecating laugh. "Obviously, you'd like me to patronize Mlle's couture house, and I'm happy to do that—I can easily divide my purchases between her and M Patou. He'd like me to be his exclusive customer, but he doesn't control me. So, consider that done—I'll come in next week and spend a lot of money, and I'll make sure everyone knows it's because of you. But what I'm interested in is something beneath the layer of clothing. Oh—there I go again—you must think I'm proposing a lesbian orgy." She laughed nervously. "No, the thing is . . . I love my husband. Not very shocking, really. But he's . . . well, he's an artist, you know. He has a great many interests, a love of novelty and beauty . . . and I'm afraid of losing him as I grow older. I've had three children, and I've sensed a slackening, a distance between us that wasn't always there." She leaned back in her chair, with her eyes closed and an expression of deep pain.

"Madame? Cerise? Are you all right?" Natalie asked with concern, after a few moments of silence.

Cerise opened her eyes and smiled, a bit vaguely at first. "Oh! Sorry, yes, I—you have no idea what I'm getting at, do you? Well, the thing is, I've heard a bit about you from a friend, the Duchesse de Chevreuse. It's simple, really—I'd like to stay youthful forever. Like you. I'd like you to do that thing you do with . . . blood." She broke off suddenly, looking paler, and fanned herself with one hand. "Sorry! I'm a bit squeamish, actually, but I'll get over it. I'm sure the thing to do is just face up to it, like going to the dentist."

"Oh, erm . . ." Sally murmured, speaking for all of them, essentially. "I think we might all need to think about this a bit. You see, we don't usually . . . well, we have, obviously . . . I mean. . ."

"What Sally is trying to say," Natalie said calmly, "is that you should think this over very carefully. It's not a light commitment, or even a rather serious one, like starting to dye your hair . . ."

"Believe me, I *have* thought about this very carefully," Cerise said. "I know exactly what I'm asking, and I'm ready."

"Really, this is a bit sudden," Lucienne said. "Would you excuse us for a few minutes, Madame?"

"Certainly, I quite understand. Why don't you take a turn around the garden and talk it over among yourselves?"

"Oh, what the hell!" Lucienne was the first to explode as they stepped outside. "I feel so put upon, so used. What is it with these rich women?"

"Hush, cherie," Natalie soothed. "Let's move a little further away." They stepped carefully along a gravel path, lifting their expensively shod feet with caution.

Lucienne sank onto a small marble bench, shuddering a bit with the chill of the stone and her emotion. "Why do these women feel so entitled, just because they have money? After that day with those ancient aristocrats, I felt so . . . soiled! I really don't ever want to do that again."

"You wouldn't have to, darling." Sally put an arm around her shoulder. "She doesn't need all of us; any *one* would do. And she's not like those creatures— she's only a little past young and really rather sweet, if a bit pathetic. I don't mind helping her."

"But is it helping?" Lucienne persisted. "She's not that old now, but she *will* be, and she'll still want to hold onto youth and beauty. It's not natural—what if her husband notices?"

Sally gave an amused snort. "When did a husband ever notice anything, especially an American one? I can just hear him: 'My wife goes to Paris, visits her couturière, and gets the most amazing beauty treatments—wonderful what they can do.'"

"Hush, Sally," Natalie said severely. "You're too young to be so cynical. I don't think there's anything wrong in giving her what she asks for—but it may not help her. If her husband is set on novelty—well, he may not even notice how young or lovely she looks. She'll still be his 'old missus.'"

"Who's cynical now?" Sally swung about with a flounce of her skirt and turned toward the house. "I'm going back in."

Back in the drawing room, Sally instigated a festive mood, refilling all their champagne glasses. "To Cerise," she proposed, "ever young and lovely!" Spying a gramophone in the corner, she quickly went through the records and selected the hottest foxtrot. "Madame," Sally held out her arms to Cerise and took the lead as they danced.

"Now, there are two things you will need," Sally said; "One, a very long, very beautiful scarf, which you will insist on wearing at all times over the next three weeks. Perhaps with a jazz or cubist pattern, something colorful. Two, a sterling silver flask which you can keep in your garter or your purse, near you at all times."

Cerise giggled. "A flask in my garter—I feel younger already! I have a platinum flask from Cartier; will that do? It was a present and I've never used it. And I have the perfect scarf—Sonia Delaunay made it for me. She gave it to me only a few days ago, and I can easily become inseparable from it." Her eyes gleamed. "So, is it really a bite in the neck?"

"Doesn't have to be, but that's the easiest and most effective. If you'd said you never wear scarves, I could have figured out something else."

"I don't, as a rule, but I will now—I do love Sonia's textiles. What about my pearls—should I put them away for a while?"

"No, I think . . . if you can manage, I've an idea it would be very good if you wore them. Pearls have a lot of power, you know, from the sea and the moon."

"Yes," Cerise said, gazing wide-eyed at Sally. "You know a lot, don't you? How old are you, really?"

Sally smiled. "Oh, a lady never tells, does she?"

Cafe Deux Magots

"Where is Sally, anyway?" Lucienne stirred her cafe crème and consulted her narrow diamanté watch. "Nine o'clock, Saturday night—I want to go dancing, like we always do."

Natalie shrugged. "If she doesn't show up in another 15 minutes, let's just go." She poured the last half-cup from her small pot of tea and downed it.

Just then, a long, dark gray Rolls Royce pulled up in front of the cafe, and Sally emerged from the deep, cushioned interior. She was blonde again and dressed in champagne-colored silk.

"Au revoir, Pierre," she called democratically to the chauffeur as she slammed the door and then, swaying slightly but gracefully, made her way to their table. "Sorry I'm late, darlings—Cerise *would* go and open another bottle of bubbly." She threw herself down in the chair beside Natalie and reached for her teapot.

"Nothing left, darling. We've been waiting for you for more than an hour."

"I know, I'm so sorry. Look, do you mind if I order a coffee or something? I've got to have a bit of a pick-me-up before we go."

"Go home and take a nap if you like," Lucienne grumbled. "I'm ready to go dancing." She leaned forward suddenly and peered at Sally. "Pearl drop earrings! They're gorgeous, and enormous. Where did they come from?"

Sally smiled hugely, pushing the sleek waves of her bob back behind her ears. "Aren't they luscious? Garry gave them to me."

"Garry? Cerise's husband? Oh, no! What are you doing there, stirring up *more* problems for that poor woman?"

"It's not like that, truly. I mean, he's not interested in me in the least. Or, he is, but only because . . . you see, it's *working*. Cerise is becoming more beautiful by the day; she's glowing. And he's noticed, in a big way —she says he hasn't been so attentive in years. You should see the pearl earrings he's given *her*! He thinks I'm giving her some special beauty treatments, and he's grateful, that's all. Well . . . and I think he thinks she and I have become 'special friends,' and he finds it titillating. But there's absolutely nothing improper between us—between him and me, I mean."

"Oh ho!" Natalie raised an eyebrow. "And between you and *her*?"

Sally smiled. "Nothing improper, as far as I'm concerned. She's very nice."

Sally began to be absent from work in a noticeable way. Mlle was not seriously annoyed, because Mme. Massey had placed a large order and had let it be known that it was entirely due to Sally's assistance and charm. But La Mèduse was in a fierce mood all week, making bitter remarks to Lucienne and Natalie. She even sent them out with Martine to do a private show for an important client, though not a "special" one, obviously.

The private view went well enough during the busy, quick changes of four ensembles apiece—Martine was on her best, most professional behavior and wasn't at all inept or clumsy in the cramped dressing room. But as the car took them back, she sprawled on the rear-facing seat, regarding them with narrowed eyes.

"How old are you girls, anyway? None of you will ever say—just like Mlle. I think it's silly, if not suspicious."

Natalie produced a light laugh. "What on earth do you mean? What does it matter exactly how old anyone is?"

"It doesn't *matter*," Martine said coolly; "I couldn't care less. But it's just normal to talk about it. Me, I'm 22; I'll be 23 next September. By the time I'm 24, I'll be getting too old for this. If I haven't had an offer of marriage here in Paris—and I probably won't—I'll go back to my village. One of the landowners is sure to want a stylish wife, even if she's a bit old. Nanou is younger than me—she just turned 21, and she has a fiancé at home. So, what about you?"

"How old do you think I am?" Lucienne asked coyly.

"It's hard to tell with you *chinoises*; you always look younger. I'd say . . . 19?"

"*Exactement*," Lucienne smiled. "You see, not so mysterious. I'll tell you a secret: I was betrothed when I was just a small child—it's the custom where I was born. I was to be married at 15, but I couldn't stand him, so I ran away."

"Ooh!" Martine's eyes widened. "Your fiancé—was

he much older?”

“Ugh, yes—and fat. A horrible old man, the town butcher. So I went to the docks, found a ship bound for Europe and stowed away. I had a tiny bundle with some jade jewelry and biscuits; it was a rough trip, but I stayed quiet as a mouse and they never found me. Luckily I had learned good French, so when I got here, I changed my name and began a new life.”

“*Mon dieu*, you poor thing!” Martine sat relishing the juicy story tidbit for a while, then turned to Natalie. “You are older, *n’est-ce pas?*”

“Oh yes,” Natalie made a comic moue. “I’m ancient —25. And since we are telling our stories . . .” she glanced at Lucienne, “I’ll tell you mine. I have no fiancé, either waiting or abandoned or still to come. I was married for two years, and then he died.” She held up a hand as if to cut off any expression of sympathy. “He died in the stupidest way imaginable. The army came to our town in Russia and recruited him, along with all the other young men his age. They went out on practice maneuvers, and he was shot, by mistake, by another new recruit who didn’t know one end of his gun from another. They sent a sergeant to tell me, a profoundly stupid man, who stood on my doorstep twisting his hat. I lost the baby I was carrying.”

As Martine stared at her, trying to find the right words, Natalie reached out and patted her hand. “So, that’s why I don’t talk about myself much.”

Lucienne practically exploded with laughter once they were alone. "That should give her enough to gossip about! Good heavens, Natalie, what a tear-jerker. I was sure you were going to give yourself away, though—do you know you used the word 'stupid' three times?"

"I didn't; it was only twice. What about you, and your small pouch of jade and biscuits! Are we really supposed to believe you survived a three-week voyage? What did you do, suck on the jade for moisture?"

"I crept out quietly at night, silly. Anyway, she bought it. She ate it all up."

"Should we warn Sally to have a story ready?"

"No, why should we? *We* managed."

January, 1929

Maison Massey

Sally stretched luxuriously and wiggled her toes, reveling in the feel of the ultra-fine linen sheets against her skin. She opened one eye to the cool light. It was just past noon, and the maid, who knew never to disturb her earlier, was across the room drawing the heavy velvet curtains. She had already set a tray, with deliciously steaming cafe crème and a segmented blood orange, on the bedside table. Sally sat up and ran her fingers through her hair, which was blonder than ever, its tone perfectly keyed to flatter her pale skin, thanks to the ministrations of Cerise's hairdresser.

"Merci, Francoise," she said to the quiet maid, who dipped her head in a vestigial bow before leaving. She was quite young, just a girl really, and rather pretty—maybe she too would like a life of immortality and glamour. Sally shook herself with a rueful smile and poured some coffee. What am I thinking, she scolded herself; it doesn't do to create too many others.

She was drinking her coffee and marveling at how even the air was luxurious in this house, warm and scented, when the door opened and Cerise flung herself across the room onto her bed.

"May I?" she asked, lifting Sally's left wrist and eying a small scar there. It was the beginning of their third week—they exchanged blood several times a day with very little ceremony.

"Go ahead—as long as I can finish my coffee with the other hand."

"I'm so glad you agreed to stay with us for this time," Cerise said when she'd come up for air, wiping a drop of blood delicately off her chin with an embroidered hankie. "Isn't it fun? I mean, I'm having so much fun —I hope you are too."

"I could get horribly used to this," Sally said, with a small gesture that took in the exquisitely comfortable bed, the beautiful room, the house and its life beyond.

"Of course, I know money can't buy everything." Cerise laughed and smoothed her skirt. She was wearing a plain, perfectly cut day dress of Mlle's, with her pearls and scarf. "Garry's become awfully fond of you, too. Do you think you could come to Venice with us?"

"I adore Venice!" Sally said immediately.

Cerise seemed faintly disappointed. "Oh, you've been?"

"Yes, but ages ago . . . when I was just a child," Sally finished lamely.

"Well, you must go again, then. The place can be magical for a child, I'm sure, but it holds even greater charms . . . when one is ready to experience them."

"You're so kind to me. But you know, in another week, our process will be complete. You and Garry may want to be alone together—you could have a second honeymoon."

Cerise lifted her string of pearls and slid a few mischievously between her lips. "Oh, we will, and we'll be very happy. But we both like to share our happiness."

Le Perroquet

"It's dull here tonight; I haven't seen anyone I want to sample," Lucienne complained, looking round the fashionable but half-empty dancefloor of Le Perroquet.

Natalie fitted a Turkish cigarette into a long amber holder and peered around the club, which seemed peculiarly cavernous and shadowy. "It's true. Perhaps we should go."

Just then, a woman in pale green satin came gliding up to their table. "Hello, you're Sally's friends aren't you? I'm Dolly."

"Oh!" said Lucienne, "yes, she's mentioned you. Im Lucienne, and this is Natalie."

The Englishwoman nodded. "And how are you, lovely ladies? Isn't this place bleak tonight?" she said, pulling a chair up to their table. "I was thinking of leaving, but since *you're* here, let's have a drink."

"Yes, let's," said Natalie. "It's so dead, at least we'll be able to hear ourselves." They caught the waiter's eye and replenished their cocktails; Dolly ordered a glass of champagne.

"Well met by moonlight," Miss Wilde said as they clinked glasses. "I mean my enormous moon face," she added with a self-deprecating laugh. "And where is our dear Sally, by the bye?"

"Sally has taken up the high life," Lucienne replied.

"Yes, or been taken up by it, " Natalie clarified. "She's staying for a while with some new friends, an American couple—the Masseys."

"Oh, Garry and Cerise. Oh dear," Dolly said with obvious dismay.

"Oh dear?" Natalie inquired.

"I'm sorry." Dolly took a gulp of her champagne. "I didn't mean to alarm you. I'm sure they're lovely people, I have nothing bad to say. I don't even know them personally . . ."

"But . . .?" Lucienne raised an eyebrow.

"Well, as everyone knows, they're generous patrons of the arts and wonderful hosts. Only . . . people around them, in their circle, don't seem to do so well. Nervous breakdowns, suicides . . ."

"Well, I wouldn't worry about Sally. She's healthy as a horse and watches out for herself. Of course, she might *cause* a few nervous breakdowns around her . . ."

"I'm sure you're right," Dolly said. "By the way, I want to invite you—and Sally, of course, if you talk to her—to a salon. A gathering of ladies. I think you would find it most interesting, and I know everyone would love to meet you. The hostess is another *americaine*—and she's another Natalie," she added, with a wink. "Miss Barney. Sunday at two, if you can. I'll write down the address."

Rue Jacob

An entire roomful of women—many of them beautiful, most of them stylish (though not always in the latest modes) and all of them interesting-looking and talking a mile a minute to one another.

"Rather extraordinary, isn't it?" Dolly Wilde smiled at the obvious amazement on Lucienne's face.

"It is! I've never seen so many women talking, rather than being mute and decorative. Not that everyone here isn't decorative, I mean."

"It's true," Natalie added. "Normally, one does not see so many women talking to each other, unless it's a sewing party with a lot of babushkas gossiping."

"Oh, we have our gossip," Dolly assured her. "Djuna writes it all up for us, don't you?" She turned to a striking, dark-haired woman seated nearby, wearing a tailored suit and a beautifully eccentric turban-like hat.

"Do I now?" she replied rather coolly, lifting her narrow eyebrows. "And who have we here?"

"Allow me to present Lucienne and—another Natalie. They are mannequins de la maison de Mlle, and I invited them because their heads are not at all empty, and I thought they would enjoy the change of scene."

"Indeed." The woman called Djuna looked at them curiously. "I think Mlle is a great genius, as it happens. Her frocks are as poetic as anything I've written. I wish I could afford to shop there—but who can?"

"Antique aristocrats and bankers' mistresses, mostly," Lucienne answered, taking a sip of the green absinthe cocktail that had somehow appeared in her hand.

Djuna burst into a lovely melodious laugh. "You're right—not a wax mannequin at all."

The next hour passed in an intense, sparkling whirl. The busy hum of many conversations, punctuated by the soft, controlled pop of champagne corks, the tinkle of ice and the pouring of tea—all suddenly seemed to hush at a new, late arrival: Sally. She was radiant in an ivory chiffon afternoon frock with floating panels, a large-brimmed hat pulled low so that just a peep of her blonde bob and her huge new pearl-drop earrings showed. She was carrying a bottle of Veuve Cliquot, decorated with a huge silver bow, and a bouquet of white roses, and a path seemed to clear automatically so that she could present these to the hostess.

Before handing over her gifts, Sally tucked the flowers in the crook of her arm and put out her hand for a handshake. "Hello, you must be Miss Barney," she said in English. "I'm Sally Lafayette. It was so kind of you to invite me today."

Clearly baffled but charmed, Natalie Barney, petite and plump and dressed *à l'amazone*, gazed at the lanky creature before her, while all over the salon, whispers and hisses were heard: "Presumptuous." "Dillettante." "Poseuse!" "Who does she think she is?"

"Well, that was rather fun, wasn't it?" Sally said to Natalie and Lucienne as they shared a cab afterward. "Although I never got to see Miss Barney's Temple de l'Amiti-ay"—she gave the words an American accent— "Her other friends kept waylaying us and interrupting."

"Oh really?" Natalie said drily. "Imagine her having *other* friends—when you are so clearly the most worthy of her affections."

Lucienne smothered a giggle behind her hand.

"What?" Sally asked, looking at each of them. "I was just trying to be a good guest. Cerise said I should bring a bottle and flowers—Americans never show up empty-handed to a party."

"Oh, of course, it's her money—that's why you can spend it like water," Lucienne said. "But, you know, you're not American, or even English. 'Hello, I'm Sally!' Everyone thought you were ridiculous, with your debutante frock and extravagant gifts."

"Well, that's just silly. Look, why are we fighting—we're not fighting, are we? I've been looking forward to spending some time with you. Shall we go get a drink? And I also want to pass along the most wonderful invitation: Cerise and Garry want us to come to Venice with them. Don't say anything—just think for a minute."

"All right, I've thought for a minute," Natalie said almost immediately. "What a terrible idea! What about work?"

"Oh, come on, you know it's slow right now. I'm sure Mlle would give us a leave of absence as long as we're back by mid-February. Think of all the wealthy women we'd be impressing as we stroll Piazza San Marco in our smart *taillures*! She might even send some new party frocks along with us. And besides . . . Venice!"

"Psh, been there. A dreary, decadent place with those stagnant canals," Natalie grumbled.

"So cynical—what's wrong with a little decadence? And Lucienne's never been there, have you?"

"No—and it's supposed to be very beautiful, isn't it? But . . . I don't know. Where would we stay?"

"The Masseys are taking a villa, with lots of room. Oh, I do wish you'd come. I don't really . . . want to be alone with them."

"Oh? Oh . . . !" Natalie rearranged her position so that she was squarely facing Sally. "Listen, ma chère, I don't think you know what you've gotten into. I thought it was a bad idea from the beginning, and I see I was right."

Sally sighed. "You can't really say, 'I told you so,' when you've never said a thing. Subtly reproachful looks don't count. But . . . I think you're right. There's something a little unstable about Cerise that makes an immortal version of her . . . well . . . frightening. It just occurred to me the other day that now she can turn others. And Garry may be more frightening. Sure, he's a mortal, but he has a level of intensity I've never seen. It's pretty clear both of them expect me to be part of a ménage à trois."

"*Bozhe moi*, these Americans," Natalie muttered. "All right, listen, ma chère, we will help you figure out how to deal with this. I make no promises, and I don't want to go to Venice, but I'll try to think about what you should do. You'd better be getting back now, hadn't you? You can drop us here and take the cab."

"Darlings . . ." Sally began, imploringly.

"I don't want a drink; I want my own armchair," Natalie said firmly. "Au revoir, cherie." She tapped on the driver's window, motioned the cab to the curb and hopped out, followed by Lucienne.

Propelled by her irritation, Natalie clicked rapidly down the block, reaching the corner before she noticed Lucienne had fallen behind. "What is it, Loulou?" she asked, when her friend had caught up; "you look so *triste*."

Lucienne, in fact, was on the edge of tears. "I hate all this discord—it makes me so tired. And . . . I want to go to Venice."

"Oh, darling, of course you do—it's a beautiful place. But we don't have to go with those people—that would just ruin it."

Maison Massey

Sally was pleased to find Garry and Cerise out when

she returned. They're dear and generous souls, she thought, but it is delicious to have some time alone. It was too early to change for dinner or even cocktails, so she slipped into silky smoking pajamas and established herself on a chaise longue in the salon.

Daydreaming, blowing smoke rings and fretting just a bit about Natalie's intransigence, she was startled when the butler showed in a guest, a pretty young man in white flannels.

"Oh. Hello," Sally said, stretching indolently. "I'm Sally. Are you an American?"

"Yes, I'm afraid so. I'm Alan Marsh—my cousin was a schoolmate of Garry's and . . ."

"He told you to look them up. You're a . . . poet? Or perhaps a painter . . . and you came to Paris because . . ."

"Because one *must*, obviously." The young man stepped forward to light the Turkish oval which Sally had fitted into her green bakelite holder. "Yes, I am a poet—or trying to be one, anyway."

"No, don't say that," Sally said, exhaling scented smoke. "You must say you *are* a poet, or you're done for." She peered at him through the monocle she'd appropriated from Edouard. "You look rather poetic —you're quite pale."

The young man blushed. "Yes, I was a sickly child, and I've never been much of an athlete. But I've never thought of that as an asset . . ."

"Oh, it is though, in certain circles. Come, sit here." She sat up straighter and patted the end of the chaise. "I won't bite." She smiled, feeling her teeth tingle.

He sat down, returning her smile a bit nervously. "Aren't you one of those vampires? Are you sure you won't bite?"

"Well . . . I might. But not yet. I know what you need —a cocktail." She sprang up, giving him a passing pat on the shoulder, and drifted over to the bar in the corner of the room. "Let's see—gin, Lillet, Pernod, lemon, a bit of cognac, a dash of bitters . . . oh look, there's fresh ice in the bucket, what a well-run household! And we need just a touch of something unexpected . . . Amer Picon, there we go, that's a lovely rosy color. I do like colorful drinks, don't you?" She plied the shaker vigorously and poured the result into two small, stemmed glasses, which she carried carefully back to the chaise.

"Cheers, Alan Marsh," she said, sitting close beside him to clink their brimming glasses.

"Cheers, Sally . . . I don't know your last name."

"Lafayette, but it doesn't matter."

"You know, I've been trying to reach Garry and Cerise since I've been here—it's been two weeks— but they're always engaged. Today I just decided to take my chances and come by. Do you think they don't want to see me?"

"Oh no, I'm sure it's just that they're frightfully busy. We're all off to Venice soon, you know."

"Venice! Oh how I'd love to see it!"

"Well, you must come then. They're taking a villa with tons of room. It would be awfully fun if you were there. You must ask Cerise to invite you."

"Oh, well, um . . ."

There were sounds from the hall just then, and Cerise herself flung open the double doors. "Sally dear, you're back!" she said with a mischievous smile that froze suddenly. "Oh. Who's this?"

"This is Alan Marsh. He's a poet, and a dear friend of Garry's cousin—I mean a cousin of . . . oh, never mind. He's lovely; I've invited him to come to Venice with us."

"Have you?" Cerise said, with a cool, quizzical look. "I see. What are you drinking—you'd better make me one. Mr. Marsh—" she veered toward where he was sitting and held out a limp hand. Unsure whether to kiss or shake it, he did neither. Cerise gave him a perfunctory smile, though it still came across as radiant. "Why don't you go and have a look around Garry's studio; he'd like that. He'll be back soon. Just through those French doors and across the garden— you can't miss it."

"Oh . . . I . . . thank you," the young American

stammered. Clearly aware that he was being dismissed, he headed out into the garden.

Sally had applied herself to the cocktail shaker again and handed Cerise a brimming glass.

"Now," Cerise said, as firmly as a large mouthful of icy alcohol would permit; "darling, I know we've become very close, and Garry and I think of you as family, we honestly do. But that doesn't mean you *are* . . . or even if you were family, that doesn't mean you can issue invitations on our behalf. We know a lot of people, and I know it must seem as if we have all Paris at our parties, but we're actually very careful about who we have join us on special excursions, like to Venice. It's true that we're taking a good-sized villa, but that's our business. You've put me in an awkward position with this young man—whom we don't know at *all.* That invitation was just for you, do you understand?"

"Of course, cherie," Sally murmured, wondering how she could ever confess that she'd invited her two friends.

En route

Two weeks later, they drove to Venice—five days on the road in Garry's enormous Delahaye, with orchids in the car's crystal bud vases.

Sally did not particularly enjoy automobile travel and sat in the back with her eyes closed and her stomach churning. At least her conscience was clear—she'd received a brief note from Lucienne ("Not coming with, sorry, bon voyage.") so she had no explaining to do to Cerise. Alan Marsh had disappeared the same day he'd come, with vague assurances that he would try to make his way to Venice and "look them up."

Which left Sally exactly where she didn't want to be, en route alone with Cerise and Garry, all three of them in handsome pale-gray wool traveling suits run up by Garry's tailor.

"Here's a nice-looking country inn," Garry said, pulling into a gravel drive somewhere near Aosta. "I know you girls won't want any lunch, with your slimming regime, but why don't you stretch your legs while I pop in and grab a sandwich?"

Cerise linked her arm in Sally's and moved toward the shade of some dusty poplars at the roadside. "Let's go over here and have a nip." She squeezed Sally's wrist.

"I'd rather not, out in the open. Better to have something from your flask. Anyway, you don't really need any more from me now."

Cerise grinned, showing the tips of her small white fangs. "I know, but it's so much nicer." With a small sigh, she drew her platinum Cartier flask from her clutch purse and took a long drink. She was delicately dabbing her chin when Garry returned.

"I had them wrap something up, so we could get

back on the road. We'll be in Turin by sundown with any luck, and we can . . ." He broke off to eye the two women appreciatively, both of them lean and leggy in their long jackets and knee-length skirts. "Whatever you're doing, keep it up—Cerise has never looked better!"

Paris

Lucienne and Natalie strolled arm-in-arm down the fashionable Avenue Montaigne, looking in shop windows. "Look at that ridiculous pot," Lucienne noted irritably, pointing out a dull green cloche trimmed with a perfunctory bit of ribbon. "I could do much better. Maybe I should take up millinery."

"Oh my dear, I don't think so—it's actually work, you know. With sleep and nightlife, when would you find the time?"

"Never mind, it's just an idle thought . . . though I may not want to stay at Mlle's forever. Well, certainly not literally!"

There was no response to this; turning to look, Lucienne was surprised to see Natalie staring straight ahead, her eyes wide, unseeing and brimming with tears.

"Darling, don't be upset—I mean, obviously, no mortal occupations are permanent for us, but I'm not making any sudden changes. We're all having too much fun—well, I'm not so sure about Sally these days, but . . ."

"No, that's not it at all," Natalie interrupted. She stopped walking and turned to face her friend. "I'm upset, or maybe relieved, or maybe confused—I've had a letter from Vladimir. He's leaving Russia. He still believes in his revolutionary ideals, but he says—or implies, really—that the situation there is . . . unsatisfactory. He wants me to meet him in Berlin."

"Berlin—how absurd," Lucienne said with an immediate Parisian reflex.

Natalie bit her lip in a way Lucienne had never seen. "I think . . . he cannot come to Paris right now. Perhaps he is being watched. But he wants to see me . . . and I want to see him."

"Oh! Well then, you must go."

Lucienne saw Natalie off at the Gare du Nord on Tuesday and spent the next week surprising herself. The atelier was basically deserted. Mlle was off in Morocco seeking inspiration, and it seemed the first time in years that Lucienne was able to fill her days completely as she chose. She found herself rising a bit earlier in the day, taking long walks, sketching, and completely relishing her solitude. A few times, she lunched at the Ritz, where the young female cook had been so kind, and she always ordered and praised the provençale seafood—she breathed in the lovely aromas, nibbled a bit and had the rest packed up to feed to stray cats. In her explorations, she found an importer of brilliant Chinese silks, which she cut and stitched into long scarves and large rosettes to embellish her plain beige or black suits.

In the evenings, she sometimes went to the cinema and once found herself next to a sweet-smelling young man who was delighted to embrace her as she took imperceptible butterfly sips at his throat. But she avoided the dance halls and nightclubs they'd frequented as a trio, and most nights stayed home reading novels and sipping bottled hemoglobin from the supply in the ice box.

However, by the second Thursday, she felt in need of a break from her own company. She slipped into some black satin and cabbed over to La Florida for a cocktail and some dancing. Sitting at a table with a slightly doctored Negroni, she spied a familiar face coming her way.

"Dolly! How nice to see you," she said, but as Miss Wilde came close, it was truthfully less nice—she was looking decidedly rough around the edges. Lucienne took in her crumpled frock, torn stocking and badly smeared makeup. "Are you all right?"

"Ah, Lucienne, how kind of you to take an interest. I'm all right, love, just a bit of a bad patch. May I just sit by you quietly for a bit?"

"Of course! Let me get you something—a cocktail? Glass of bubbly?"

"Don't fret, love, I'm fine." She sat, rather heavily, with none of her usual grace.

Just then, a young man whom Lucienne had been eying as eminently nibble-able came over and asked her to dance. After a glance at Dolly, who nodded enthusiastically, Lucienne accepted and they glided off across the polished floor. They danced well together; a hot foxtrot and a maxixe were followed by a tango, during which Lucienne was able to get a quite satisfactory taste of her partner. She returned to her table to find Dolly asleep with her chin propped on her hand, drooling slightly.

"I'm awake," the Englishwoman said abruptly, rousing herself mid-snore. She opened her eyes wide and looked at Lucienne for a moment. "Lucy darling, I wonder if I could ask something of you—I need to get away . . ."

"Away?"

"She's thrown me out. Miss Barney. Or maybe I've thrown myself out. I've been sleeping . . . here and there. But I need . . ."

"Oh." Lucienne was doing a rapid mental calculation of what it would take to make the flat presentable, un-incriminating. "Of course you can stay with us— with me—for a while."

"You're too kind. But actually what I mean is, I need to get out of Paris for a while. Have you ever been to Venice? Would you like to go?"

They went back to the flat, where Lucienne went in first and reconnoitred. Being a naturally tidy person, she had left nothing noticeably amiss. Dolly had a bath, slept in Sally's bed and was amazingly fresh the next day, and not the least bit dismayed that there was no food on hand. Lucienne outfitted her with some of Sally's more loosely cut things—Dolly was a tallish, large-boned woman—and by late afternoon, they were dressed, packed and at the station.

Dolly already had her first-class ticket and insisted on paying for another. Lucienne was still quite in the dark about what sort of straits Miss Wilde was in, but finances did not seem to be a problem. Dolly ordered a bottle of champagne from the steward once they'd settled in their compartment, and as they clinked glasses she looked at Lucienne earnestly.

"I'm so glad you're here, darling—we're going to have a marvelous adventure, I know. But I must warn you, I may be rather odd at times. As I told darling Sally once—how fun to be wearing her clothes!—we all have our secret lives. But Lucy dear, if I get off at one of our stops and don't come back to the train, just go on without me. I'll catch up, somehow."

Paris - Berlin

Through the many hours on the train, Natalie found herself reading, over and over, the ending of

Vladimir's letter:

"I realized, Natalie, that the only way to endure immortality is to work, as I've always worked, for the good of the people— and to see you, at least every so often. May I keep seeing you, now and then, please?"

Directions followed, if she should choose to heed them—he would be at the Cafe Metropol every evening from five to eight, for the next three months, or until she came.

Vladimir was paler and thinner, but he looked well, intensely handsome, in fact. As Natalie approached his table—until this moment, she hadn't quite believed she was going to see him, despite his precise directions—he stood and smiled at her, radiating a warm, passionate glow. She stopped a few feet away, just looking at him, and then they were in each others' arms, holding each other like long-lost family. They ordered some red wine and sat close together, looking almost constantly into each others' eyes, a classic vignette of reunited lovers. At one point, Vladimir started to talk about Russia, and Natalie put a finger on his lips.

"Don't tell me about that yet—I just want to look at you. You look amazingly well. I was so worried, after . . ."

"Were you?" He gave her a searching look. "I was never quite sure what your intention was, that day.

Not that it matters, now—I'm so grateful for the gift you gave me. Of course, I wouldn't have survived if it weren't for your friend Lucienne. How is she, by the way?"

"Lucienne? She's very well, but—I don't understand. I know she went to see you in the hospital. I couldn't go, I was too . . . ill. Out of my mind, really. But she said you were going to be fine."

"And so I was, after she helped me." He told her about the transfusion. "I think I would have died without her blood."

"Bozhe moi." Natalie went paler than usual. "So you're not really 'mine.'"

"Vampires, mortals—none of us really belongs to another, do we?" Vladimir smiled gently. "The most important thing is that we will always be friends."

"Yes," Natalie sighed. "Vladimir, I'm so sorry I didn't . . . handle things better . . . I never meant for you to suffer . . ."

"The suffering was necessary. I went to some very dark places in my soul. And when I went back to Russia—it was very difficult at first, learning how to live this life—you might say I became more a 'man of the people' than I'd ever been." He grinned, showing a glimpse of fang.

Natalie's brow furrowed. "Oh Vladi, I don't know if you can forgive me for acting so thoughtlessly."

"It has been painful, often, I can't deny—but I thank you for the pain, the blood, the deeper understanding. For eternity."

He was smiling broadly, which Natalie found odd until she realized he wasn't looking at her but at someone behind her, a beautiful dark-haired girl who came up to their table and perched on an empty chair with a quizzical look.

"Natalie, this is my dear friend Theresa. Theresa, this is my old friend, Natalie, from Paris."

Theresa looked at Natalie with good-natured curiosity. "Vlad, why do you call her your *old* friend? She looks younger than me! What age are you, Natalie, eighteen?"

Vladimir laughed and put an arm around Natalie's shoulder; after a minute, his other arm wrapped around Theresa. He looks comfortable being with two women, Natalie thought, too comfortable. They made polite conversation for a few minutes like any new acquaintances, the hidden currents of blood between them left unspoken.

"Paris . . . such a romantic place," Theresa said at one point. Her eyes were fixed on Vladimir, and she did not seem to be thinking of Paris at all.

"I should go," Natalie said, slipping out from under Vladimir's arm. "I want to go have a shower at my hotel."

"I'll walk with you," Vladimir said quickly. "Just give

me a minute; there's something I have to talk about with Theresa." He turned toward the young woman; their heads were already close together and the effect was unbearably intimate.

"No, please don't bother—I'm fine. I'll see you another time."

"Tomorrow. I'll be here."

Paris - Venice

For the most part, their train journey could not have been more pleasant. Dolly had her quirks, certainly, like opening champagne at any time of day, including with their breakfast coffee, but she was a charming companion, always ready with amusing observations and intricate, entertaining stories. She looked extremely elegant in Sally's wardrobe, with a well-groomed freshness that made it hard for Lucienne to believe she'd seen her so scruffy only two days ago. Even their visits to the dining carriage, which Lucienne had been apprehensive about, were agreeable. After cocktails, Dolly would be completely absorbed with her hearty dinner, taking only the briefest notice of Lucienne, though she jocularly named her "Mlle Biftek" for her habit of dining on small, bloody steaks.

Next afternoon, they were due to arrive in Mestre, the last stop before their arrival at Santa Lucia station in Venice. Dolly had again been most delightful all through a long bubbly breakfast that segued into a peaceful sunny afternoon. They sat across from each other, reading, wearing dark glasses against the bright light. ("It doesn't do to get all squinty, darling," Dolly said, handing Lucienne an extra pair.) They pulled into Mestre around three, and Dolly announced she was going to stretch her legs on the platform.

"Don't get lost, darling," Lucienne said with a smile.

"Do you want to come? You can keep me out of trouble."

Lucienne laughed and yawned, snuggling into her plush seat. "Oh, I don't think so, I'm so comfortable." Surreptitiously, she touched her flask; she was looking forward to having a nice, long drink without having to sequester herself in the lavatory. "See you in a bit."

It was one of the longer stops, but 45 minutes later, Dolly was nowhere in sight, and Lucienne was now regretful and alarmed. Despite Dolly's warning at the start of their trip, she'd shown no signs of any odd or unpredictable behavior. She'd 'stretched her legs' at other stations and Lucienne, seeing her walk up and down deploying a long amber cigarette holder had realized it was her tactful way of enjoying a smoke without filling their compartment with fumes. But now—where on earth was she, Lucienne wondered, scanning the rapidly emptying platform. The whistle blew, doors slammed, and the train emitted its first loud chuffs and slowly began to move. And then, at the far end of the platform, two running figures came into view: Dolly, followed by a man. Even from a distance, Lucienne could see that Dolly was dreadfully disarrayed, her dress torn and one shoe either missing or broken, making her gait uneven but still fast enough to keep ahead of her pursuer. But not fast enough to catch the train, which was just starting to pick up speed. Lucienne hesitated only a moment and then pulled the emergency cord.

The conductors were ferociously cross, but the sight of a lady passenger—and one known to tip lavishly, at that—in very obvious distress, mollified them. Her attacker had fled at the first sight of uniformed personnel and Dolly was helped, breathless and bleeding from a gash on her arm, to her compartment.

"Oh Lucienne, ma chere fille, you shouldn't have done that," she gasped, leaning heavily on the doorframe. "But I'm glad you did."

"Let's get you cleaned up. And then I think you'd better tell me what's going on."

Dolly smiled faintly. "But my dear, I've told you—or maybe that was Sally—we all have our secret lives."

Venice

The palazzo was exquisite—crumbling a bit here and there, but that only added to its antique elegance. A serene morning room faced a quiet canal, and they breakfasted there each morning before delicious days filled with long walks, sumptuous museums and chic cafes, followed by glittering evenings of parties, music and midnight gondolas back to their own private dock. This morning found the three of them in matching white silk pyjamas, Cerise and Sally wearing dark glasses to mute the daylight from the lace-curtained windows. Garry, who was irrevocably skinny, ate heartily; Cerise and Sally had long cool glasses of delicious blood orange juice (winking at each other as they added "tonic" from their flasks), copious pots of coffee and violet- or carnation-scented cigarettes. Cerise, who had never smoked before, had taken it up to help quell her desire to let her fangs out and feast at inappropriate times. These times were so frequent that she now had an enormous collection of beautiful cigarette holders to match every nuance of her wardrobe and mood; this morning it was mother of pearl with silver filigree.

"Sally," Garry said, folding his morning newspaper, "could you come into the library when you've finished breakfast? There's a manuscript I'd like your opinion on."

"Oh, er, of course—though I'm no expert, on anything really." She glanced at Cerise with unspoken inquiry.

"I don't suppose it's anything I need to see—Garry's old papers make me sneeze. You go ahead, darling; I have a massage scheduled."

"Take your time; finish your coffee." Garry went in through the French doors.

He sat writing at a huge ebony and elm desk, wearing a jazzy-patterned silk dressing gown. "Come over here, Sally dear. I want to show you something." He laid down his fountain pen and straightened the sheets of paper.

"All right, but if it's poetry, I warn you I don't know the first thing about it," Sally said, crossing the room hesitantly.

As soon as she was within reach, Garry grabbed her wrist, which was still bruised from Cerise's frequent nibbles. She winced and he dropped it immediately, but put an arm around her waist.

"I'd never want to hurt you, dear Sally; I care for you too much. I know that you and Cerise have been doing . . . things. There's no way a beauty tonic could produce the amazing change in her. And I want to do those things with you too." With his free hand, he pulled his belt loose, and his robe fell open, revealing his slender, naked body sporting a vigorous erection.

Sally drew back, trying to willfully summon a blush to her pale cheeks. "Oh, Garry. Is that the 'manuscript' you wanted to show me? I'm sorry—I'm very fond of you too, but what a dreadful cliché."

"No, no," he hastily wrapped his robe again. "I don't mean to rush things. Here," he handed her a sheet of paper. "I want you to read this. Take your time. I've been thinking about this for a long while, and I can wait."

Garry's pen strokes were clear and decisive, and the paper was of the highest quality. But the words turned her stomach: *"We, Garrard Massey, Cerise Callahan Massey, and Sally _______"* (followed by spaces for three signatures), *"being of sound mind, hereby declare that we love each other so deeply and ineffably that, having once consummated that love, we will have no need to live out our lives into middle and old age. We intend to end our lives, by our own or each others' hands, freely and willingly, on this day of ___________, 1929."*

"Isn't it silly that I don't even know your surname? This is just a draft, of course; we'll be sure to fill it all in properly."

Sally backed away slowly, not wanting to take her eyes off Garry. However, he merely stood smiling mildly, arms crossed, looking at her with a pleased, hopeful smile.

"Garry," she said carefully, "I do care about you very deeply, and I'm enormously grateful for all the kindness you and Cerise have shown me. This . . ." she gestured vaguely toward the paper which she'd laid back on the desk, "this is so . . . I need a little time to think, to get ready . . ." She was backing toward the door; Garry nodded and smiled reassuringly.

"Of course. As I said, I can be patient."

Just as Sally reached the door, though, he sprang forward, crossing the room unbelievably fast. "Don't go," he said urgently. "Please don't go. I want you, now."

"Garry, please, I can't." Sally twisted painfully in his grasp. "Please let go, you're hurting me."

"I don't want to. Don't make me hurt you." He pushed himself between Sally and the door.

Gathering extra strength—she could feel her fangs coming out—Sally grabbed his shoulders and flung him back, away from the door, so hard that he fell against a bookcase. She heard what sounded like a cascade of heavy volumes and Garry swearing, as she slipped through to the foyer.

Her decision—not really a decision but an undeniable impulse—was that she had to leave at once. She didn't dare run upstairs to get her things and risk being trapped by Garry, or perhaps even worse, have to explain anything to Cerise.

Thankful for her hosts' slapdash ways and their rather relaxed Italian help, she grabbed up a light wool coat that had been flung over a hall chair. On the table near the front door was Cerise's clutch purse, and she grabbed that too before slipping out, closing the heavy door as quietly as she could. She didn't like stealing from her hostess and friend, but she'd need a few lire to get away somewhere. She could always send Cerise's things back later.

Without looking back at the palazzo, summoning all her strength, Sally ran. Down cobblestone alleys, through small quiet squares, across bridges. Good thing it's just a myth that we can't cross water, she thought with a fleeting smile. She didn't feel safe stopping until she'd crossed half a dozen canals and reached an obscure and perfectly unfashionable district of small workshops and laundry-hung tenements. Gulping deep breaths, she sank onto a bench outside a tiny church, shivering slightly, but only from the chilly stone, not the proximity of holiness (another myth, she thought wryly). She wrapped Cerise's coat around herself more tightly; shoving her hands in the pockets she found, in one, a pair of thin kid gloves and in the other, a good-sized packet of folded banknotes. This was fortunate, because Cerise's purse, which she now opened, held no money apart from a few coins. There were other useful contents, though, which she made use of: a comb, mirror, lipstick, powder and a long narrow scarf, which she tied jauntily around her neck, hoping to make her ensemble of coat, pyjamas and satin slippers into something resembling an avant garde fashion statement, rather than clear evidence of her hasty escape. Smoothing the slightly too-small gloves over her long fingers, she sat up straighter, squared her shoulders and gathered her thoughts. There looked to be enough cash in her pocket for a third-class train ticket back to Paris, if she could figure out how to get to the station.

Sally had felt invisible while running, but now, walking briskly and attempting to appear purposeful, she felt eyes on her from all sides. Her face grew tired from the effort of directing fierce and stony glares at men who assumed they knew what pyjamas under a coat meant, alternating with sweet smiles at frightened children clutching their mothers' hands. Her Italian was not very good—she'd been relying on Garry's fluency, she realized—and the Venetian dialect was further confounding, but she finally managed to compose an intelligible question for a blue-uniformed policeman.

"The train station? Santa Lucia?" He launched into a long, detailed answer, much of it incomprehensible, but the gist was clear; she would have to go to Piazza San Marco to catch a water taxi.

San Marco at mid-day, the heart of fashionable tourist Venice, was just where Sally did not want to be, but there seemed to be little choice—not knowing the train schedule, she wanted to get to the station as soon as she could. Walking straight across the piazza toward the quai seemed too exposed, so she kept to the shadowy arcades along the perimeter, though these had their own perils, as clusters of foreigners, mostly English and American, browsed the charming shops and sat in cafes. Two or three times she heard her name called, by people she'd met at parties—she forced herself to remain calm, flashing a bright smile and a brisk wave to convey that she was delighted to see them but was on her way to a pressing engagement. She had just decided that it would be better after all to head out into the piazza when she again heard, "Sally!" but in a particularly urgent and very familiar voice.

It was Lucienne, waving frantically from a cafe table, well inside the elegant Caffe Florian. Sally realized Lucienne could not have spoken loudly enough to call her in a normal way; the voice had gone directly to her mind. Dear, beautiful Lucienne—and beside her was Dolly Wilde, looking very chic in a cream suit of Mlle's, or rather, of Sally's.

Over a couple of cognacs, Sally gradually calmed down enough to describe some of her predicament. Lucienne had never seen her friend anything less than unflappable and was shocked at her terrorized behavior, the way she ducked into the corner of the banquette when anyone passed close. Dolly, however, was perfectly serene and accepting; crises were part of life, as far as she was concerned.

"But you can't leave," Lucienne exclaimed in disappointment; "we've just gotten here."

"Oh, but she must, don't you see," Dolly said with calm sympathy. "What a horrible situation, though I can't say I'm entirely shocked, from what I know of those people."

"What do you mean?" Sally looked a bit wild. "Why didn't you warn me?"

"Oh my dear, you weren't listening to anyone. Never mind. The thing to do is take the Paris train that leaves at six—there's an earlier one, but it's much slower. We should have one more drink, and then you can come with us to our pensione, and I'll return some of your wardrobe which Lucy was kind enough to lend me. You really shouldn't travel in pyjamas," she smiled. "Then we'll see you to the station."

Sally groaned softly and put her head on the table. "I just want to get away now."

"I know, darling." Lucienne tried to hide her shock at seeing the state her bold friend was in. "But Dolly's right. Imagine if someone were to recognize you and see how poorly dressed you were. Word might get back to Mlle, and she'd never forgive you."

Sally raised her head with a rueful smile. "I thought I'd put myself together rather well—I'll bet pyjamas for daywear will be *everywhere* by next season. All right, one more drink and we'll go to your pensione. Dolly, can I borrow your—I mean *my*—hat?"

Sally felt it first as they left the cafe, but she assumed it was her own hyper-sensitivity, until Lucienne and Dolly exchanged glances. There was a nervous, urgent buzz of conversation spreading from the tables closest to the piazza, with a crackle of newspaper pages turning.

"What on earth is it?" Dolly wondered aloud and strode into the square to find an urchin peddling papers. She returned with a folded special edition of the *International Herald-Tribune*, and her always pale face was paper white. Without speaking she showed them the headline: "American Socialites Dead in Apparent Suicide Pact."

Beneath a file photo of Garry and Cerise, beaming at a charity gala several years back, ran a brief article which was clearly withholding many facts. Found today by a maid calling them for lunch,   Garry dead, blood everywhere, exact cause of death still being investigated, Cerise missing and presumed dead, apparent suicide note being studied by experts. And toward the close, "A young Frenchwoman, known only as 'Miss Sally' and believed to be an intimate friend and houseguest of the couple, is being sought for questioning."

"Mon dieu," Sally whispered. "This cannot be happening. I have to disappear."

Sally was pacing, as well as she could in the over-furnished pensione room, smoking furiously, reading and re-reading the creased newspaper with its maddeningly brief story. She paused mid-step, chewing on Lucienne's long ivory cigarette holder.

"Where the hell is Cerise? She can't be dead, can she?

Though I suppose if Garry shot her . . . Anyway, they don't have my last name!" she exclaimed, eyes wide. "When I get on a train and they check my passport, they can't prove it's me!"

"Maybe not, but how many young Frenchwomen named Sally do you think will be traveling today? They'll at least take you in for questioning."

Sally crumpled suddenly into a chair, head in her hands. "You're right—what a disaster! And it's only a matter of time before they learn all the details. The servants only knew me as Signorina Sally, but all those people I met at parties—someone will remember . . . Oh Loulou, I was such a fool to get so involved with them. Oh, poor Cerise. Poor mad Garry. If I'd known it was going to end like that, I should at least have grabbed some more valuables, enough for first class." She laughed, ruefully. "Dolly tried to warn me, if only I'd listened. Where is she, anyway?"

Lucienne shrugged. "One of her mysterious errands. She said she was going to get supplies—food, maybe."

"It's hard, isn't it, spending so much time with mortals. The occasional meal is fine, but they're *always* . . ."

A key turning in the lock interrupted her, and Dolly opened the door, startlingly accompanied by a thin, shabby-looking man of curiously non-descript appearance and hard-to-determine age.

"Hullo dears, got your clothes on? Don't worry, Paolo is completely trustworthy. He's here to help."

Paolo, thus introduced, said nothing. He was carrying a battered valise which he set down on the nearest bed and snapped open, removing a slightly crumpled, brown, man's suit jacket. He approached Sally, looked her up and down carefully, and held out the jacket, clearly signaling that she should put it on.

"*Bene*," he said, nodding at the fit of the shoulders and sleeves. He unpacked the rest of the valise and handed Sally a pile of clothes—men's underwear and shirt, all slightly grayed with age and imperfect laundering, brown trousers and vest to match the jacket. Suppressing a hint of squeamishness—she could tell the clothes were clean even if they didn't look it—Sally retreated to a corner screened off by the wardrobe door.

When she emerged, to quiet applause from Dolly and a squeak of amusement from Lucienne, the still taciturn Paolo gestured her to the seat at the dressing table, where he draped a towel over her shoulders and, quite skillfully, deployed small sharp scissors to give her the shortest haircut of her life.

"Goodness, I thought an Eton crop *was* boyish," Sally said, running a hand over her head.

Paolo said something in Italian to Dolly, who nodded and knelt beside Sally at the dressing table. "Darling, you've got to take off your makeup," she said, offering some cotton pads and cold cream, "and then I'll help you with your tie. Hmm . . . one bit of illusion," she added, once Sally's face was bare. Taking up a small brush and her pot of kohl, she added a bit of bulk to Sally's fine eyebrows and a faint shadow along her jaw and upper lip. "There. Now try the shoes—Paolo brought two pairs."

"He's . . . a sort of angel," Sally said in wonder. The second pair fit almost perfectly.

"You don't know the half of it. He's got you a fake passport too."

"But, who is he?"

"He's my drug dealer. He knows the way around everything here."

Sally's eyebrows shot up, as if Paolo had been described as a white slaver. "What does he want in return?"

Dolly laughed. "Don't worry—I'm a good customer, and we're old friends. You can send him some money from Paris. Now, you should get to the station. Go with Paolo; he'll help you stay inconspicuous." She smiled again at Sally's uncertain look. "Really, he *is* an angel."

The valise was packed, minimally but convincingly, with an extra shirt and a pair of socks. Sally pocketed her money and inspected her new passport. It was French, and her name was Jean Vallotin. A slouchy fedora completed her attire, and Paolo tucked a pack of cheap cigarettes into her breast pocket.

Dolly explained, "Smoke as much as you can, to make your voice hoarse, and try to have a cigarette in your mouth when you need to answer any questions—then you can just grunt." She kissed Sally's cheek and then carefully wiped her lipstick away. Lucienne gave her a long hug.

"Au revoir, cherie—bonne chance!"

As they stepped out into the dusk, Paolo again gave her one of his unnervingly appraising head-to-toe looks. Sally looked back at him with a questioning frown, which made him smile widely.

"You'll do," he said. "Here, I'll take your bag until we get near the station. We need to walk fast." He led the way through a maze of streets, where Sally was relieved to see neither tourists nor policemen, just ordinary working people shopping or heading home. She had no trouble keeping up with Paolo's stride, and before long, the bulk of the station loomed ahead.

Paolo stepped into the doorway of a closed shop and set down the valise. "*Allora, il mio ragazzo . . . .*" He slipped a cigarette out of a pack in his pocket. "Got a light?"

Sally patted her pockets in confusion. Paolo pulled a box of matches from his own pocket, lit up and then tossed the box to Sally. "Keep 'em." She realized this was her cue to light her own cigarette and did, suppressing a cough as she inhaled the harsh tobacco.

"I won't come in with you," Paolo said. "The ticket counter is just through there and to the right."

"I appreciate what you've done for me. I'll be sure to send thanks and some money after I get back."

"Eh," Paolo waved her words away. "Signorina Dolly has helped me when I was in a tight spot—I am happy to help her friend."

"But truly, I am so grateful. I'd like to . . ."

"Lower your voice," Paolo interrupted gruffly.

Sally looked around, startled. "There's no one around," she whispered.

"I don't mean quiet—I mean, more *maschile*."

"Oh, right," Sally said in her deepest register, a light tenor. "Well, thanks then, Paolo." She clenched her cigarette in her teeth, picked up the battered valise and gave a sort of salute.

"*Va bene*," Paolo said as he turned and melted away.

Stazione Santa Lucia

Sally strode briskly to the ticket window, waited in a short line and was crushed to find that the direct train to Paris had left twenty minutes ago. The next one was at midnight. Discouraged, she purchased her third-class ticket and trudged to the station cafe for an espresso, remembering to keep her voice gruff as she ordered. A crisply uniformed policeman sat at one of the tables. Sally tilted her hat slightly lower and forced herself to slouch past him to a corner seat, where she slumped over her cup in what she hoped was an inconspicuous way.

He's just here for a coffee; there's no reason for him to suspect me of . . . anything, she told herself, just as the officer—rather young and good-looking—finished his drink, got up and walked past her table, giving her an interested if passing glance.

Merde, I'm not cut out for this undercover stuff, Sally told herself. She busied herself with lighting another of her vile cigarettes and tried to occupy her mind with composing a history for her persona, Jean Vallotin. I'm a . . . salesman? Improbable, I look too young to be sent abroad. Why would I have come to Venice—and look at my soft hands. I'm a student, that's it, on holiday, looking at art, maybe visiting a cousin . . . The espresso took effect and Sally began to feel more hopeful. She was Jean, a respectable Parisian youth though without much money, on a brief improving jaunt to Italy where she'd . . . *he'd* . . . also visited a cousin . . . homeward bound. She finished her coffee and cigarette and rose with an almost jaunty step, practically whistling, for a stroll round the station.

Lounging by the newsstand, reading an illustrated magazine, a man—very well-dressed but with a somehow shifty gaze—watched her pass with unmistakable interest.

Hm, Sally thought. Normally, I would think, *Watch out for that one.* But he can't possibly know I'm a girl, can he? He must be someone who simply takes an interest in the passing scene. Or perhaps he's some sort of petty criminal, looking out for a mark. In any case, how refreshing not to have to think about sex.

The station, though large, was not supplied with many diversions: cafe, newsstand, waiting areas. There was a first-class restaurant, for which she had neither interest nor funds, and which probably required possession of a first-class ticket. And there was a special ladies' waiting room, which appeared quiet and comfortable—just where she'd like to curl up, she thought, peering longingly through the glass door. But she must remember the point of this exercise and not think about how much she yearned for a hot bath and her own silky clothes. She looked quickly away from the ladies' lounge door and caught the eye of a young man about her age, who winked as he passed. Oh dear, now she was a voyeur!

She tried a bench next—hard enough that there was little chance of dozing off—and then decided she'd better acquire something to read, or at least hide behind. Approaching the newsstand, she saw the same loiterer, and to her dismay he was now reading today's paper, a late edition which carried Garry and Cerise's pictures on the front page. Relax, idiot, she told herself; Even if you weren't in disguise, there's no way a random stranger would know who you were. As she walked past him she glanced his way with what she hoped was a neutral, civil half-smile, and after purchasing a French paper, pretended to be immersed in it as she headed back to a bench.

The French daily had not yet picked up the Massey story, she saw with relief. She turned quickly past the fashion pages and folded the paper open to the sports news. She was congratulating herself on her cleverness when, to her horror, the lounging man from the newsstand sat down beside her.

"You're French," the stranger said in French, with a glance at the newspaper. "That explains it. Got a light?"

Sally quickly shook off a moment's paralysis and dug in her pocket for her matches. She was about to strike one when she remembered Paolo's action and handed the box over. Men didn't light cigarettes for each other. Or did they? This man didn't shake out the flame but held it out toward her, gesturing toward her pocket. "Are you smoking?"

"Er, sure, thanks," she said, quickly pulling out a cigarette and accepting his light before he handed the matches back.

"So, how's your team doing?" The man indicated her newspaper.

"Oh," Sally gave a short laugh, keeping her voice gruff. "To tell you the truth, I'm so tired, my eyes aren't even focusing. I just . . ."

"Wanted a paper to hide behind? I know just what you mean." Taking the paper from Sally, he opened it out as if he were going to point out a news item. "Is it true what they say about French boys?" he said as he grasped her thigh.

"No!" In her surprise, she forgot to be gruff at first, but quickly collected herself. "I'm afraid you are very much mistaken, sir," she said solemnly in her deepest register.

Far from being embarrassed or offended, the man at her side looked at her with what appeared to be extreme amusement. Then he stood up, made a mocking half-bow and said, "Pardon, *mademoiselle*. I didn't realize you were *une vierge*." Touching his hat in sarcastic salute, he strolled away, turning back once to grin at her.

Confused and shaken, Sally stood up, grabbed her valise and started walking rapidly and blindly, pushing through one of the exits. Outside in the cool evening air she felt calm enough to smile over the encounter —the man hadn't seen through her disguise, she realized; he was just taunting a young man with being too "miss-ish" to respond to his advances. So much for not having to think about sex!

She pulled out her flask and took a long drink, sighing with satisfaction.

"Hey, brother," said a cracked Italian voice nearby, and a ragged, stooped, elderly man stepped from the shadows. Despite his thick dialect, his meaning was clear: "Could you spare a taste of that good stuff?"

"Oh, er . . ." Sally realized the 'grandmother's health tonic' line she usually used might be less credible in this context.

The clochard was tactful about her hesitation, however. "That's okay—how about a cigarette?"

Gratefully, Sally insisted he take two—he lit one and carefully placed the other one under his cap before slipping away.

The young policeman from the cafe walked past and gave her a more-or-less routine glance. Her flask was still in her hand and Sally suddenly realized she didn't know if she was violating some statute about drinking in public. She pocketed it quickly, took an ostentatious breath of fresh air and went back into the station.

Inside the echoing, high-ceilinged hall, Sally again wondered how she was going to pass the next several hours. She now had to avoid the newsstand, where her recent companion had again taken up his spot. She had lost her newspaper in the scuffle and didn't want to present herself, sitting unoccupied, as a target for further unwanted company. Lost in thought, she was passing the doors to the first-class restaurant when a woman coming out almost collided with her. Tall, buxom and wrapped lavishly in scented gray furs, she was a well-preserved grande dame of fifty or so, moving with an imperious air of entitlement. She seemed about to deliver a scathing rebuke when she took in Sally's appearance, and what she saw appeared to change her scowl to a smile; she raised her eyebrows and said in a flirtatious tone, "You must watch where you are going, young man—we could have ended up in quite a compromising position."

"*Perdone, mi scusi, signora,*" Sally stammered, remembering belatedly to lift her hat.

"Hmph." The woman narrowed her eyes, seeming about to take offense again. "Oh, you're foreign, aren't you. *Français?*"

"Oui, Madame." Sally found herself, as if it were dictated, tasking the woman's hand and raising it to her lips. "Jean Vallotin, *étudiant, à votre service.*"

With a warm, rich laugh, the woman switched to French. "You may call me Contessa. Come and have a drink—I see I've frightened you half to death." She placed a gloved hand on the door of the restaurant.

"But Madame . . . la Contessa . . . was just leaving?"

"Oh, I was just too hot. Here, take my furs. Come,

M. Vallotin." Loading Sally with her furs and not even looking back to see that she was followed, the contessa re-entered the restaurant.

Over glasses of burgundy, it was decided that Sally—Jean—should accompany the contessa, traveling first-class to Berlin, departing at nine. "Really, I must insist," the contessa decreed, in between chapters of her life story and her pressing concerns. "Frankly, my dear, between the pederasts and the thugs, a gently reared youth like you doesn't stand a chance in third. I suppose when you came out to Italy you were with your tutor and it all seemed a great lark, but trust me, on your own you won't find it so jolly. Where is he, anyway, your tutor—staying on to pursue his 'research'? Well, we all know what that means."

After the strain of hours of keeping her wits fine-tuned, Sally found it supremely restful to be in the contessa's company. She was so forceful and sure of herself; she supplied all the conversation—all Sally had to do was agree. Berlin instead of Paris? Why not? It was as good an escape, or better, as no one would be looking for her there. And hadn't Lucienne said that Natalie was in Berlin? Perhaps, somehow, they might meet. In any case, the contessa seemed prepared to take Jean under her wing and pay his way —a perfect way to elude any connection with the Massey affair—in exchange for merely his . . . company.

Venice - Berlin

Sally had, of course, traveled first class before, but she'd never been in such a large, luxurious private compartment. The contessa had a sort of suite that must have occupied half a car: a huge sitting room with its own private dining table; two bedrooms and two baths; plus a small maid's room. The maid had already boarded and unpacked all of her mistress's travel requisites and favorite things for the overnight trip. Champagne was chilling in an ice bucket on the table, flanked by an array of elegant nibbles (on the contessa's own gold-rimmed, monogrammed travel porcelain), as well as framed photographs and a large bouquet of red roses in a silver vase. Two silky-furred pekingeses, named Milk and Honey in English, sat together on a velvet sofa, looking around with the smug air of cosseted pets.

"Pooky and Mooky, did oo miss Mamma?" the contessa cooed, dropping the handbag, muff and cigarette holder which encumbered her to embrace them. The amber holder fell to the floor with an audible crack which made Sally cringe and stoop to collect it, but the contessa shrugged. "Don't bother, I have dozens. Come, darling Jean, you must meet my beloved doggies."

The dogs could smell Sally's true nature, of course, and shrank away from her. The contessa fussed over them for a bit. "Silly doggies, what's wrong? You usually love mamma's beaux. Really, they adore young men," she went on; "They roll over for them like complete sluts—but perhaps they can tell you're a *gentleman*. You are, aren't you, Jean, despite your awful clothes? What happened, did your tutor steal your good suit? We must get you some new outfits in Berlin."

Sally hoped she was being only as taciturn and abashed as any young man in this predicament would be. Presently, the contessa asked her to open the champagne, and the situation became easier to deal with as the contessa subsided onto the sofa, glass in hand and dogs on her lap. There was still an hour to go before the train departed, but Sally could only agree that it was a good deal more comfortable in this lavish suite than roaming the station, trying to avoid police, men on the make and prying eyes. The only eyes she had to deal with here, the contessa's, were already half-closed, as the older woman savored her Veuve Cliquot.

"Jean, would you be an angel—find me a cigarette and a holder, in my bag."

"Of course, signora la contessa." Sally rooted in the bag as directed and found the requested requisites.

"Come, sit by me, my dear, and tell me all about yourself." The contesssa patted the velvet cushion beside her.

Sally found it surprisingly easy to invent a history:

genteel but impoverished parents, a wealthy uncle who took an intermittent interest in Jean's education, a desire to accomplish something in art or *belles lettres*, though of course the family wished for something more practical, such as law or business. She was starting to feel that she really knew her character rather well and was quite pleased with her performance when the contessa reached over and gave her knee much the same sort of squeeze she had gotten from her admirer in the station.

"That's all very well, Jean, but you haven't told me what I really want to know—what about your *education sentimentale*, your *petits amours*, your girlfriends?"

Sally felt the fizzy sensation she sometimes experienced in lieu of blushing, but the answer came to her almost immediately. "Ah, signora la contessa, a gentleman does not kiss and tell."

The contessa laughed delightedly and gave her knee another squeeze. "I knew you'd say that." She leaned in, positioning herself for a kiss, which Sally had no choice but to give. She tried to make it forceful but not insistent, long enough but not too long, an end in itself rather than a prelude to further action.

Sitting back, Sally played "overwhelmed" in what she hoped was a believable way. "Will you excuse me for a moment . . ." she paused, subtly glancing toward the doors that led to one of the bedroom-bath suites, "my dear contessa." The older woman beamed at the endearment.

Sally was careful to lock the door before taking a deep drink from her flask—which was distressingly close to empty. Running the taps and occasionally splashing a bit for verisimilitude, she stared at herself in the mirror. Mon dieu, the woman's a complete vamp, utterly focused on what she wants. Am I like that? she wondered, widening her eyes and allowing her fangs out for a moment. The train shuddered suddenly and made a series of sounds and small movements; they were getting underway. Sally retracted her fangs and composed her face—how naked she felt without lip rouge. The cosmetic 'stubble' which Dolly had applied looked a bit smudged now, unconvincing at close range. She carefully wiped away all but a shadow at the jawline. Then she combed her minutely short hair, patted on a bit of 4711 water and returned to the contessa.

Her patroness had also been composing herself—she turned to Sally with a Sobranie in a long onyx and gold holder, waiting for a light.

Jean lit her cigarette, poured them both more champagne and sat in a chair facing the sofa with a wide smile, raising a glass to toast, "Our journey."

The conductor entered the compartment after a polite knock; the contessa managed the exchange and upgrade of Jean's ticket with minimal fuss, and the conductor merely smiled and said, "Ah, *francese,*" perhaps with a faint wink, upon examining Jean's passport. Sally let out a deep, relieved breath as the door closed—she had left Venice.

As the train glided through the evening, Sally found she had a genuine, growing admiration for the contessa. True, she was a bit imperious, a bit vain— and quite obsessed with her ridiculous dogs—but she did not simply rely on her position and wealth; her steady stream of conversation showed charm, curiosity and intelligence, making her companion feel like a sought-after guest rather than a stray or a gigolo. Floating above the situation, distanced by the effects of the champagne, Sally felt a sort of professional admiration for this really rather plain, middle-aged woman who cast a considerable glamour.

Champagne and hors d'oeuvres segued seamlessly into a small luxurious dinner served by the maid and a steward: consommé, filet mignon and stuffed mushrooms, with a famously excellent wine. Sally ate carefully, relishing the rare beef and tolerating the other elements. Presently, after a long postprandial chat, the contessa pushed back her chair, stood and returned to the velvet sofa, patting the spot beside her.

"Jean darling, come sit here and make love to me. You would like to, wouldn't you? I don't think you're one of those Greek-style boys, although I find I can talk to you almost like another woman."

Sally stood and bowed. "À votre service, madame la contessa." She realized she'd known her escape ticket, and the luxurious safety of this trip, would have to be paid for, after all.

"You should know, madame . . ." Jean paused, caressing the contessa's cheek, "that I like to take things very slowly. *Mille baisées, s'il vous plaît.*"

"Ah, you French are so romantic," the contessa said with a good-humored sigh. "Just make sure I don't fall asleep before we get to the point."

A long interlude followed; Sally kissed as she never had before, discovering an unexpected repertoire of osculation. She did not neglect caresses and compliments, and now and then, as a breather, poured them each a glass of champagne from the new bottle which seemed to have magically appeared at some point.

The hour grew late and at one point, the contessa wriggled impatiently. "Jean. You *will* take me, won't you? You're not just a tease . . . or a fairy . . . or a virgin? Here, let me help you." She reached for Sally's trousers.

Jean pounced, forcefully, pinning the contessa's shoulders against the sofa. "I don't need any help." Without thinking, the fangs came out, and Sally began to feed. She pulled back after a minute, not going too far.

The contessa looked up at her with wide, unfocused

eyes. "Oh, Jean darling. Oh, you're marvelous. Don't stop!"

Sally took a few more sips, helping her benefactress into a light swoon. Then she loosened the contessa's clothes, covered her with a light shawl, kissed her drooping eyelids and retreated to the guest bedroom. She had not yet begun to undress when she heard a small sound from the sitting room and looked in: the maid was fussing about, gently patting the contessa's cheeks. Wordlessly exchanging smiles and gestures with the maid, Jean picked up the unconscious woman—lighter than her imposing bulk would suggest—and carried her to her own bed.

It was mid-morning, bright and cool, when the maid tapped at Jean's door with a cup of coffee. She said something, obscured by shyness and a regional accent, which Sally guessed meant that the contessa was waiting.

The motion of the train through the night had thrown Sally into a deliciously deep sleep, but it was briefer than she would have liked, and her head still swam a bit from the unaccustomed amount of food and wine. But after inhaling the coffee's fragrance, she washed and dressed again in Jean's shabby clothes, adding a handsome dressing gown she found on a hook. She crossed the drawing room to the contessa's bedroom door and knocked with trepidation.

"Come in, darling Jean!" The contessa's voice was warm and vigorous; she sat up in bed wearing a lavishly ruffled, rose-colored peignoir and looking quite radiant. "Come sit by me, *caro*." She extended her hand for a kiss and patted the satin coverlet. "I'm sorry to have to wake you so early, but we reach Berlin in about an hour—in fact, I'll have to start my toilette in a moment. I just wanted to see you, to say how magnificent you were last night. I confess, I may have been a bit tipsy and a bit drowsy—the details are more vague than I would like—but I feel utterly marvelous. For such a young lamb you seem to know quite a lot about pleasing a woman."

Sally smiled, still a bit dazed, and kissed the contessa's hand again. "You see me as a young innocent, but I assure you, parts of me are very ancient. I am delighted to have pleased you, madame. It has been an enchanting journey." With a bow, Jean left her to dress.

Berlin

Freshly bathed, lightly scented with vetiver and with a "close shave" faintly shadowed at the jawline, Jean Vallotin began to dress—cream-colored silk-knit underwear, a hyacinth-blue shirt with gold and opal cufflinks, the trousers of a beautifully-cut gray cashmere suit. Before the mirror, Jean carefully arranged the neckwear which, born of necessity, had become a signature style, already being emulated by the most modish Berliners: a soft foulard ascot tied under the shirt collar, just peeping above the top button with a hint of color and pattern, and a wide four-in-hand tie of rich, iridescent brocade below the collar, secured with a gray pearl stickpin and tucked into a snug waistcoat.

Sally had devised the double neck-cloth system after realizing what a giveaway her slender throat and complete absence of adam's apple might be. Now, slipping on her double-vent jacket, smoothing it down, arranging her pocket square and selecting a boutonnière from a vase of pale chrysanthemums, she smiled as she remembered how desperate she'd felt to get back into girl's clothing on their arrival in Berlin. She'd had it all planned—her ever-so-gentlemanly and heartfelt little speech to the contessa before a lingering kiss on the hand, a bow and goodbye . . . until she'd spotted her photo on the front page of every paper at the station newsstand. She didn't even need to lean close to see her likeness, with a blonde bob and gauzy frock, or to read the headlines: "Parisienne femme fatale sought in Massey deaths!"

Luckily, the contessa was too preoccupied in supervising her mountain of luggage and reading messages to give much attention to the newsstand or to Jean himself.

Finally, she turned to her traveling companion: "Jean darling, you *must* be my guest here. Take the hansom back to my townhouse—do make sure they're careful with my luggage—and make yourself at home. And I want you to visit this shop" (a name scribbled on a page torn from her notebook) "and get yourself some clothes—everything you need. Put it on my account. I insist! It will give me great pleasure. Let them fit you out completely. I have to deal with some business in the country for a few days—such a bore —but *you* should enjoy Berlin. Au revoir, my sweet; I'll see you soon."

There had been no choice, really, but to agree. And life, these past few days, in the contessa's grand townhouse, had been nothing but agreeable.

Sally smiled again at Jean's flawless reflection before picking up a pale gray homburg, gray suede gloves and an ivory-topped walking stick and heading out for a stroll.

Three days had already been enough for Jean to adopt a routine: a French or English paper and a packet of Sobranies from the corner newsstand, and then on to a deeply shaded sidewalk table at a chic cafe on Kleiststrasse. Coffee, pastry, cigarettes in a short, pale-amber holder and the news occupied an hour or so—longer if one of the giggly young ladies for whom Jean raised his hat chose to sit and chat.

A stroll followed—always in the shade, perhaps into a gallery or shop, sometimes accompanied by one or two of these giggly young women. Sally, though she tried to be as taciturn as possible (sometimes pleading linguistic shortcomings) had become more accustomed to using the deepest register of her voice and, with a natural understanding of what would please young women, was a quite effective flirt, to her own amusement. She also knew perfectly well how to keep things light and non-committal. By early afternoon, she always headed back to the townhouse alone, to freshen up.

Taking care of her specialized needs proved surprisingly easy. On her first evening in town, she slipped out late, wearing the shabby old clothes she'd been so eager to rid herself of. She walked steadily away from the crowded center of town, until the air cleared and she was able to follow her nose. She'd done the same thing on first arriving in Paris, years ago, and just as she had then, she soon found what she was looking for—a small butcher's shop with a yard in back where a red-glazed lantern burned. The gruff but helpful butcher sold her several stone bottles of fresh blood, "for a special soup my grandmother makes."

In the privacy of her large, comfortable room, Sally was able to relax and nourish herself at leisure. As far as the servants knew, Jean lunched out and then returned for an afternoon nap, which was indeed how Sally spent the rest of the afternoon.

Evenings began, pleasurably, with a maid knocking gently at the door and then bringing in a decanter of cognac—clearly thought of as essential to a gentleman's preparations. Jean was approved of by the staff, being quiet, courteous and extremely undemanding (unlike *some* of the young men the contessa had installed). What they didn't realize was the extent of the houseguest's accommodating nature —the morning outings, although enjoyable, were primarily to allow the maids to clean the room, and to avoid the gossip that sleeping til late afternoon would have entailed.

Downing a last swallow of cognac, Jean winked at his reflection, impeccable in white tie and tails, a red carnation the only spot of color. The tailor had suggested the option of a more modern, less formal, dinner jacket, which could be worn with a homburg or boater, but upon consideration, Jean opted for conservative evening dress, wanting to be correct to the point of invisibility. Sally found that with some adjustments, the high wing collar and the cut of the coat provided both flattery and camouflage.

Cafes, cabarets, salons and soirées—Berlin's fabled nightlife did not disappoint. In a tiny club where women dressed as men, featuring a brilliant, velvet-voiced chanteuse, Jean was scrutinized with excited interest, but ultimately dismissed as "echt mann." In other tiny clubs where men danced with men, Jean danced with a few, perhaps led one outside to whisper under a streetlight and take a surreptitious sip, but left disappointingly early. In vast cabarets, to a soundtrack of unintelligible political satire, Jean lounged at a balcony table with a party of vivacious young things, drinking champagne, sniffing white powder and nibbling necks here and there, as they roared with laughter. On thronged sidewalks, Jean strolled slowly, examining details of dress and footwear, perhaps inviting a green-booted woman to step into an alley for a brief grope and gulp.

The early-rising staff would raise amused eyebrows and smile discreetly, as the young man let himself in at dawn.

The fourth morning in Berlin, Jean received a telegram from the contessa: She would be back at the weekend (it was Thursday now) and hoped Jean would wait for her arrival, if at all possible. Sally carried her coffee into the small, paneled dressing room and pondered. Her escape from Venice with the contessa had been so timely and fortuitous that she'd hardly questioned the nature of the implied relationship—she was staying here in this luxe townhouse (with beautiful new clothes and a pocketful of spending money) as if she were a young gigolo picked up on a whim. With the contessa away, it was a delightfully comfortable situation, but soon the mistress of the house would return and so would complexity.

Sally selected a shirt and tie from Jean's supply—the tailor had been insistent that the contessa would want him to have a dozen of each. Today she chose a rose-striped shirt and a magenta tie, reasoning as she tied her supplementary ascot that the daring colors would only reinforce her masculine credibility. She reflected on the now double nature of her masquerade, her passing in society as someone she was not. After years of presenting herself as a normal, mortal young woman (moving in whatever sphere allowed her to be most independent and, ideally, fashionable), a few days of playing at being a young man about town was refreshing and only barely a challenge.

The housekeeper smiled and the parlor maid sighed as M Vallotin left the house: *Such* an attractive young man, and so well-dressed and well-mannered. Obviously his clothes were on the contessa's account —she always wanted her companions nicely turned out—but he wore them with such flair and originality. A magenta tie, a rosebud in the buttonhole! And always so polite and cheerful— though he seemed a touch preoccupied this morning.

Aware of his audience, Jean turned down the sidewalk swinging his walking stick jauntily, but his thoughts were troubled. Should he stay until the contessa's return, or plead pressing business of his own and leave by tomorrow?

The shady tables at his customary cafe were taken, so he continued down the avenue to another place he'd been wanting to try, a comfortable, old-fashioned spot. Settling in with a pot of coffee and the paper— the Massey story seemed to have faded from international notice, Sally was pleased to see—Jean gradually became aware that he was being observed. It was a familiar sensation by now, and not the least bit of clairvoyance was needed to guess that the gaze fixed on him would belong to a young woman. Jean remained immersed in the *Berliner Tageblatt* and allowed her to approach. Bolder than most, she sat down at his table and angled herself to peer into the gap between newspaper and hat brim.

Forced into politeness, Jean half-folded the paper and removed his hat, saying in rudimentary German, "Good morning, miss; can I help you?" whereupon the young woman tilted her head, peered at him and burst out laughing. "C'est toi!"

"Natalie!" It was more the habit of the last few days than presence of mind that kept Sally's vocal register low. Quickly, she placed a warning hand on Natalie's and leaned in close as if for a passionate tête à tête.

"Talia darling, I'm *so* glad to see you. *Don't* say my name, I'm on the run from a frightful situation in Venice, and I'm seriously incognito. My name at the moment is Jean Vallotin."

Natalie leaned back, grinning hugely. "Jean, dearest, you look so very handsome! Finish your coffee and then come with me—I know a place where we can talk."

"How did you know it was me?" Sally asked, a bit

anxiously, sitting on the lumpy bed in Natalie's cheap hotel room. "I seem to have passed perfectly everywhere . . . unless people are just humoring me."

"Oh no, not at all—you are flawless as a young man, I'm sure of it." Natalie still found it hard not to smile at her sheer joy in having found Sally, but she sensed that her mirth was upsetting her friend, and she tried to suppress it. "No, I was sure you were a very handsome young man, but something—the shape of your head, the set of your shoulders, your nose—was so familiar. Then, when I looked really closely, I saw those little freckles on your left cheek that show up when you don't wear powder . . . So, tell me all about this . . . situation."

Natalie hadn't been reading the news; Sally brought her up to speed, and then Natalie told her about meeting Vladimir. "He's—well, he's brilliant as a political thinker, an organizer. His goals are admirable. But personally . . . he's a bit of a shit. Maybe it's just that he's new to being a vamp, but he's got this girl, Theresa, and probably a half-dozen others more or less on tap. Each of them thinks that she's the only one to share something very special and deep with him."

"Well . . . isn't that what *we* do, more or less?" Sally challenged. Natalie shrugged.

"When he wrote to me, he seemed so desperate to see me, but he hardly seems to care that I'm here. I think he just wanted me to give him my blessing and to let me know that he's happy to have been turned. Though, in a way, he's still angry at me—I admit, I handled things badly. He never fails to point out that he would have died without Lucienne's help."

"Sounds messy and unpleasant. Why have you stayed?" Sally asked.

"Oh, I don't even see Vladi much, but it's interesting here, isn't it? I've been enjoying myself. And what about you?"

Sally grinned. "Jean's been quite the popular man about town. But now I have to figure out what to do about the contessa."

It was late, and the cabaret felt somehow tired, but Natalie insisted they had to stay. "Really, Jean, you of all people will love this performance. I've been here almost every night. Bodo is too brilliant to miss."

"All right . . . if you're sure we shouldn't move along."

"Darling Jean, don't tell me you don't love Das Polonisches Club! All the romantic young men look like Chopin, and all the brilliant young women look like George Sand."

"Yes, I know—the boys are all intense and passionate like Vladimir, and the girls are all comparing collar buttons. And they're all thinking, what is a perfectly fashionable but rather dull gent like me doing here? Honestly, I haven't seen anyone

I'd want to bite, if I were starving, in the last hour."

"Patience, mon vieux," Natalie said, laughing at her friend's discomfort. "Ah, now—look!!"

Eugeniusz Bodo, squeezed into an hourglass corset and heavily made up under a blonde wig, took the stage. The orchestra woke up as it dug into the hot arrangement, and a luscious throaty voice—perfectly poised between both genders and the distillation of the pure concept of sex—began the most marvelous song: "Seksapil."

Bodo was tall and broad-shouldered, but it was impossible to think of the singer as anything but "she." She projected an aura of feminine irresistibility that made whatever lay beneath her sculpted gown irrelevant. More than that, Bodo had a magnetic sparkle that left no doubt the performer was the most desirable creature in the world—and at the same time, deliciously self-aware and self-mocking, fully conscious of the delightful absurdity of the audience's response to the artifice on display. The song, itself an irresistibly endearing "ear worm," was all in Polish, except for the refrain, "Sex Appeal," but the bouncy rhythms, chewy consonants and piquant delivery made it clear that it was a witty celebration of the singer's charm. At the end, Jean could only leap to his feet and join Natalie and the rest of the audience in shouting, "Brava!!"

"Alors, you're right, she's *formidable*. "Geniusz indeed!" Jean said when the performance was over.

"But now, perhaps, we can move on?"

"Ah, but here is Vladimir! I've been dying for you to see him," Natalie said. "Vladi!" she waved. "And Theresa! And . . .?"

"This is Greta," Vladimir—sullen, soulful and pale, just as Sally remembered him—introduced a young blonde who was clearly part of his entourage.

"Vladi!" Natalie was still effusive. "Did you catch the show? Isn't Bodo divine?" (This was answered with a shrug.) "Vladimir, ladies, this is my friend Jean, from Paris."

There were greetings, bored and disaffected on both sides. Jean kissed the hands of Vladimir's companions, who clearly had eyes only for the form of romantic intensity the Russian was purveying. Champagne was ordered; Jean settled back with a sigh. Natalie was in a tête à tête with Vladimir—who had looked gratifyingly annoyed to find her with a male friend. Jean overhear the contessa's name, and a few minutes later, Vladimir's hand was on his arm.

"Come smoke a cigar with me, old chap. Ladies, you'll excuse us for a few minutes?"

They made their way through an overcrowded saloon and then out to the sidewalk. Jean declined a cigar and took out his own cigarette case and a short ebony holder.

"Jean Vallotin," Vladimir said with a smile, looking his companion up and down as he blew a smoke ring.

"So pleased to meet you. If I'm not mistaken, we have much in common."

Jean looked more closely, trying to read Vladimir's eyes. "If you mean the affections of dear Natalie, I assure you, we are only friends."

The Russian laughed heartily. "No, no, dear fellow—I am not hinting at any jealousy. I owe a great deal to the beautiful Natalie, but . . . both of us have moved on with our lives. Still, without doubt, we will be important to each other . . . forever!" Vladimir grinned in a particular way which showed a bit of fang, and then pulled a silver flask from his pocket. It was far from subtle, if one knew what one was seeing. He offered the flask inquiringly to Jean.

"No, thank you. I have my own."

"Aha, I know you do. But actually, there's a reason I wanted to talk to you—we always recognize each other, don't we, old man? no need for guessing games —but seriously, Natalie says that you know—rather *well*, I understand—the Contessa Montenegro. A great lady. My dear fellow, I would be more grateful than I can say for an introduction. The contessa is legendary, you know. If I had her backing, the doors she could open . . . there's no telling what I could accomplish. I'm sure Natalie has told you all about my work."

Jean smiled with startling radiance. It was so simple. "But that can be arranged quite easily. Why don't you and Natalie come to tea at the contessa's townhouse, Saturday at five."

The contessa's return, Saturday morning: a whirlwind of furs, flowers, messages, scent, packages and pekingeses going mad with excitement. Eventually, though, everything was in its place—the contessa and Jean in the private sitting room (with Pookie and Mookie on a loveseat), with a light repast, a pot of coffee and a bottle of champagne at hand. The contessa sank into a sofa with a happy-to-be-home sigh.

"Don't sit down just yet, darling Jean—I want to drink you in! How well you wear that nice suit. I hope you enjoyed your visit to the tailor."

"You've been generous beyond measure, madame. I have never dreamed of such beautiful clothes."

"It's a pleasure to see you in them—you're a born dandy. Now, why don't you open the champagne and tell me all about your adventures. I hope you've been enjoying our *Berliner lüft*."

Jean felt able to answer quite truthfully, "It is the most exciting city I have ever encountered."

The contessa beamed and questioned further, and Jean was happy to supply selected details of the past few days and nights: the floorshow at the Europahaus, the colorful crowd at El Dorado, the extraordinary cocktails at the Eden Bar, the Kit Kat

Club with its table telephones.

"The other night, I saw the most extraordinary performance, a Polish actor . . ."

"Eugeniusz Bodo! Oh yes, he's quite famous, and divinely talented. Who would think anyone could capture the essence of the opposite sex so well." To Jean's amazement, the contessa stood up and did her own, rather credible rendition of "Seksapil," projecting a glamour that belied her age and travel-weariness. She broke off with a laugh. "That's all the Polish I can manage."

They sipped and nibbled and chatted through another hour or so. With some trepidation, Jean confessed that he'd invited guests for tea, assuring her they could be put off if she was too tired.

"Nonsense, my darling. That's exactly what I would like—meeting some of your young friends. We can both have a little nap before then and be fresh as daisies. I do like a bit of a lie-down in the afternoon, don't you?"

"Oh yes," Jean answered, truthfully and enthusiastically, having gotten up earlier than usual to greet the contessa.

"Well, come along then, darling." The contessa rose, and pulled Jean up into an embrace. "Come and make love to me—and then we can have a lovely little sleep. Darling . . ." she took Jean's hand firmly and led him toward her bedroom, "I can't wait to see you by daylight." She reached for Jean's cerulean tie, murmuring, "So handsome . . ."

Jean laid a hand on the older woman's. "My dear contessa, there is something I have to tell you . . ."

"Oh my sweet, don't give it a thought. Did you have some *petits amours* while I was away? What could be more natural? But I'm sure, as a well-bred young gentleman, you took proper precautions—I'm not bothered in the least. After all, you're here *now*, that's what matters."

Shirt buttons were being undone; there was no way around it. "I'm so sorry, madame—I have to tell you . . . I'm not a man."

The shirt was open; the contessa paused, her hands on the silk undershirt. Smiling, she shrugged. "Oh well—nobody's perfect!"

Sally knew that Natalie would be perfectly charming —her centuries of experience supplied her with effortless manners for any occasion. But Vladimir was a surprise. Obviously he had a great deal of appeal to women—hence Natalie's initial attraction, bordering on obsession, and his present entourage of pale, infatuated girls. But she had never seen him like this—polished, elegant and at ease. His energies might be devoted to proletarian revolution, but he seemed perfectly happy amusing the contessa in her exquisite drawing room.

Following their afternoon "lie down," which was the closest thing to genuine human passion Sally had experienced in years—really quite astonishingly thrilling—the contessa had amazed her further by declaring that "mere details" made no difference in her feelings for Jean. The contessa expressed no curiosity about what had led Sally to present herself *en travestie*; she was not asked to reveal her real name or circumstances. She simply remained Jean Vallotin, *etudiant et jeune homme*. The contessa understood very well that she herself was a mere "interlude in a young man's life," and that Jean would doubtless need to resume his trip back to Paris at some point, but she hoped they might spend a few days in each others' company, and she would "always treasure the sweet memories . . ."

So, rested, bathed and freshly dressed in a smart afternoon suit, Jean sat comfortably sipping tea, a bit bemused, while Vladimir proceeded to charm the contessa.

The little dogs, however, were a problem. They had become just barely able to tolerate Jean, but now the presence of two additional vamps threatened to drive them wild. Natalie had the presence of mind to announce that she was allergic—she even managed to produce a convincing sneeze—and with much ado, Pookie and Mookie were sent off with the butler.

Vladimir took advantage of the disruption to re-seat

himself beside the contessa. Along with removing the dogs, the butler had brought a tray of aperitifs to fortify their teatime, and the hostess now applied herself, rather gaily, to pouring out little drinks for each of them. Vladimir leaned in intimately to clink glasses with her: "To Madame la Contesssa's eternal youth and beauty," he toasted, with an appallingly indiscreet wink which the contessa was luckily too charmed to notice. The two of them continued to trade murmured comments, confidences and compliments, while Jean and Natalie chatted politely, now and then raising an eyebrow at the seduction underway.

"*Such* a fascinating young man," the contessa said later, as she and Jean had a small dinner à deux. "The Russians are a remarkable people, don't you think? And Vladimir—so brilliant and impassioned! With the right support, he could be a real hero of his nation."

Not knowing quite what to say, Jean produced a neutral smile—possibly too neutral.

"Oh, look at you, you're jealous!" she laughed. "Not that you've any right. You and I both know we've been merely a diversion for each other. Perhaps after all it is time you were heading back to Paris, cheri. Perhaps with your little friend, Natalie."

"I thought you wanted us to spend a few more days together, Madame la Contessa?" Jean said carefully. "I am so grateful for your kindness . . ."

She produced her rich, throaty laugh. "Oh, Jean darling, don't worry—you've sung for your supper quite beautifully. You have no debt to me. You can set out tomorrow, if you'd like. I'll be with my dressmaker most of the day anyway, and then I'm dining with Vladi at l'Âme Slav."

Sally showed up at Natalie's room the next day with two suitcases full of haberdashery—the contessa wanted Jean to keep all the clothes and "wear them with pleasure." It was a warm day, and she was wearing the vest and trousers of the gray suit with an open-collared shirt and a soft neck-cloth. She hadn't taken the time to execute her usual meticulous details of artifice, and her appearance was ambiguously androgynous and by no means unattractive.

"I've been given the boot," she told Natalie, recounting the contessa's conversation.

"And some very nice brogues," Natalie punned with a grin. "They look deliciously comfortable. Do you think you'll go on dressing *en travestie*?"

"I suppose I may as well—I have all these lovely clothes, and they are rather fun to wear."

"Mm, I can see that—you *are* a dashing fellow, Jean. But do you want to leave Berlin yet?

"Not really . . ."

"Oh, I was hoping you'd say that. Well then, let's

share a room and stay on a while. We're not expected back in Paris until mid-February anyway. But we'll have to move." Natalie pulled out her own suitcases and began flinging clothes into them.

"Move?"

"This may not be the most high-class establishment, but they won't take kindly to my suddenly acquiring a boy friend. Don't worry, we can just go across the street. We'll check in as newlyweds."

Sally raised her eyebrows.

"Or brother and sister, if you prefer, but I don't think they'd buy it. We look nothing alike."

Sally, stripped to silk underwear and sprawled on the bed in their new room, threw a pillow at Natalie. "That was a clever idea of yours, Mme Vallotin—the newlywed thing. They won't think it's odd if we're in bed at all hours."

"Yes, well. I hope it works out, with this cozy matrimonial mattress. I was forgetting how you thrash and snore sometimes."

"I'll try my best to be a still as a corpse." Sally stretched luxuriously and took a long drink from her flask. "Come along, my lovely bride—finish your unpacking later. Let's take a nap."

It was dusk when Sally woke; the room was full of purple shadows and the glare of streetlights came from the gauze-curtained windows. Natalie was already up, sitting at the dressing table. Sally rolled over, took a swig from her flask and then burrowed into the pillows for a few more blissful minutes. The sheets were coarse and the mattress lumpy—in fact, compared with the exquisite guest quarters she had recently inhabited, the room was really rather squalid —but the relief and freedom of being safe and private here with Natalie, not having to hide the most profound part of her nature, so much deeper than mere sex . . "Oh the luxe of it," Sally murmured.

"What's that, darling?" Natalie turned toward her. Sally propped herself up on an elbow, and then sat straight up, eyes wide.

Natalie had been busy with her russet-toned eyebrow pencil, thickening her delicate brows and drawing a perfectly elegant pencil mustache onto her upper lip. She was wearing one of Jean's piqué-front evening shirts with his formal, grosgrain-striped trousers, and had already tied a perfect butterfly bow with one of the freshly laundered white ties. She had pomaded her hair into small stiff waves, with an almost imperceptibly tiny chignon at the nape of her neck.

"Would you mind doing my links, darling?" Natalie approached the bed with arms outstretched.

Sally stared, speechless. "You look . . . ridiculous," she said finally.

Natalie's face fell, but then she turned back toward the mirror and her eyes flashed. "No I don't!"

"No—you're right. Actually, you look magnificent. But . . . the trousers are a bit long on you."

"Pff. I'm barely two inches shorter than you. So, they'll break a bit low—I promise you, no one will be looking at my feet."

"I suppose. But your hair—it looks amazing, and I don't know how you got your chignon so small, but still—unless you *want* people to know you're a girl . . ."

Natalie turned to the mirror again, then picked up a hand mirror and studied her profile and back view. She sighed. Virtually alone among women of fashion, she had never bobbed her hair. Now though, she opened one of her cases and took out the tiny scissors from her sewing kit. "Here—let's have it off then."

Sally took a sharp, shocked breath. "Are you sure?"

"Of course. Just do a neat job. Here, let me put a towel over my shoulders."

"But . . ."

"Don't worry, it's only hair. It will grow back."

"But—what will *I* wear? I've only the one set of evening clothes."

Natalie laughed and gestured toward the armoire.

"Silly—pick one of my frocks!"

Sally frowned at her reflection. "You know what Janet Flanner said about Parisiennes—by day they look like boys, by night like female impersonators." Mascara-enhanced, her eyes were huge in her cropped head; her painted mouth looked odd to her, and she was acutely aware of her legs below Natalie's black satin dress.

"Who's this Janet and what does she know? You look gorgeous."

"A friend of Dolly's. It's a good thing this frock has an up-and-down hemline; you are *not* just two inches shorter than me. And won't the hotel people notice what a different couple we are now?"

"They won't give us a glance now that we've checked in and paid for the week. Here, do you want to try a bandeau on your hair?"

"Argh, I *do* look like a boy!"

"The most beautiful boy! Who cares—let's go turn the town upside-down. We'll switch back tomorrow."

Sally watched Natalie settle the silk top hat on her sleek red head. She wrapped herself in a coat and took her friend's arm. "I say, Nat, you *do* look handsome. All right, let's go."

As they waited for the elevator, Natalie said, "I wonder how Lucienne and Dolly are doing. If you know the name of their pensione, I could send a telegram."

Sally reached over and tapped Natalie's throat. "Sotto voce, old thing. Make your voice deeper, or I'll have to do all the talking."

Natalie coughed and cleared her throat. "Mon dieu, I forgot. Is this better?"

Sally shrugged. "Pas mal. Be sure you don't mention my name if you send a telegram." Her eyes widened suddenly. "What am I doing—I can't go out like this. I'm meant to be incognito."

Nat tugged the wide green satin bandeau a bit lower. "Relax, cherie—this is Berlin. No one knows you here."

As it happened, they had to leave the first nightclub they looked into, when they spotted Vladimir and the contessa. "We look perfect, Nat darling—but not good enough to fool people we've slept with," Sally observed.

"No matter. There's no end of fabulous nightclubs. What about the Wintergarten? It's just up this way."

"Oh yes, I love that place; the band is divine."

The club was crowded and noisy. Sally and Nat squeezed through the crowd, intent on finding a table, unaware of the ripples in their wake.

"Isn't that . . . isn't that Jean Vallotin?" a young Berliner-about-town said, nudging his world-weary girlfriend.

"Who?"

"That dapper French fellow who's been making the rounds for the past week."

"Oh, *Jean*! You mean, just heading up to the mezzanine? Now, that can't be him, he doesn't have red hair."

"No, not the redhead—I mean, with him, in drag."

"You're joking, surely . . ." She lifted the monocle which hung on a silver chain down the front of her black dress and put it to her eye. "I see what you mean, though . . . the profile, the jaw line . . . it *does* look a bit like him. He *almost* makes a pretty girl. But no girl could have such long legs."

"He must have been inspired by Bodo's performance."

"Yes, but . . . Bodo is a true artiste; he creates such a convincing illusion. Jean's doing all right for a brief entrance, but no one would be fooled for very long."

"You're going to wear out your monocle, Dagmar, if you keep staring like that. Why don't you just go up there and take a closer look?"

"Maybe I will." The monocled blonde made a point of drifting casually up the mezzanine and wandering past the new arrivals, who had found a snug table and settled in with cocktails. They weren't speaking to each other, just sipping quietly and listening to the jazz band. Dagmar bumped lightly against their table, hoping to provoke a response, but the girl in the green bandeau just looked up with a half-smile as Dagmar excused herself, and the red-haired young man nodded wordlessly.

"I'm *sure* it's him," Dagmar announced on her return. "And what's more, I think the fellow with him is a girl."

"The French—they're so kinky."

Venice

Lucienne adored Venice, but she was starting to wonder how much longer she could stand it. Her long walks, from late afternoon to late evening, had taken her across most every bridge and into every square, from grand to tiny, bustling to forgotten. She loved the overarching atmosphere of faded elegance and cosmopolitan chic—much as in Paris, she felt that people were appreciative yet incurious. In short, it was a good city for solitude, but she was growing weary of being alone. Like her, Dolly slept into the early afternoon and they breakfasted together, usually sitting over coffee in the Piazza San Marco and watching the diverting scene for an hour or two. But after that, Miss Wilde would be gone for the most part, off on mysterious errands relating to money or drugs (or more prosaically, translating jobs). Lucienne would return to their room a bit before dawn to find Dolly in bed, nestled in quilts, embracing her pillow like a lover.

Dolly was sleeping particularly late, impossible to rouse this morning. They'd been in Venice for almost two weeks, and Lucienne decided they must have a talk about their plans. She left a note asking Dolly to meet her at Florian's.

Settling in at their usual table, Lucienne drew off her gloves. She was wearing black-trimmed beige crepe with black accessories. Waiting for her coffee, she could feel eyes on her from a neighboring table and ventured a careful glance under the small, crimped brim of her cloche. A dark-haired young woman, with a pale olive Italian complexion, prominent eyes and very red lips, was staring at her quite frankly. Though her features were plain, there was something about her that made one want to keep looking. And then there were her clothes. She wore a black knit dress that looked almost shrunken in its snugness, with a scrap of striped scarf at the throat and an odd little cap pinned to her wispy short hair. A huge brooch, of strange abstract design but unmistakable quality, made it impossible to think she was either poor or dowdy.

"Pardon, mademoiselle—you are quite right. I am staring at you." The woman spoke slightly accented but excellent French. "But only, I assure you, because you are so perfectly chic. *Vous permettez?*" Without waiting for an answer, she took the empty seat at Lucienne's table and leaned in to study the sleeve of Lucienne's jacket. "Forgive me, I am so rude," she said, after a moment. "It's just that I am fascinated by how she does it. It's Mlle, n'est-ce pas? From the rue Cambon?"

"Yes. I'm one of the mannequins de la maison."

"No wonder! I wish you worked for me; I imagine anything you wear becomes beautiful. So simple, so . . . *slouchy* and yet . . ." Studying Lucienne's ensemble, she trailed off. "I am Elsa Schiaparelli," she said abruptly, putting out her hand.

"Lucienne Leung. Oh—you have an atelier in Paris. Those trompe l'oeil jerseys! I love those. I'd wear one if . . .if I could."

"Well, *you* at least have an excuse—but you would think the rest of fashionable Paris was under contract to Mlle too. If I don't do better next season, I'll have to close the shop; I can't compete with her empire."

"Mlle has spent many years building up her clientele —she works very hard," Lucienne said loyally.

"And yet, it hardly shows," the other woman said, still studying seams with fascination. Qualifying her ambiguously critical remark, she added, "I mean, she makes it look effortless."

Lucienne was beginning to find the intense scrutiny

uncomfortable and was relieved to see Dolly approaching.

"Mlle Schiap," Dolly nodded pleasantly to the visitor. Lucienne was hardly surprised; Dolly knew everyone. "Excuse us, please. Lucienne my dear, we've got a telegram."

February, 1929

Berlin

Pajama-clad, short-haired and scrubbed as a pair of young boys, Natalie and Sally lounged on their *lit matrimonial,* sipping a liquid breakfast from their flasks.

"That was ridiculously fun the other night, wasn't it?" Sally said. "People didn't know what to make of us."

"That woman Dagmar!" Natalie laughed. "I'm glad she finally came back and talked to us. I thought her eye was going to fall right out with her monocle from staring so hard. You were perfect—you didn't give away a thing—but I know she was still suspicious. Was she one of Jean's conquests?"

"No! I mean, I may have flirted with her a bit, but she's always with that fellow, Fritz."

"Well, I don't know . . . I don't think she'd mind a stolen moment with Jean."

"Not worth the risk—I can't see Jean getting into a fist fight. The best thing, though, was all the people who hardly gave us a passing glance. Or if they did, and had any doubts . . . they didn't care! That's what I love about Berlin."

Natalie stretched luxuriously. "What about tonight? Shall I be Nat again? I must say, I enjoyed it---but I'd also like to go out with Jean and drive all your admirers mad with jealousy. Or we could be *two* gents out on the town . . ."

"Only the one set of evening clothes, remember," Sally cautioned.

"Oh, what of it. You could wear the gray . . ."

"I most certainly could not! *Travestie* is not the same thing as incorrect dress!"

There was a tap at the door just then. "Message from the front desk," a voice called, somewhat apologetically.

"You answer the door, Jean darling, you're more presentable," Natalie whispered, diving under the covers.

Sally grabbed Jean's dressing gown and opened the door a cautious crack.

"Excuse me, *mein herr*," said the bellboy. "There is a caller for you. A . . .lady gives you this note. The concierge didn't like to just send her up. She is . . .*chinesische*."

"It's Lucienne! Please do send her up, immediately."

Kisses, embraces, laughter at the pleasure of seeing each other, and mutual admiration. Lucienne was amazed to see Natalie's shorn head.

"You should see her in tails!" Sally said with a wink. "But tell me—how are things in Venice? Are they still looking for me?"

"I don't think the local police are very worked up about it," Lucienne said. "It's an inconvenience that these Americans had to die in their jurisdiction, but I think they'd just as soon declare it a clear case of suicide."

"Which it was!" Sally interjected.

"Yes, of course. Anyway, from reading the local papers, I have the sense they're ready to just wrap it up. But then, there's this." Lucienne opened her carryall and unfolded an *International Herald Tribune*.

Sally snatched the paper from her and began to read, her eyes growing huge.

"I'm doomed!" she cried, flinging it down. "I'll have to fake my own death, move to Tibet and see you in thirty years or so."

"Oh come on, darling," Natalie said. "It can't be that

bad.”

“Well, actually, it might be,” Lucienne said soberly. “There’s some relative of the Masseys’, a cousin or something, who is calling for a full investigation. He’s offering a reward for any information that can lead him to Sally.”

Sally, sunk in an armchair, head in hands, groaned. “Oh my god—that Alan Marsh fellow; he knows the family somehow, he must have got them involved . . . I don’t know what they think I can tell them. What a disaster! I suppose I should have gone to the police as soon as I heard Garry and Cerise were dead . . .If only I didn’t have quite so many secrets to keep.”

“Don’t be stupid, you did exactly the right thing,” Natalie said forcefully. “There’s never anything to be gained from being interrogated.” Her expression, momentarily haunted, suggested she spoke from personal experience.

“Oh, what’ll I do?” Sally moaned again.

“Well, for the moment,” Lucienne spoke up brightly, “you can stop wallowing in self-pity and show me some of the fabulous nightlife I’ve heard so much about! Why don’t we just stay put for at least a few more days and see which way the wind blows, so to speak.”

“You’re right,” Natalie concurred. “Berlin’s an ideal place to re-invent oneself—which our darling ‘Jean’ has done quite well already.”

"Ladies," Jean, impeccable in white tie, ushered his lovely companions ahead of him into the Europahaus. Natalie in ivory and Lucienne in tangerine created a subtle stir as they moved through the crowd, and Jean was happy to be relegated to the background.

They'd hardly been seated before Natalie was swept off to the dance floor. "Let's fox-trot, darling," Lucienne said urgently; "otherwise that fat sweaty gent is going to ask me, and I'm not ready for that just yet." They took to the floor, but before long a different gent (less fat, less sweaty; "I think I can manage") cut in, and Jean was momentarily un-partnered. But it was only a moment; a beat later, a young woman glided into his arms, a lithe small figure in black satin, with a sleek black bobbed head.

Jean had the confusing sensation of dancing with Sally—with herself—before realizing why the girl was so familiar. "Louise!"

"I'm sorry, do I know you? Or are you a cinema fan?" She looked up at her partner, bright searching eyes below her straight black brows. "Oh . . .!" she gave a small gasp. "I think I *do* know you!"

"Jean Vallotin, à votre service, mademoiselle," Jean said; then leaning in toward her ear, murmured, "Yes, you know me, but I'm undercover. Please don't give me away."

Louise snuggled into her partner's arms and smiled contentedly. "What a good dancer you are. Will you invite me to your table for a glass of champagne?"

Louise was at the club alone, explaining, "I came with my director, but he left in a huff when I didn't want to do a tango with him. He's a terrible dancer, but he wanted to show me off for some free publicity, and I just wasn't in the mood. You know, I was a dancer before any of this other nonsense, and it's important to me how I dance, and where, and with whom." Lifting her glass, she flashed her radiant smile at Natalie and Lucienne. "I was so glad to find your friend Jean—a perfect dancer and a real gentleman." She squeezed the black-trousered knee beside her. "Can we take another turn? Ladies, you won't mind if I borrow your escort again?"

They danced close together to "Star Dust." Louise leaned in to murmur, "Please say you'll invite me back to your rooms. I simply must know what is going on."

"There's nothing going on, my dear," Jean produced a bland, affable smile, "except that we're having a most agreeable time dancing together. I should be going soon."

"*Please*. I want to help." Louise looked up at Jean intently, and he was struck by the seriousness of her straight-browed face.

"I'm not sure you can help . . . but yes, all right, come back with us for a nightcap. Have you eaten dinner?" Jean added, remembering mortal etiquette.

"Oh," Louise said vaguely, "I had a nibble earlier. I don't really do big dinners in the evening, unless I have to." Jean smiled and once again, recollecting their first meeting, had to remind himself that Louise was a vamp only in the colloquial sense.

Natalie and Lucienne were happy to have Louise join them for the rest of the evening, as they went on to two more cabarets. They were less thrilled about inviting the actress back to their rooms. They had ended up watching Bodo's last show of the night, and under cover of Louise's rapt fascination with the performance ("Fantastic! He's like the Polish Mae West!"), held furtive negotiations. "You persist in thinking she's one of us," Natalie whispered.

"No, I know she's not but . . . I trust her. She says she wants to help me, and I think perhaps she can, somehow."

Lucienne shrugged. "We'll give her an hour chez nous—after that we call her a cab and say good night."

"So tidy—I hardly recognize the place!" Louise said with a smile. She crossed the room and commandeered the sole shabby armchair. "Okay, let's get one thing straight. I know you're all vampires." She turned a long, steady look on each of the three faces, each of which froze in careful neutrality. "Don't ask me how I know, I just do—you're vampires in the real, ancient, immortal, blood-sucking sense; not the femme fatale movie star sense. And it doesn't bother me a bit, because you're all really swell girls—smart, gorgeous, fun and free-spirited, just the kind of women I can be friends with. But look at it this way: I know your deepest secret; I've known since the first night we met, and I would never breathe a word to anyone. I know what you are, and I'm here, knowing you would never hurt me. I trust you, and you can trust me. So, I really want to know why Sally has turned into Jean, because it doesn't strike me as just good old lesbian crossdressing fun. If you're in trouble, I want to help."

It turned out that Louise had been following the story in the *International Herald-Tribune*, so she knew at least half of it. Sally filled in the rest.

"The thing is," Sally said, pacing the room barefoot in her trousers and undershirt, "I've been having a fine time playing a man-about-town, but I can't keep it up forever. And now it looks as if they're not going to give up on trying to find me."

"But you were completely blameless in the Massey business—why not just go to the police, answer their questions?" Louise said, frowning. "Oh! I see, you can't do that because you *would* be hiding something, and they'd know it. You're good, you can pass perfectly with most people, but they'd have some crack investigator with a sixth sense, and then they'd never let it go. You're right—you can't talk to them. But *I* can."

"Why would you be involved?" Lucienne asked. "I mean, from the police point of view. That would just raise further questions."

"Not if I was who they're looking for—Sally."

"But—what you just said, how they'd have some extraordinarily gifted investigator there. *You'd* be hiding something."

"No, you don't understand, that's not how it works. I *would* be Sally Lafayette, innocent Parisian model. Not every film critic agrees, but I really am an actress."

Over the next days, after Louise left for Venice, Sally could hardly sleep at all. Although she knew the sensible thing would be to lie low, she found herself out every night, all night, feeding ravenously and indiscriminately. Her bloodletting was never lethal, but she was vicious in a way she'd never been before, a casual cruelty enabled by the dark anonymity of Berlin's midnight streets and the creatures she found there: venal, money-hungry, indifferently depraved or deliciously masochistic. She wore Paolo's shabby suit from Venice, not caring about bloodstains or alley-grime, pockets stuffed with banknotes to press into the hands of her willing victims. She no longer cared about passing as a man or about any sort of elegance; there were innumerable humans ready to yield to the urgency of her lean body, hungry eyes and razor-sharp teeth.

Finally, deeply, dreamlessly asleep—no idea how many days later—Sally was gently but firmly wakened by Lucienne. "Come on, darling, we're going."

Befogged and empty-eyed, she submitted to being stripped and washed. "Look at these scratches," Natalie hissed softly. "Better wash them well; who knows where she's been."

Eventually, clean, groomed and presentably dressed in Jean Vallotin's smart gray suit, she allowed herself to be shepherded by her friends to the train station.

Berlin – Paris

"MYSTERY MODEL COMES FORWARD: 'I WAS SCARED BUT I'VE NOTHING TO HIDE.'

"Caught up in the glamorous high life of the hyper-wealthy, Parisian Sally Lafayette (a professional mannequin for the house of Mlle) thought it was all good fun, until the terrifying day when Garry Massey proposed a suicide pact. Speaking in heavily accented but excellent English, she told me in this exclusive interview, 'I became a close friend to Cerise [Massey] first—she wanted to know how to dress better, and I think she was lonely actually—she needed a friend of her own, apart from her husband's circle. We had lovely times together, and then Monsieur Garry became very friendly to me too—but not in any improper way. He was kind and generous and very funny. They invited me to go to Venice with them, and it was a great treat, something I'd never have been able to do otherwise. It was a wonderful experience, seeing the beauties of the city, until that morning . . .' Here, the charming young French girl struggled to control her tears.

" 'When Monsieur Garry told me that we should all kill ourselves so that we could be together forever, I knew he had taken leave of his senses. I don't know why this happened, but I was terrified. He tried to block the door and grab me. Also, he tried . . . well, he tried to take liberties, too. I got away from him and I simply fled and did not look back. It was the most frightening thing that has ever happened to me. And then when I saw the papers . . .' Here, the beautiful blonde broke down completely. 'I was so shocked, and so saddened—what a senseless waste of two fine people's lives. But I was so scared. I didn't know what the police would think, when they knew I was there in the house and then ran away. I should have stayed and tried to stop them, but Monsieur Garry was so strong, so determined . . .'

"This interviewer would have found it inhuman to ask for any more from the poor girl—after she had wept on my shoulder for some time, we concluded our session."

Natalie, the last of them to read the story, folded the

paper crisply and leaned back against the scratchy plush seat. Outside, pretty milk-chocolate-colored cows grazed on green hillsides, ignoring the Paris-bound train.

"Well, it looks as if Louise gave a perfect performance—you were right to trust her. But *bozhe moi*, Sally, don't you *ever* do something like that again!"

"Says the woman who turned her lover into a socialist vampire Casanova," Sally retorted with a grin.

Natalie gasped indignantly. "I don't even know which part of that to deny first!"

Sally laughed benignly. "Oh, don't bother, Nat darling. I just mean, we're none of us perfect. Well, except perhaps Lucienne . . . but we just need to carry on and do the best we can. Truly, I couldn't have managed without your help, both of you. I've been out of my mind—I don't know how you managed to get me dressed and onto this train."

"We could never have managed without Dolly's help, too," Lucienne said. "You're lucky she's so well-connected. I've had a letter from her at poste restante. She apologizes for letting me down—silly woman, she hardly did that—and says she'll see us back in Paris. *And* what about your contessa—she certainly made things easier for you. Not to mention supplying your divine new wardrobe." She patted the gray-wool-trousered knee beside her. "Oh, by the way, we put that awful old suit in the wastebin."

"No! I wanted to save it as a souvenir! All right, I'm joking," she added, at her friends' gasps of outrage. "Listen, I need to stretch my legs. Care to join me for a stroll to the cafe car?"

Lucienne stood up. "I'd like that. You know, it's rather nice having a handsome male escort. Coming, Natalie?"

"Sure, why not."

They made their way along the swaying corridors, down the length of two cars to an etched glass and mahogany door. As they entered the cafe car, a tall, sallow-skinned man in dark glasses and a well-cut black suit stepped aside to let them pass and then left the car. Lucienne, in the lead, seemed to stiffen and hesitate.

"Darlings, I just realized I have a bit of a headache. I'm going to go back to our compartment and lie down for a few minutes."

"Oh, poor dear—would you like me to escort you back?" Sally offered.

"Such a gentleman!" Lucienne smiled. "No, don't worry, I'll be fine. If I feel better, I'll come join you here; otherwise I'll see you when you're back. We can't miss each other—there's only one corridor!"

Lucienne hurried back the way they'd come and spotted the black-clad figure at the far end of the next car. She sped up, almost running, glad of her short, pleated skirt and happy no one else was in the corridor. Still, it was hard to catch up; she passed her own compartment and kept going, finally coming up behind her quarry just as he opened the door to the next car.

In the loud, rocking junction between the cars, he turned to her, lowered his dark glasses and gave her a long, searching look.

"You?" Lucienne breathed.

The man smiled with intense pleasure. "Come," he beckoned, and opened the door to the next car.

Lucienne stared in astonishment. Instead of a corridor lined with compartment doors, the car was a huge, elegant room stretching into the distance. The floor was covered in thick, pale carpeting, and the furnishings were completely different from anything in the rest of the train—sleek, burnished, almost monochromatic and embodying the utmost in luxe modernity, with a distinct flavor of the far east. Pervaded by subtle incense and filtered light, even the air felt expensive.

"Uncle Yu," Lucienne said, with a bow of deep respect, "I'm speechless. I never expected to see you again—much less here, and now."

With a laugh, her host led her to a settee covered in pale gold silk. In a galley halfway down the car, she glimpsed the discreet movement of an attendant.

"Liu Shien, beloved great-niece," he said now, continuing to gaze at her with satisfaction. "Of course you could not have expected to see me 'here and now,' as you so charmingly put it. When you last saw me, a world away and a long time ago, you were a very young girl, and I was an exceedingly ancient man." He again smiled deeply, and apart from the good-humored crinkles around his eyes, his skin was flawlessly smooth below sleek black hair. "But, as you know, some of us are not required to age in the usual way. Tea?"

With a degree of self-effacement that was almost supernatural, the attendant had placed a tray with an exquisite tea set before them and had silently withdrawn.

"You are understandably confused," Lucienne's uncle said as he poured the steaming fragrant brew into paper-thin porcelain cups. "After we gave you our gift, freeing you from the fate of an arranged marriage and an ordinary life . . ."

Lucienne's vision went dark for a moment; she felt she was going to faint. "Wait a minute," she gasped, "what are you talking about? What gift, what do you mean *we* . . .?"

The older man made a brief sound halfway between

a remark and a throat-clearing. "Ah, of course, I mean *Luc*, your mysterious poetic lover. *He* gave you the gift, of course, but it was all part of our plan."

"I don't understand you—whose plan?" Lucienne demanded.

Her uncle ignored the question. "Do you remember seeing me the night you left? I gave you some money for the trip."

"Yes, of course, that was kind of you, and you were right to tell me to leave immediately. I wanted to wait, and that would have been . . ."

"Unwise," he said gently. "I am sorry you were not able to say goodbye to your parents. Even though they would have sacrificed you on the altar of respectability—still, I'm sure you loved them and they you, in their way. But," he looked closely at Lucienne, who seemed lost in thought, on the edge of tears. "did you never wonder at how easy it was to get away, and to make your way in Paris?"

"Easy? It wasn't easy—my journey was so long. First that . . . place in Shanghai, and then Casablanca, learning to live as I am . . . The money you gave me wasn't nearly enough to get to Paris, not until I'd earned the rest, sometimes in rather distasteful ways. Did you know that?"

Yu smiled ambiguously. "But it was easy once you reached Paris."

"Easy? I had nothing; I had to look for work . . ."

"For all of three days." Uncle Yu smiled. "Of course, you are poised, elegant and perfectly beautiful—why shouldn't you walk into the top fashion house in the world (which you'd never even heard of before; how on earth did you find it?) and be hired on the spot?"

"I suppose it *was* a lucky break."

The older man leaned back against his silk cushions and reached for a jade cigarette box, which he offered to Lucienne. She shook her head. He took a carved ivory cigarette holder from an inner pocket of his suit and in a moment, exhaling, laughed gently.

"My dear Liu Shien, I have been watching over you all your life. Do you think it's by mere chance that we are on the same train? I know all about your 'career' and your friends. They are nice enough girls. *Lucky*, isn't it, that you were able to find friends of your own kind? But you've been living, more or less, in squalor —not what someone of your breeding and station deserves. And it is unnecessary. It's time for a change. I have a proposal for you."

Approaching Paris

"We're in France—oh, at last!" Sally sighed. "I can feel my blood tingling, can't you?"

Natalie raised an amused eyebrow. "*Nyet*, I don't think so—but I don't have as much French blood as you, only what I've tasted over the years. But where the hell is Lucienne?" They had met Lucienne in the corridor on their way back from the cafe car; she'd said her headache was better and she was just going to have a coffee. Now, more than two hours had passed. "Why must she choose this moment to be inscrutable?" Natalie complained.

"Hush, you know she doesn't like that word. She's not usually so mysterious, our darling friend . . . but you're right, where is she? We should be getting our things together; we'll be at Gare du Nord in less than an hour. Here, I'll pull down our bags."

"Didn't Loulou have a little green train case? I don't see it," Natalie noticed.

"Hm. Do you suppose she . . . met someone? Someone fascinating enough to go off with for a bit?"

"Did she have the case with her when we saw her in the corridor?"

"I didn't really notice—I was just so glad her headache was better. She could have had it in her hand, I suppose."

"But when could she have met someone?" Natalie persisted.

"Oh, I don't know," Sally said, a bit impatiently. "But you know, despite being the youngest of us, she is a grown and capable vampire, perfectly able to take care of herself. She knows where we are and when we're arriving in Paris—if she chooses to be otherwise occupied, that's her business. If she doesn't show up when we reach the station, we'll just take her things back to the flat."

Rue Cambon

"You asked to see me, Mlle." Sally stood before the sleek macassar and ivory desk in her employer's inner sanctum.

"Sit down, Mlle Lafayette—and please appreciate that you are being asked to sit, rather than being summarily dismissed. I *should* terminate your employment here—and I *will* if I have any reason to suspect that people are coming to gawk at *you* rather than at what you are wearing."

"Mlle, I cannot tell you how sorry . . ."

The couturière silenced her with a look. "More than any other mannequin, Sally, I think of you as the face and form of this house, the ideal representative of my style. Your behavior has been . . . extremely regrettable. However, the fact that no news item about you has failed to mention both your elegance and my name in the same sentence is a mitigating factor. And this photograph of you is very good." She picked up a clipping from her desk: Louise, serious and beautiful, with a blonde bob. Mlle studied the photo for a moment. "Not quite your most characteristic look but *tres jolie*. This cream-colored georgette frock you wore—we are deluged with orders for it. *Alors*, Sally, you may go now—oh, and grow your hair out a bit; I don't know why you've cut it so very short."

March, 1929

Rue St. Honoré

"Oh, I'm desperately bored," Sally complained to Natalie, two days later, as they strolled along the rue St. Honoré after an afternoon of fittings. "I was so eager to be back in Paris, but—fittings, showings, demurely displaying clothes all day and then a few hours of nightlife—is this all was can do?"

Natalie gave her a sharp look. "I don't know what you want, *ma chère*. We have the easiest job in the world and our freedom by night. Would you rather be on the run from the police? Is that it—you miss the danger and uncertainty?"

"No, of course not—or, well, maybe yes, in some ways. Maybe I'll go out as Jean tonight, while I still can. You know, Mlle wants me to grow my hair longer."

"Oh yes, me too; La Mèduse told me. It's funny, though—she told me *she* thinks we look *tres chic*, and Mlle likes the look too."

"But then . . .?"

"Apparently Mlle is afraid that half the women in Paris will copy us, but their husbands will hate it, and they'll blame her. So it's strictly a business decision." Natalie reached up and touched her cropped head with a sigh. "Let's both go out as boys tonight. I know, don't tell me, only one set of tails. I don't care —I'll wear the gray suit and a beret and be your bohemian friend."

Place de l'Opéra

They dressed, taking nips from their flasks and egging each other on into an extravagantly flamboyant mood, though they were careful to keep their attire sedate, without showy accessories. As they stepped out into the full-moon night, breezy and fragrant, Natalie and Sally took long strides in their sleek trousers, heading for Montparnasse.

"I feel so wild tonight, Nat—what shall we do?"

"Boeuf sur le Toit? Le Jockey? Let's prowl about til we find an amusing set."

"All right, but I don't want to end up at one of those artists' brawls. What about someplace nicer— spectacle and champagne, gambling, elegance . . .

Where would Gaston and Eduouard go?"

"Well, they like the Ritz, of course. But this time of night, maybe the Casino de Paris?"

"That's it, about face, *mon vieux*. We want the high life."

Nat sighed in exasperation. "You are absurd, mon cher Jean. As you'll be the first to remind me, I'm not properly dressed."

"Well then . . ." Jean adjusted his top hat with a restless gesture. "Let's go and stand outside the Opera. It should be finishing in about half an hour— we'll watch the people coming out, and if we see anyone especially delicious, we'll follow along wherever they're going."

It was a mild night, perfectly pleasant in the Place de l'Opéra. The handsome pair of young boulevardiers lounged against a low railing, took nips from their flasks, gave handfuls of coins to accordion players and gypsy flower sellers.

"Look, they're starting to emerge," Jean noticed, standing up straighter and clutching a bunch of violets.

"There's a fun-looking set," Nat observed. The striking, well-known artists' model Kiki, wrapped in an impressive fur cloak, appeared to be leading a mixed group of avant-garde artists and their wealthy patrons toward the cab stand.

Jean was still scanning the crowd on the steps. "Natalie, look! I think it's Lucienne!"

"Ahem, not 'Natalie,' if you please—oh! Yes, it's her."

Clad in a shimmering gold lamé gown, their friend stood with a tall, older Asian man who was helping her into a sumptuous brocade coat. The watching pair nodded to each other and moved into position to follow Lucienne and her escort. Happily, they were proceeding on foot, not arm in arm but chatting intently, and heading in the direction of the Cafe de la Paix.

"What are they doing now?"

Jean sighed. "Just talking. She has a red cocktail, *naturellement,* and he has a glass of bordeaux, I think. Stop asking me."

"Well, I can't keep turning around," Nat complained. "We're supposed to be inconspicuous, but I don't know why we had to pick such a remote corner. What's the point of having followed her? I wish we'd just gone to Montparnasse for a good time."

"Oh fine, let's go then. Wait—she's coming this way."

Lucienne was indeed heading toward their table, her golden glamour almost unbearably bright.

"Well, *gentlemen,*" she greeted them. "What the hell are you doing here?"

"Lucienne, *cherie*!" Nat had risen and was kissing her on both cheeks. "Mightn't we ask you the same thing? We've been so worried."

"Yes, we didn't know what to tell Mlle. You may or may not still have your job," Jean added.

"Don't be silly—I sent a telegram to Mlle. And, well . . .I thought you'd understand. You must have noticed I took my train case. I was going to be in touch soon." Lucienne sighed. "You'd better come and meet my uncle."

Liu Yu was tall and extremely elegant, wearing a precisely-cut, hyper-modern dinner jacket that made Jean feel overdressed in tails, and Nat (in gray flannel with slightly too-long trousers) feel shabby. It didn't help that Lucienne herself looked exquisitely womanly in her golden gown, which fitted her like a glove. In any case, Lucienne's uncle looked right through their masculine guise and before a word had been said, bowed over each of their hands.

"You must be Mlle Natalie, and you are Mlle Sally. I am enchanted—and you look quite chic in these new fashions. Liu Shien has told me all about you."

Monsieur Yu, as they thought of him, ordered a round of drinks: "Blood and Sand, I think," he proposed, with the faintest suggestion of a wink. Clearly, he was one of them, but his discreet small-talk gave nothing away. After a half-hour or so, he turned to Lucienne.

"Well, my dear, we should be going. We have a busy day tomorrow. Ladies . . ." (annoyingly, he seemed to stress the word) "It has been a great pleasure." He inclined his head in another small bow.

Lucienne gave them each a brief hug, somehow affectionate and cool at the same time. "I'll call you soon," she said quietly. She took her uncle's arm, but turned back for a moment as they began to move away. "Please don't mention to Mlle that you saw me."

"Well." Natalie stared after them. "That was . . ."

"Appalling. What a jerk. And her uncle's no prize either. Come on, Nat, let's go home—no more adventures for this chap tonight."

Natalie sighed. "I suppose you're right. I feel so . . ."

"Foolish? Crushed? Insulted?"

"Sad. I thought Loulou was our friend; I thought we were an inseparable trio."

"Never say never, with immortals."

En route

"So, where *are* we going, Uncle Yu?" Lucienne asked. She only knew that the train was headed south and that he'd told her she didn't need to pack anything.

Also, they were in a regular first-class car, not his private rolling apartment; the journey would not be long. "I was hoping we could stay in Paris for a while. I missed it so much while I was traveling—and I love seeing *your* Paris."

"How the other half lives?" Yu said with a gentle smile. "Don't worry; I think you will like this at least as much."

A long black Hispano-Suiza with a uniformed driver met them at the Cannes station. As they spun briefly through town, Lucienne had just time to glimpse the chic, striped awnings of Mlle's summer boutique— now shuttered closed—before they started up a winding road out of town.

Set among formal gardens, back from a semi-circular drive, an immense casino rose palatially before them. The driver opened her door and a crisp-liveried young man appeared at once to shield her with a parasol until they reached the shelter of the entrance marquee.

"Heavens." She turned to her uncle. "You didn't tell me we were going to Versailles."

"Not quite. Though I suppose I *am* a sort of sun king here." On each side of them, lined-up staff members bowed with deference.

Rue Cambon

"Three days? The country? When you've just returned from your scandal-ridden jaunt to Italy?" Mlle was seething; Sally stood perfectly still, her head bowed slightly. Her hair had grown out to a neat chin-length bob and was black again.

"I've had all my fittings, and nothing needs alteration. You have my word, I'll be back Thursday, a full day before the showing. I wouldn't ask but . . ."

"Yes, yes, I know—your grandmother. And just when Lucienne has to be nursing her bedridden uncle." She peered at Sally closely. "I always thought you girls were more . . . unencumbered. I've a good mind to dismiss the lot of you. All right—go. But I want to see you here at ten Thursday morning, ten sharp."

Charroux

The woman Sally called her grandmother was not a relative in the family sense, but they were closely tied by blood. Mme LaSalle was the oldest living member of Sally's original vampire clan, and they had known each other for more than two centuries. Sally was extremely fond of the old lady (who had preferred an elderly form for the last hundred years) and they wrote to each other regularly. Mme LaSalle's last letter had been very brief, saying only that she had something of the utmost importance to discuss, and

Sally found it alarming enough to make plans for an immediate visit.

Sally stepped off the train and began walking briskly into the quaint village of Charroux. The little house near the edge of town was just as she remembered it, neat and unremarkable behind a lush, shady garden. She realized she must not have been there in 30 years, but not much seemed to have changed.

She heard a firm footstep after her knock; the door flew open, and she was enfolded in a tight hug against grandmère's tall, lean body, so like her own.

"Sally, ma chère fille, come in, let me feast my eyes. So, this is the latest mode?" She shrugged. "I can't say I'm impressed—but you wear anything well, beautiful girl. Look, I've dressed up for you, too!"

Sally, who had been focused on her grandmère's face and the warmth of her welcome, now took in her whole figure and squealed with delight. *"Vous êtes une Merveilleuse!"* In the avant-garde high style of 1795, Mme's gown was diaphanous and classical, trimmed in red ribbons. A striped turban topped her short curls. "Oh," Sally sighed. "Les Merveilleuses, les Incroyables . . . what a terrible and wonderful time."

Mme LaSalle poured them each a glass of her special cordial, concocted from several types of blood and a selection of local herbs (there really was a "grandmama's health tonic") and they sat by the fire in her cozy parlor. They talked for a while of old times and new, of the Incroyables and the Dadaists, the *philosophes*, the great salons, the *grandes horizontales*. This was a ritual, Sally knew—an expression of their pleasure in each others' intellect, their shared history, their quickness of thought and association. She sipped her drink, savored the old woman's company and waited patiently to learn why she had been summoned.

Abruptly, but exactly as expected, Mme LaSalle cleared her throat and changed the subject. "Sally, my dearest—when you last saw your *cher maitre* . . ."

Sally closed her eyes, feeling herself instantly plunged back to that moment. Jacques Grandin, the great, ancient and immeasurably learned vampire who had turned her, trained her and mentored her for so long, was dying by his own choice. He lay on a sunstruck bed beside an open, south-facing window, and the steady exposure had withered him day by day. At the end, he was skeletal and almost transparent, but still clear-minded and calm. Sally knelt beside him to receive his final words: "I cannot survive my disillusion with the Enlightenment. But *you* must find a way forward. If men must be stupid, perhaps the wisdom of women will find a new way . . ."

Grandmère nodded, as if she'd heard the dialogue within Sally's head. "He was bitterly disappointed in humanity, as you know. He believed so fervently in progress, understandably, when you think of the trajectory of his life—from the dark ages to the

Renaissance, and then on, after the setbacks of the Reformation and all that nonsense, to the rationalists, the Enlightenment. That was his apogee, and he thought it could last. But the excesses of the Revolution, the Terror and above all, the resurgence of superstition, prejudice, irrational stupidity . . . it broke his spirit."

Sally bowed her head, dry-eyed but deeply sorrowful. "I understand—but I also think he must have been very, very tired. I find there is always cause for pessimism and despair. This last war was terrible! But there is also always the vigor and beauty of life itself —until one is too tired to feel it." She sighed. "I still miss him. I'm so grateful that *we* still have each other, you and I."

Mme LaSalle reached across suddenly and grasped Sally's shoulder. "My dear, you must prepare yourself. I will not be here much longer."

Sally stood up so quickly she almost knocked her glass to the floor—she caught it just in time. "No! What are you saying?"

"Sit down dearest—come, sit by me. I am not . . . tired in the way Jacques was, as you correctly analyze. I still have my vigor; I still enjoy a beautiful moonlit night, and our correspondence—and now seeing you here today—is pure joy. But as you know, as you have always known, I have the gift, or curse, of second sight. Be thankful you are spared that. I see such dark days ahead that I do not think I can bear to be here much longer. Another five or ten years perhaps . . ."

"Years? So you won't do anything right away?"

The older woman smiled. "No, nothing immediate. But I wanted to let you know now. A year is just an eyeblink for us."

"But, what is happening?"

"I can't tell, exactly. This last war, as you say, was dreadful, and there is worse to come. There will be a great deal of human suffering and human evil, especially here in Europe. There are those who say vampires are evil, but what is coming will far outweigh anything the worst of us might do. You should be prepared—it may be necessary to leave France. And stay well away from Germany."

"Oh, but Berlin is the most exciting and tolerant city in the world! I must tell you all about my adventures there; I couldn't say too much in my letter . . ."

"I'm glad you enjoyed it, but I must strongly advise against going back. You might do well to think of leaving Europe altogether."

"Grandmère, *you* should leave, if you feel so strongly about it. There's no need to think of ending your life."

"But, ma chère, I have always been, above all, *une française*. Where else could I possibly live?"

"What about . . . Canada? Don't they speak French there?"

The old woman snorted scornfully. "They may *call* it French. *Non*, I'd rather die."

Sally laughed, in spite of herself. "So intolerant."

Grandmère folded her once more into a long embrace. "I am too old to start over in a new place, my dearest. But you—you must."

Casino Imperiale

Lucienne's head buzzed with all she had learned in the past five days and nights. She had shadowed croupiers until she understood the rules of a dozen different games of chance—not just the official rules, but the hidden rules beneath the rules, which insured the immutable truth: the House always wins. That truth was well concealed under a thick, shiny veneer of luxury, glamour and amusement; the patrons appeared to bask in a rosy glow of well-being. For most of them, this extended through the end of their stay, when they cashed in their chips, pleased with their modest wins or ruefully regretful of their trivial losses. Only a few departed in serious distress—disheveled, hollow-eyed, sometimes struggling against the brawny guards who escorted them firmly away. Lucienne quickly learned to spot the ones who were likely to reach this denouement; often they showed signs of desperation from the beginning, whether this took the form of giddy high spirits or grimly determined play. She was not surprised to hear about the ensuing suicides—several each year—but she was disturbed and saddened.

"It seems such a waste, Uncle—allowing them to destroy themselves like that."

"Not to worry, my dear. If you see any that you fancy, just say the word and they will be turned over to you."

Lucienne turned away to hide her grimace of disgust; she didn't want to be rude to her uncle, but she couldn't refrain from speaking her mind. "I can't live like that—and you don't have to, either. Perhaps long ago it was the only way for us to survive, but we have choices now. We can co-exist with humans."

"Of course we can," he answered with a laugh. "Just as the wolf can co-exist with the flock of sheep. I'm just saying, if you see a nice wooly lamb you want . . ."

"Please, stop."

Uncle Yu caught Lucienne's wrist as she moved to cover her ears. "Listen, my dear. You seem to have some youthful illusions about our nature—it's normal enough; you are young, after all. But eventually you will come to understand: we are predators, obligate carnivores like any creature that hunts. Do you think it matters whether you drink blood from a silver flask or from the throbbing neck of a struggling—or willing—victim? It's only a question of style, or taste." Tenderly, he smoothed her hair and squeezed her shoulder. "I did not mean to upset you. We will talk another time, my dearest niece. Tonight we open the new Jade Room; you will want to be well-rested."

Lucienne looked herself over in the full-length mirror and had to admit she was pleased with the dress Uncle Yu had ordered: a *qi pao* of luscious green silk damask that hugged her curves with elegant flattery—so different from the casual breezy chic of her Paris wardrobe. "I am a goddess," she told herself, with only a hint of mockery, as she leaned in to put on a pair of tremendously long jade drop earrings. She had been extravagant with her eye makeup; only her small red rosebud mouth and severe bob were more modern than mythic.

Lucienne's role at the casino was, she reflected, not so different from what she was used to chez Mlle: she represented the house. From the private second floor, there were five different grand staircases descending into various salons and gaming halls—her evening generally involved one grand entrance after another. She'd make a sort of royal progress across each room, dispensing beneficent smiles or mysterious aloof glares, as the situation demanded. Her uncle had gifted her with a foot-long, white jade cigarette holder, which she had found useful as a distancing mechanism in the event her discreet gestures of flattery or encouragement were misunderstood.

Flattery and encouragement, to keep the high rollers rolling, were called for tonight in the ultra-exclusive new Jade Room, but Lucienne had also learned to spot behavior that could be problematic in any way —rudeness, lack of personal boundaries, cheating fellow players or doing suspiciously well. She only needed to murmur a word to one of the ubiquitous, inconspicuous, dark-suited security team, to have a guest removed from the room or even ejected from the club. However, enforcing standards was not to her taste, nor was it really her job.

"Your presence here," Uncle Yu had told her, "is to embody the ineffable, to preside as a muse or goddess would. I want people to leave feeling they didn't just go to a casino and spend some number of francs, but that they had a sublime experience."

The young man at the roulette table caught her eye first because he was terribly attractive, with dark eyes and a lock of hair that kept falling untidily over his forehead, despite his otherwise impeccable grooming. He had a faintly exotic look—Spanish, perhaps, or even Turkish—and a quietly fierce intensity that intrigued her. She drew nearer and saw that he had a huge heap of chips. Just as she bestowed the full radiance of her "winning" smile, she was horrified to see him push the entire stack onto a single number, the black nine.

When he lost, apparently, everything, his eyes went blank and black. He stood up and stumbled blindly away from the table, heading out to the balcony through a curtained French door. Lucienne followed, with a sense of dread.

She was prepared to find him climbing the balcony rail, but he was only standing near it, struggling to light a cigarette with violently shaking hands. Lucienne helped him steady his flame and accepted a light for her own cigarette.

"Did you lose it all, just now?"

"All of my inheritance, along with a big loan from my best friend. I'm done for. As soon as I finish this, I'm going over the rail."

"Don't," Lucienne said, laying a cool hand on his.

"Why not?"

"You're too pretty, for one thing—I'd hate to see you broken. Anyway, it's not as far down as it looks; you probably wouldn't be killed."

"Ah." The young man considered this seriously. "I suppose you speak from experience."

"Unfortunately, yes." They were quiet for a few moments. "I suppose you want to marry your sweetheart," Lucienne said. "You'll tell me that she doesn't care about money, but her father won't give his permission unless you're rich."

He opened his eyes wide. "How could you know that?"

"I'm wise beyond my years—and I'm older than I look," she said lightly.

"Are you going to tell me I'm wrong—that I should just run away with her?"

"Oh, no. If she was willing to run away with you, it would have already happened. No—you are done for. Especially after word gets out about what you've done here."

"Then, what am I to do?" The young man's voice was choked with anguish.

"I don't know. Weren't you going to kill yourself?"

"Yes, but . . . Can you help me? Or can I help you?"

Lucienne now produced the smile she'd been saving up since she first saw him—wide, wicked and full of promise. "Perhaps," she said.

Rue Cambon

La Mèduse entered the dressing room briskly, without knocking. "This is most irregular, Mlle Lafayette, but I will permit it just this once, as it appears to be some sort of emergency: there is a telephone call for you."

Sally followed her to her office; La Mèduse indicated the telephone and discreetly withdrew. Her mind still full of the visit to her grandmère, Sally was startled to hear Lucienne's voice.

"Sally, you've got to help me. I have to get out of this place; it's killing me."

"Lu darling, what on earth—where *are* you?"

"It's the Casino Impériale, not far from Cannes . . ." Lucienne trailed off, and Sally could hear a deep muffled voice in the background. Lucienne resumed in a bright, social tone. "Thank you so much; the party sounds lovely. I shall have to check my diary and call you back."

"Loulou, don't 'phone me here; leave a message with our concierge . . ." Sally began, but the line was already dead.

Casino Imperiale

"Uncle Yu." Setting down the telephone on her desk, Lucienne turned to face him. "I'll need to go up to Paris soon, for a little while."

"For a party?" He smiled. "I wonder that you have the energy—you've seemed so lackluster the past few days."

"I *should* go to this party. I'll see lots of useful contacts; it's a wealthy crowd. And . . . your *salon de beauté* here is quite good, but I'd like to see my favorite hairdresser. And pick up some of my clothes at the flat."

"Those drab rags? When you have an exquisite new wardrobe? Anyway, don't lie to me—I know you just want to get away. Poor little Liu Shien—did your new plaything break? Don't fret, you'll soon have another."

Lucienne stood up and backed away from her uncle, keeping her eyes on him as if he were a dangerous animal. "Please stop."

Liu Yu laughed indulgently. "Come now, don't tell me you've never killed one before."

"Actually, he was my first. I'm very tired, Uncle; I'm going to rest."

"Lucienne." He put a hand on her shoulder, regarding her with concern. "I should have warned you—what happened was not your fault. I've given you . . . more power than you have had before. It will take some getting used to. All right, dear one, go and rest now."

Stretched on her satin coverlet, Lucienne closed her eyes and saw Alain, as he'd been . . . . was it only a few days ago? The young man had been lovely: gentle and playful, with a sweet, spicy taste. He was clever too—he'd studied engineering and had ideas for all sorts of useful inventions.

"Silly boy, if you'd gone to the patent office and invested that loan from your friend, instead of coming here . . ."

"Then I wouldn't be here right now." He raised his head from her bare feet, which he'd been kissing and nibbling with pleasing thoroughness.

Lucienne leaned over and stroked his warm shoulders. "True. Come here, you spicy morsel; I want to taste you again."

He was tangy and tender; he was willing to please, but he seemed to lack stamina. After three days of sport, he had begun to fade—he weakened, became unable to speak and finally fell into a deep slumber from which he did not awaken. At last, his breathing ceased. Lucienne was aghast; she had not drained him, had not tried to turn him. She thought they were only playing, well within the bounds of what he could live with. Clearly, she was wrong. The chambermaids discreetly removed the young man's body. Lucienne had not spoken of it with her uncle, but obviously he knew. Shocked and distraught, she had hardly been able to move through her evening duties. Her mind revolved around a thought which she could hardly keep herself from voicing aloud: I didn't do it right. I broke him.

Lucienne dreamed about playing chess with Alain, with kisses as forfeits for every captured piece. Though she felt he would win the game, she had just taken his queen when her eyes flew open. A man was standing at the foot of her bed, his head inclined curiously.

"Alain?" she whispered. The room was too dim for her to see any details beyond a slender, male form. There was no answer. A strange intuition stirred. "Luc?"

"Do you want me to be Luc? Do you miss him very much?" the man said.

"Uncle Yu? What are you doing here? What are you talking about?" Lucienne sat up quickly, her throat dry.

"There there, dearest niece, don't be alarmed," he said gently. He sat down at the foot of the bed and leaned forward just a bit to pat her hand. "Dear Liu Shien, you have been such a help to me here, as I knew you would be. But I should have thought before bringing you here—it's an isolated world, not what you are used to. You are young, lonely and bored; you need excitement and romance. If you want Luc, I can be him again. I have been him before."

Lucienne could only stare, speechless. The outline of her uncle's lean face, with its sharp cheekbones, seemed to imprint itself on her vision, merging with a memory. Finally, she found her voice. "Please. Leave my room."

Ile St. Louis

It was dusk on the Ile St. Louis, in the park behind Notre Dame. "I don't know what to do, Natalie,"

Sally complained, walking restlessly backward and twisting her hands with anxiety. "I want to go right now, but La Mèduse will have my head if I miss any more work. I guess it will have to be this weekend."

Natalie squeezed her arm. "Don't fret, the weekend will be soon enough. We'll need time to prepare."

Sally looked at her sharply. "*We* will?"

"You don't think I'd let you go alone? That uncle of hers is not to be trifled with; he's an old one, very powerful. I sensed it as soon as we met him."

"Easy for you to say Saturday is soon enough; you didn't hear her voice."

"I know, cherie, but the only way we can help Loulou is by being strong and ready."

"What do you mean, exactly—do you know ways of dealing with 'old ones'?"

"I know a thing or two and I can teach you . . . But another thing that worries me is how we get in."

"I've checked the train schedule. We go to Cannes and take a taxi to the casino."

"And you think they just let in anyone who comes to the door? Two unaccompanied young women— unless they're dripping in diamonds and furs, and well-known socialites to boot—are likely to be turned away. They won't want gold-diggers or tarts on the premises."

"Hm." Sally turned thoughtful. "Then we go *en travestie.*"

"Interesting . . . we *could* do that . . . although as you recall, M Yu saw right through us."

Their stroll had taken them around to the front of the cathedral, and just then a woman emerged from one of the doors—a woman in black, with a very round, white, familiar face. "Dolly!" Sally called. "Over here!"

With hugs and kisses of greeting, they repaired to a bench to talk. Dolly, without seeming evasive, managed to brush past their questions about where she'd been since Venice and instinctively divined that they were troubled about something. "Lucienne in a tight spot! The poor child. I'd never expect it of her —ah, but family can be the worst, sometimes. How can I help?"

"I'm not sure you can, darling, unless you know anything about the Casino Impériale. We want to go there and rescue her, but apparently it's frightfully exclusive; they might not even let us in."

"Oh my dears, I know just the person to help you with that. She's a great friend of mine—an Indian maharani. She's terribly rich and grand, but perfectly nice and great fun—you'll love her. And she's a dedicated gambler; I'd be surprised if she isn't already well known at this casino. We'll go with her, as her entourage."

"And, it's just that simple?" Natalie raised a skeptical eyebrow.

"You'll see; it is."

The Ritz

They met Indira (as she insisted they call her) the next night, for cocktails at the Ritz. Dolly wore gray satin, Sally and Natalie their usual black. The rani was radiant in a sari of amethyst chiffon. Though its style was timelessly traditional, her modern taste was evident in every detail: silver trim instead of gold, delicate-strapped silver dance shoes embellished with gems and a stunning parure of platinum and diamonds, including a jeweled bandeau and a tiny stud at the side of her nose. She occasionally employed a monocle hung on a delicate silver chain.

Indira's musically-accented French was excellent and her humor delightful. After a couple of rounds of martinis, as Indira began an amusing, self-mocking complaint about how bored she'd been since her pet lieutenant had returned to his regiment, Dolly seized the opening and brought up the subject of an expedition to the Casino Impériale.

"Oh, I have been so much wanting to go there again; it's a magnificent place. I insist you all come with me. I hear they have an enchanting new hostess, the Jade Goddess of Luck. What fun we'll have, won't we, Benvenuto?" To Sally's and Natalie's astonishment, she opened her silk evening bag and brought out a small tortoise, which had evidently been sleeping within. He put his head out as his feet touched the table and took a few slow steps. The gems affixed to his shell glinted attractively in the light.

"Leave it to me," Dolly said, after Indira had gaily bid them farewell. "I'll have your outfits ready Friday night, and we'll meet back here for Saturday lunch; then we'll set out for Cannes."

"Lunch?" Sally asked, anxiously. Dining out with wealthy friends was clearly one of Dolly's great pleasures; it was impossible to tell her that meals were an annoying encumbrance. "Will we be able to get to the station in time?"

Dolly laughed happily. "My dears! The whole point is to make a grand entrance with the rani. We're going in her car, of course."

Dolly's apartment

"Another masquerade," Sally murmured, as they headed over to Dolly's rooms. In talking it over, she and Natalie agreed there was really no way to conceal their identities from the apparently omniscient Uncle Yu, but arriving as members of the maharani's entourage, in the shadow of her glitter, would at least buy them some time.

Dolly met them at the door modeling her own traveling ensemble, a simply-cut dress and matching coat in pale green raw silk.

"Very nice," Natalie said. "You must be the lady companion. And what have you got for us—are we in sarees? I've always wanted to try one."

"Are we the junior wives?" Sally giggled.

Dolly picked up two dark bundles lying on a chair. "Private secretary," she said to Natalie. "Don't let me forget to give you your spectacles." Handing the other to Sally: "Lady's maid."

"You love putting me in horrible clothes—it's Venice all over again!" Sally protested.

"That *was* my idea, actually—but I knew Indira would be appalled. She thinks you're charming and wants you there as her friends, not her staff. And anyway, my dears, nothing succeeds like excess."

"Is that one of your Uncle Oscar's lines?"

"It might be—but it's mine now. What I mean is, the maharani's so soignée, it won't do for you to be dowdy; you'd just draw more attention. So, here we go—rose chiffon for Natalie and buttercup georgette for Sally. I'll show you how they go on."

With squeals of delight, the mannequins shed their frocks and applied themselves to learning the art of sari-wrapping.

"Lovely," Dolly said approvingly, stepping back.

"Now the finishing touches. She gave them each a huge silk shawl, matching their sari colors and edged in silver brocade. "Over the head and the left arm. Hold it in place with the other hand—which will have a dazzling great bracelet for further distraction." She produced these, bright with peridots, aquamarines and pearls.

"We look stunning," Natalie said, gazing in the mirror with fascination. "Who are we?"

"Oh, it doesn't really matter, when you're with the maharani," Dolly said. "People will assume or guess whatever they want—you might be friends, or daughters-in-law, or half-Eurasian cousins. You'll see."

En route

Lunch at the Ritz was a giddy blur, with lots of champagne. Natalie and Sally didn't even have to pretend to eat; it was assumed they were too excited. But what Sally found most interesting was the reaction to their group. In their flower-garden colors (Indira wore lilac), filmy scarves and dazzling jewels, they drew the attention of the whole room, but that attention was curiously non-specific and un-inquisitive, as if deflected by the surface glitter of their exotic appearance. Dolly was right—they were spectacle, nothing more.

And their arrival at the Casino was the same thing,

writ large. Although the rani's elegance and poise had been notable from the moment they met her, Sally and Natalie had not had occasion to witness the full power of her commanding, regal presence. Of course, the immensely long, silver Hispano Suiza, with its custom hood ornament, a bejeweled cobra, amplified the effect. As the driver pulled into the semi-circular gravel drive, they were immediately surrounded by a deferential crowd of attendants standing by to unload and transport their copious amounts of luggage. Again, as they went through the grand entrance doors, Sally noticed the curious sense of deflection of the attention directed their way, as if they were enveloped in a radiance too bright to look at directly. There was a further stroke of good fortune. As the rani signed the register, the manager apologized profusely: M Yu was not there at present to welcome her personally. But he would certainly greet her that evening.

"Lovely," the rani replied graciously, echoed inwardly by her young companions. Safe within the dazzle of her royal glamour, they retired to the maharani's lavish double suite.

Casino Imperiale

Sally and Natalie had just awakened from a deep afternoon slumber, sipping from their flasks and murmuring their appreciation of the luxuriously comfortable room, when there was a gentle knock at the connecting door.

"I've brought your evening saris," Dolly announced and spread the shining cloth on the nearest bed. Heavier and stiffer than the ones they'd worn for their arrival, these were ornately trimmed and even paler in color, ice blue and mint green. "I'll be in silver, and the rani in cream. You know, don't you, that white is the color of death in India? So you see, just like Mlle, the maharani has made mourning chic."

Natalie noticed, as they made their entrance down a grand staircase into a glittering salon, that she no longer felt enveloped in a protective cloud of radiance. Now it was as if a pure white spotlight fell directly on the four women. The immense, crowded room went almost silent at their arrival, and people drew back to create an unencumbered path. From the far side of the salon, a tall dark figure approached them: Uncle Yu, in impeccable evening clothes. And, just behind him, in high-collared, form-fitting scarlet silk, Lucienne.

Indira smiled brilliantly. "So, it's you at last, old friend!"

Uncle Yu bowed deeply over the hand she extended, and Lucienne (to Sally's and Natalie's amazement) dropped into a graceful curtsy. "Maharani, you do us the greatest honor," Yu said. "Please allow me to present my niece, my right hand in this establishment, Mlle Leung."

"Enchantée, my dear," said the rani, while Lucienne bowed wordlessly.

Yu's eyes, lowered deferentially for a moment, now flicked over the rest of the group. "These two young ladies I am well acquainted with—ha ha, again in fancy dress! I approve; this is much more fetching than those ensembles I saw you in last. And this must be Miss Wilde." He gave Dolly a brief courteous bow; unruffled, she smiled coolly.

"And now, your highness, my house is at your disposal. Name your pleasure: a bit of dinner? Cocktails? Or may I show you the gaming rooms?" Uncle Yu and the maharani, with Dolly at her elbow, moved forward, chatting amiably. Lucienne slipped back beside Sally and Natalie. Her red-painted lips stretched into a wide smile.

"What a surprise to see you here! Why have you come?"

Sally glanced at the group ahead of them to see that they were out of earshot and leaned closer to her friend. "We're here for you, darling Loulou. On the telephone you sounded so desperate . . ."

Lucienne gave her a wide-eyed look and then laughed musically. "Telephone? I can't think what you mean. I'm in my element here—I never want to leave."

"Cherie," Sally whispered urgently, "obviously you

can't talk freely here. Is there somewhere we can go?"

Lucienne gazed for a moment in the direction of the groups ahead, and they heard the maharani announce, "Actually, I am quite ravenous—I believe I shall fortify myself in the restaurant. Come along, Miss Wilde. Will the young ladies . . .?"

"They mentioned, ma'am, when we were dressing, that the journey had quite destroyed their appetites."

"Oh, I expect they'll just want a cocktail, then." The rani glanced back toward them and waved gaily. "No matter, we'll meet up later."

"Did you just use telepathy on the rani, and Dolly?" Natalie asked, as Lucienne led the way through an archway to another broad staircase.

"Just a bit. Why not?"

"Why not!" Sally was indignant. "We don't do that sort of thing."

"Really?" Lucienne looked amused. "Who's *we*?"

The bar was huge and sleek, an assemblage of chrome and frosted glass with multiple levels wrapped in tubular railings. There was almost no one else there, but Lucienne settled them at a table on its own small mezzanine, like a miniature ship's prow, as far as possible from anyone else. Either her commanding charisma, telepathy or a slight inclination of her head brought a waiter instantly to her side. She placed an order and then sat quite still, smiling in an oddly vacant manner, until a round of Blood Bronx cocktails had arrived.

The waiter withdrew; they clinked glasses and then Lucienne started talking, almost as if a switch was suddenly turned on.

"So, my darlings—I'm so pleased you've come to visit, and in these *amusing* costumes. I don't blame you; one needs a break from Mlle and her endlessly subtle, tasteful modes. I have the most marvelous wardrobe now; I don't think I'll ever want to go back to dressing *à la garçonne*." Opening her scarlet silk clutch purse, she fitted a pale green cigarette into a long jade holder and swiftly deployed a Cartier lighter. Exhaling scented smoke, she asked brightly, "How long would you like to stay?"

"Lucienne, you can drop the act now; there's no one anywhere near us." Sally leaned forward. "Ten days ago, you phoned me and said, 'I've got to get out of this place; it's killing me.'"

"I said that? How preposterous!"

"It's you who are preposterous, cheric," Natalie said sternly. "I know, it was Sally who received your call, but I saw how it affected her. Clearly, you were dead serious when you telephoned her, and now . . . Now, I think you have been bewitched."

"Ugh, I don't believe this!" Lucienne said in exasperation. She gestured brusquely, and almost at once, another round of cocktails appeared. "Drink up darlings—don't waste any, they're expensive. Then I want to show you something."

Lucienne unlocked a red lacquer door with ornate brass hardware, opening off a wide, thickly carpeted hallway in a quiet upstairs wing. "This is where I live now," she announced, ushering them inside.

The sitting room was spacious and lovely, a landscape of shimmering silks in green and gold. The fresh scent of flowers and ferns from several large bouquets mingled with the woody notes of aromatic logs burning in the fireplace. Cozy chairs and sofas, bookcases, a gramophone and a gold-lacquered bar all proposed their pleasures.

"Come, this way." Lucienne led them through a small but exquisite dining room. "I have a personal chef, should I want a bowl of . . . soup. And, for guests, of course."

Next was her bedroom, hung with peach-colored velvet drapes and flatteringly lit with gold-shaded lamps. "You're welcome to stay; there's plenty of space." She gestured toward a pair of divinely comfy-looking chaises longues. "And this is my dressing room."

"Alors, *now* I'm jealous," Natalie said, taking in the massive closets, the multiplicity of mirrors, shallow drawers, shoe racks, tiered glass shelves of cosmetics surrounding the vanity. "This is bigger than our entire Paris flat!"

"The bath is through here." Lucienne opened a door to reveal a glorious expanse of turquoise tile, with a tub the size of a small swimming pool. "And, this way . . ."

She opened another door to a short hallway, leading to a second sitting room. It was almost the twin of the first, with its fireplace, flowers, bar and cozy seating, but this room was decorated in rose and silver, and was filled with people. There were four men and three women; some quite young, others older, all quite attractive, all dressed in silken loungewear—and all marked by a pallid glamour that showed all too clearly what Lucienne had been up to with them.

A murmuring cry went up: "Darling mistress, you're here!" and Lucienne was surrounded with coos and caresses.

When she was done greeting each of her pets, Lucienne announced, "These are my dear friends and fellow vamps, Natalie and Sally. I want you to make sure they feel extremely welcome."

A rustle of excitement swept the room, and both guests immediately found themselves surrounded by two or three ardent admirers.

"Aren't they lovely?" Lucienne smiled indulgently, stroking her two nearest companions exactly as if they were silky-furred cats. "The clientele here is quite exclusive, and I have my pick of the absolute cream. Don't I, creamy?" She nuzzled the delicate-featured young woman beside her.

Sally gently disengaged herself from a brother and sister, identically ice-blond, who had snuggled beside her. "Lucienne. Will you please come and talk with us in another room?"

"Not right now, darling. I only have a few more minutes of break; then I need to get back to the gaming rooms. I *do* work here, you know. I can meet you back here in about two hours."

"Not here," Sally said sternly. "Natalie, let's go."

"Oh, all right," Lucienne said. "I'll see you back at the downstairs bar at eleven."

"Natalie!" Sally raised her eyebrows. A muscular, fortyish man was massaging Natalie's neck and shoulders; her eyes were closed in pleasure but she opened them at Sally's insistent voice.

"Yes, I'm coming," she said dreamily.

They argued all the way back to their room, with Natalie maintaining that their friend was simply going through a normal phase: "She's younger than us, remember. Didn't you have a period of purely amoral hedonism?"

Sally shrugged. "Sure, a century or so ago. But, the

way she said, 'It's killing me.' I can't forget the anguish in her voice. If I only knew exactly what she was talking about."

"It was Alain—she broke him, and she felt terrible about it."

Natalie and Sally whirled about at the low, unexpected voice behind them. A small pale gamine, in yellow silk pajamas, had noiselessly followed them from Lucienne's suite. "Hello, I'm Aimée. I didn't mean to startle you, and I didn't really mean to eavesdrop. It's just . . . .I could tell you love Loulou, and I do, too. All of us do. We'd like to help her."

Natalie recovered herself first. "Should you even be here, talking to us?"

The girl—she was quite young—laughed. "We're not prisoners. We stay with Loulou because she's so wonderful, but we're free to come and go. I can hardly imagine being apart from her . . . but I'd also do anything for her to be really happy. And you are right," she turned to Sally; "Lucienne is not happy. She is charming and fascinating, we delight in her company of course, but she cannot forgive herself for Alain. I was the first one after she . . . after that ended . . . .so I know how she was. The others didn't see her then."

They had reached the door of their room. "Come in, please, if you'd like," Sally said. "I want to hear more. Who was this Alain?"

Aimée arranged herself gracefully on a divan, shrugging the open neckline of her loose shirt away from her throat in an ambiguously unconscious gesture. "Alain was—like the rest of us, I suppose—a handsome person unlucky at cards. There are choices one can make, here, if one is too deeply in debt. But he must have been . . . not very strong. Loulou blames herself, but I don't think it could have been her fault."

"He died?" Sally asked.

Aimée nodded. Again she moved in a way that caused her neckline to slide down, inviting them to notice her delicately marked throat, long and pale below her bobbed hair. But Sally looked away, and Natalie frowned and closed her eyes, thinking of Vladimir. After a moment, Aimée consulted her tiny wristwatch. "I should go; I want to bathe before Loulou's next break."

"It's like the Versailles of gambling," Sally said as they wandered and explored the magnificent casino, until it was time to meet Lucienne again.

Natalie nodded. "Lavish doesn't even begin to describe it. This place is beyond luxury."

There were deeply "Oriental" spaces filled with jade and ivory carvings, rosewood furniture, billowing incense and golden Buddhas, while other salons were purely French, adorned with gilded chairs, crystal chandeliers, crowds of flowers and mirrored walls. Some rooms were silken and serene; others dim, intimate and smoky. Everywhere, though, there were attentive attendants, ready to direct, assist and pamper; and everywhere there were laughing, giddy, gambling guests, all evidently in the best of spirits. The two young women, still in their elegant evening saris, were offered innumerable glasses of champagne and trays of hot morsels; were constantly invited to join games of baccarat, piquet, chemin de fer, vingt et un, or simply to bet on thrown dice or coin tosses.

"Is it time to go down to the bar yet?" Natalie whispered. "I'm running out of ways to say, 'No thanks, maybe later.'"

They found a gilt-balustraded staircase that seemed like the one they'd taken earlier, but the lower level they reached looked completely different—yet another series of elaborately decorated gaming rooms, but these were all empty and silent. They were crossing a huge, French-style hall, when Sally stopped with a gasp.

"What is it?"

"That doorway at the far end—something moved. There's someone there."

"Or rather, *here*," said a voice behind them. They whirled to see Uncle Yu. "It is a mirrored wall, of course. Someone once called my humble establishment 'The Versailles of Gambling.' Look, there we all are." He put his arms around their shoulders and swiveled them slightly, so that the three of them appeared as a distant reflection. "Isn't it ridiculous, the nonsense one hears about vampires not showing up in mirrors? How could we shave, or part our hair? How could you ladies apply your exquisite *maquillage*? Come, let's sit over here. I am glad to have caught up with you, at last."

"Yes, we should talk," Sally said, more boldly than she felt.

Yu sat between them on a blue silk settee, turning back and forth to regard them with amusement. "The little model girls, always playing at dress-up."

Sally felt herself bristle, most of all, for some reason, at the word "little." Liu Yu was not a large man—he was lightly built and no taller than she was. "How we dress is immaterial. You know who we are—devoted friends of Lucienne's. We're here because she asked for our help. You are holding her here against her will."

Natalie, on the other side of Yu, was frantically trying to catch Sally's eye with the unspoken message, 'Careful, chérie,' but Sally was oblivious.

"And what do you say, Mlle Natalie?" Yu asked.

Natalie only shook her head, and Sally spoke up again. "I would ask the same—what do you say, M Yu? Clearly, Lucienne has become a valuable asset to your establishment, but have you actually asked your niece if she wanted to trade her independent life in Paris for her role here?"

Uncle Yu began to laugh, loudly enough to attract the attention of one of the casino's ubiquitous servitors. Responding to a wordless gesture with amazing speed, the waiter brought a tray of glasses, with decanters of whisky, bitters and blood. Yu mixed himself a drink and indicated his guests should do the same. Sally poured herself a small, neat whisky; Natalie waved her hands to decline.

Turning to Sally and touching his glass to hers, Yu said, "Listen, ma petite. I was once young and idealistic like you."

Sally's face framed an objection, but he put a finger to his lips and continued. "I thought it was possible to be an ethical vampire, to live among mortals doing no harm to the innocent. But over time I came to know—as you will know, if you live long enough—that it cannot be done. *She* knows." He turned to Natalie with a long, pointed look, and then back to Sally. "And my dear Liu Shien has learned: in the long run, it cannot be done. We cannot have what you naively call an independent life. We *depend* upon a steady supply of nourishment. Sure, you can lead *la vie bohème*, hoping that you have enough chance encounters with charming young poets and musicians to add up to a square meal—or you can take matters into your own hands and secure your future, as I have done for myself and for Liu Shien. You two would be welcome to join our staff as well—you should think about it."

"Work here? Acquire the 'security' of a string of half-alive blood slaves? I don't think so," Sally said scornfully.

"Sally, don't be rude. M Yu is making a most generous offer." Natalie stood, and Sally did likewise, towering over the slight old man, feeling as if she'd just been released from a sort of paralysis. "We will think over what you have said most carefully," Natalie said formally. "Until later, M Yu."

They left the salon, retraced their steps to the main floor and this time easily found the staircase leading down to the Bar Moderne. Sally felt as if a tight physical restraint was loosening with every step they took away from Uncle Yu's presence.

"Natalie, what's going on? What does he do that made me feel so trapped? Is that what's happened to Loulou?"

"Hush, darling, I'm thinking. I've got some of it figured out, but . . ."

They'd seated themselves at one of the chrome and glass tables, and a waiter arrived almost instantly with two Blood Bronx cocktails.

"I guess we've become regulars, and I guess they're

used to customers who always order the same thing." Sally shrugged and raised her glass to clink with Natalie's.

"Yes, that's it!" her friend exclaimed. "There's an old bit of vamp lore—it used to be common knowledge among us: if all the blood you drink comes from a single source, or if it's all the same . . . what they used to call the same *strain*, which I think corresponds to what we now call blood-type . . ." She trailed off thoughtfully.

"And, what then?"

"It creates a cycle of dependency for the vamp, so they can't leave that one source. Not without great effort, anyway."

"So, you think . . .?"

"I'm guessing it's better than casino odds that all of Lucienne's little friends have the same blood-type. She implied that she has her pick of the clientele, but I wouldn't be surprised if the old man does some pre-selecting. He's been feeding her since she took up residence, and if it's always the same strain . . ."

"She's trapped?"

Natalie nodded. "I think that's at least part of it. He is powerful and very old; he may have a whole arsenal of entrapments. But we can try to loosen that bond, at least. Do you have your flask with you?"

Sally grinned and patted her garter. "Always prepared.

Shall we order a drink for our friend?"

Lucienne had changed her scarlet brocade for ivory, which virtually matched her pallid skin. Her eyes looked particularly dark and huge, dilated and almost drugged, as she glided ghostily toward them.

"Darling!" Natalie cooed. "You must have been working hard. Come, sit down—we've ordered you a drink."

Lucienne slid into a seat, aiming perfunctory air-kisses in their direction, and accepted the glass gratefully. "Thanks. It does take it out of me, dealing with the public—even if it's a pretty rarified public." She took a sip of her cocktail and grimaced. "Ugh, it tastes odd." She sipped again. "Not bad, though. So, what else did you want to talk about? You think I should leave here and return to *la vie bohème* in Paris?"

Sally suppressed a shudder at Lucienne's echo of her uncle's words. Before she could speak, Natalie answered gently, "No no, chérie—in fact, your uncle has made us a generous offer of positions here, too. We're going to think it over, but we may be joining you."

"Really? How . . . interesting. I mean, it would be fun to have you here, but . . ." Lucienne took another sip of her drink. "But wouldn't you miss the cafes, the nightclubs, the walks by the Seine?" She stared at them, her eyes brimming, and then shook her head.

"I don't know what's come over me. Paris is lovely, of course, and I'll visit sometime, but it's perfect here. I have everything I need. You should join me; we'll all be so happy."

"Well, we *will* think it over. Finish your drink, darling," Sally said, trying hard to hide her dismay.

"No thanks, I don't want any more—it tastes a bit off."

Natalie was watching her with narrowed eyes. "You're right, the drinks aren't as good now—must be a new bartender. Let's go—you can show us a few more of the sights before you go back to work."

Natalie stood and moved swiftly to the end of the room, where silvery satin drapes swathed the tall windows. "Is there a terrace through here?" She parted the curtains to reveal a pair of French doors. "I'd love a bit of fresh air."

There was a terrace, beautiful and inviting, despite its access having been hidden—an expanse of white marble, bounded by a low balustrade, shining in the moonlight. A fresh breeze, scented with night-blooming flowers, wound about them.

Sally stretched her arms wide and took a deep breath. "Oh, *this* is lovely. Now I can see why you like it here."

Lucienne turned her face to the almost-full moon and inhaled the fragrant air. "I didn't even know this was here," she said, faintly puzzled. "Sally, have you got your flask? I'm so thirsty all of a sudden."

The gardens, just a few steps down from the terrace, were lovely in the moonlight. Red roses so dark they looked black, and white ones like small moon-faces, were too cool to release their aromas, but jasmine and orange blossom filled the olfactory space. Sculpted camellia shrubs, clusters of peonies, low beds of violets and primulas, with water trickling unseen below dark distant trees—the farther they moved from the brilliantly lit casino, the more Lucienne, sipping from Sally's flask, came alive.

"I don't know why I've never come out here; it's so lovely. It makes me miss the Luxembourg gardens, though—there's no one else walking here."

"Lucienne, darling, listen. You haven't come out here because you haven't wanted to—or haven't been able to—leave the casino. Your uncle has been using enchantments on you." Briefly, Natalie explained the blood-type dependency and then went on. "I'm sure there's more than that, too. There's a very simple but powerful magic in the air ventilation system inside the building—it must affect everyone, not just you. Why else would people want to sit at the gaming tables round the clock?"

"Yes . . . perhaps you're right, Natalie. But there is something else. I . . . have to stay here, even though I can see now that I don't entirely want to. I have to atone; I've done a terrible thing." Lucienne sank down onto a bench, burying her face in her hands.

Her shoulders shook with sobs.

Sally was immediately beside her, cradling her in her arms. "You can tell us, chérie." She was about to say more, the name 'Alain' on the tip of her tongue, but caught Natalie's warning gesture.

Lucienne wept for several long minutes, but finally, haltingly, began to tell the story. "I never meant to harm him, but really I was thinking entirely of my own pleasure. After I—I killed him, I have to say it— I felt I had lost, or perhaps killed, a part of myself as well, the part that can think I am basically a good person, in spite of everything."

"Oh Loulou darling, you *are* still a good person, or you wouldn't suffer so much about this. But staying here, the way you are living . . ."

"It will eat your soul," Natalie said quietly. Lucienne stared at her for a moment, and then nodded.

"But how can I get away? Even apart from magic and blood-types—and the sheer, effortless comfort and security of living here—he is my uncle. And my . . . oh, *mon dieu* . . . he is Luc."

"Luc? You mean . . ."

"Yes, Luc, the demon lover who haunted my youthful nights and who made me the evil vampire I am today." There was a ghost of a smile on Lucienne's lips. "He is both my revered uncle, to whom I owe all obedience, *and* the vampire who made me, to whom I belong, body and soul. I can't leave. But *you* should—

you should go as soon as possible, before his hold on you strengthens."

Natalie turned her head away from the pain in Lucienne's voice and face, her eyes squeezed shut. When she opened them, she started at the sight of a pale figure walking toward them, seeming to float with the languid yet rapid progress of a ghost. A ghost with a round pale face, sleekly coiffed hair and an elegant silver gown.

"Dolly!"

"My darlings! I didn't think I'd be lucky enough to find all three of you together—but we always meet happily by moonlight, don't we? Isn't it the most beautiful night of all the world? These gardens! But, sad to say, I've actually come to drag you away from this, back indoors—there's something you really must see. The maharani is going to play against old Mister Yu himself, for very high stakes, apparently."

They hardly had time to finish greeting each other or to absorb this news when one of the casino's ubiquitous functionaries appeared out of the darkness, and out of breath.

"Mlle Liu! Your presence is requested in the Imperial Jade Salon, immediately!"

Lucienne nodded severely and sent the young man off, but when he had gone she inhaled sharply. "That's bad, when he has to send someone for me. I'm meant to anticipate what will be needed, always. I must go."

"We're right behind you. Just lead us to this Imperial Jade Salon," Sally said firmly.

After the moonlit gardens, the wash of light indoors was dazzling, and the salon they reached was particularly brilliant. Chandeliers, hung with translucent slices of pale jade, filled every corner with illumination. The few notes of darkness stood out in sharp relief: black keys on the white piano, ebony sections of the roulette wheel, pips on cards, and M Yu in a long robe of black brocade. He was, as they entered the room, bowing low over the maharani's outstretched hand.

"Oh, Indira," he murmured; Lucienne was startled to hear the tenderness in his tone.

"Oh, Yu," the maharani replied, smiling fondly with equal sentiment. "So, it has finally come to this."

"I have wanted you for so long, my dear. What has it been—decades?"

"Oh, probably centuries," she answered lightly. "All right then—I accept your stakes. We will play three rounds, and if you win . . . I am yours. If I win . . . I claim a prize of my choosing."

Yu bowed. "Certainly, my queen. Anything you ask. The choice of game is, of course, yours. What would you like—poker? Baccarat?"

Indira was silent and thoughtful for what seemed a very long time, until a smile lit her features. "What about . . . the Old Game?"

"As you wish," M Yu said with a bow, solicitously seating Indira on one side of a square gaming table. He waited while she arranged herself—her mother of pearl cigarette case, a pearl and sapphire-studded holder and a crystal ashtray to her right; her tiny, jewel-sparkling tortoise Benvenuto, looking sleepily out from his shell, at her left. Yu then took the seat opposite her and beckoned to Lucienne.

"Come and shuffle for us, my dear," he said affably, but he took her hand as she reached for the cards. "So cold! Have you been in the gardens? Never mind, let Marcel do it." A young Asian man in a crisp white jacket moved forward and took up the cards. He cut the seals on six new decks and began the lengthy, thorough process of shuffling them together.

"Madame, the first deal is yours. Please begin."

Sally was baffled by card games—she recalled endless, bored eighteenth-century hours faking her way through them—and this one seemed to be some particularly complex variant. Lucienne was, of course, familiar with all the casino's offerings, but from her tense, wide-eyed attention, there was clearly something out of the ordinary as the first round got underway.

Natalie watched the action with a maddening opacity that suggested she knew exactly what was going on, and Dolly turned away, unable to bear the tension.

The maharani handled the cards with elegant ease, sliding them into place with seemingly casual flicks of her fingers. She had beautiful hands, Sally noticed, smooth and strong, her long, oval-nailed fingers sparkling with a half-dozen large rings.

Once they both had their cards, Indira's eyes grew huge and veiled, like a wide misty night sky, as she considered the variables. Benvenuto was still half-sheltered in his shell; the maharani reached out a finger and stroked his back, which surprisingly seemed to rouse the little reptile, so that he trundled over to the two face-up cards, coming to rest at the nearest, the nine of diamonds.

"Silly creature," she smiled. "He thinks we are playing Newmarket with Spinado." Still considering, she placed a violet-scented cigarette in her holder. A waiter appeared instantly with a light, and she inhaled slowly before picking up a card and stating her bet, with a brilliant smile at Yu.

Through the several moves that followed, Yu did not return her smile; he appeared deeply apologetic, even distressed, as he turned over his winning hand.

"No matter." Indira shrugged eloquently. "Perhaps I

will be yours after all."

"Would that be so dreadful?"

"Hardly. Your deal, my friend."

M Yu handled the cards like weapons: they shot like darts from his fingers. Once each card had reached its target, he grew deeply silent and still, as if far far away. A moment later, he seemed to re-emerge, with a clatter of social energy.

"Take your time, my dear," he said gallantly. "Let us have something to drink. Champagne?" A waiter hovered at his elbow with an ice-bucketed bottle almost the moment he spoke.

"I should prefer an Aviation," Indira said; another waiter rushed away and returned only a few minutes later with a moonstone-colored cocktail of gin, maraschino, violet and lemon. "Thank you. How delicious," the maharani said, sipping carefully while she studied her cards with the keenest attention.

She requested another card, which he slid over to her with a smile, and then both of them fell silent for a time, until M Yu declared.

Indira sighed, "Yes, I suppose one must." Resting her chin on one palm, she watched Benvenuto make his way across the face-up cards until he came to a rest. Then she sat up straight and placed her bet. Yu nodded his acceptance.

"Thank you." She smiled, laying down her cards. "My round, I think. And the deal returns to me."

Yu's face darkened alarmingly. Lucienne, standing behind him, opened her eyes wide as if something had physically struck her. But Yu contained his palpable rage, and Indira serenely sipped her cocktail before gathering in the cards.

"We're even, now. This is the decisive round," the maharani said—quite unnecessarily, but she seemed to want to talk. "Tell me, my old friend, why did you never marry? I'd have thought you'd want a line of sons to inherit the empire you've created. Not that your exquisite niece isn't worthy . . . Forgive me, it's just my idle curiosity . . ."

Natalie was watching M Yu's ageless face as the deal, and the maharani's prattle, went on. She felt she could see waves of volatile emotion moving like storm fronts behind his eyes. She exchanged a glance with Lucienne that clearly indicated she also felt the roiling danger building up in her uncle.

Sally was mesmerized by the maharani's beautiful, deftly moving hands. She realized again how imperfectly she understood the game and wondered whether she was even capable of following the swift movements. It looked as if Indira had dealt Yu an extra card, then had realized her mistake and taken it back. But Yu would surely have spoken up if anything were amiss.

Indira paused for only a moment to examine her cards and then resumed her line of conversation. "Your niece Lucienne—such a beauty—is she your sister's child, or your brother's? I only ask because 'niece' is such an imprecise word; in our language the difference is always clear . . ."

Lucienne could hear him roar 'Enough!' in her mind's ear, but with clear effort, Yu pulled himself back from an outburst. "My dear Indira, please allow me a moment of contemplation. We will have ample time to chat after the game." He frowned at his hand for a moment, and then his expression cleared. "One more card, please."

Indira slid it across to him, noting his satisfied glow. She studied her own cards briefly. "Hmm, what to do. Help me, Benvenuto." She touched her talisman lightly, and the little animal moved straight toward the second face-up card, the ace of clubs. "Yes, I thought so." The maharani nodded. "I shall offset."

"No!" This time, Yu failed to restrain himself and roared audibly; his hand shot out and swept the tortoise from the table.

The maharani was not the only one of them to gasp at the clatter of tortoise-shell against marble floor. Her eyes flashed and her nostrils flared. She pressed her lips together tightly before speaking. "Miss Wilde, would you be good enough to see to Benvenuto, please. M Yu, I offset, and I believe I have the winning hand."

"Not yet, your royal highness. I shall also offset. Another card, please."

"Very well."

Dolly returned to the table cradling the little tortoise in her hand. There was a visible chip at the edge of his shell, but his limbs were active and his blinking eyes hardly more bewildered than usual. The maharani opened her bag, and her pet crawled in.

Lucienne had begun to feel very strange; she pressed her hands to her temples but soon realized there was no way to keep Yu's will out of her head. Under his direction, she began to stare across the table at Indira, projecting a fierce, dark and convoluted energy that was sure to destroy all clarity of thought in the older woman. But when she met the maharani's gaze, it was as if there was a wall of flame behind her eyes.

"Show your cards, please. Here are mine," Indira said calmly.

"Sorceress! Cheat! Monster!" Lucienne heard her uncle shriek, so clearly that it took her a moment to realize his voice was only in her mind. The others heard nothing—they only saw the black-robed gentleman lay out his cards with an ironic bow and a rueful smile.

"You have won, madame. Name your prize."

Lucienne took her leave of her uncle the following afternoon in his office. It was not necessary for them to speak, but they observed the formalities:

"I have appreciated this priceless opportunity. I regret that I must leave to fulfill other commitments."

"It has been a joy to have you here for this time, and to see how skillful and wise you have grown. You will always have a place wherever I am, whenever you choose."

"I know."

He placed his hands on her shoulders in a formal embrace. For a moment, his features wavered and she saw her first love. "I am within you, always," he whispered.

Lucienne gazed at him for a long few seconds; then she squeezed her eyes shut, drew back and left.

En route

The maharani, despite having been up gaming far into the night, had risen early and had enjoyed several more hours of pleasure and dazzling luck. By late afternoon, she was well-satisfied and ready to depart. Under Dolly's capable organization, their substantial quantities of luggage disappeared into the Hispano's capacious trunk, and the five women settled into lavish seats for the trip back to Paris.

The maharani unlatched a small hatch concealed in the armrest beside her. "Benvenuto's traveling compartment," she said with a smile, and opened her bag to allow her tiny companion to seek out the even cozier space for a long nap. "Now," Indira said, as the driver pulled out onto the main road, "who wants a cocktail?"

The small sleek bar, with its silver and rosewood fittings, held more than seemed possible. With the deft movements of long practice, the maharani mixed a round of Negronis and handed around the sterling travel cocktail glasses.

The maharani's guests sipped gratefully and, after some generic pleasantries about the loveliness of the car, the day, their stay, fell silent.

Indira looked them all over—she put in her monocle for a moment—and smiled benevolently. "Well, that was fun. It is truly a first-rate casino. But I am glad your uncle allowed you to quit your job, my dear." She reached across and patted Lucienne's knee. "You were clearly frightfully bored there. Better to be in Paris, surely."

Lucienne looked away for a moment, then met the maharani's eyes. "I cannot say how grateful I am, madame, that you would take up my cause—and at your own risk . . ."

"Oh, don't be silly, my dear—I was in no danger.

Your uncle and I have always understood each other."

"Still—he takes things very seriously. To think that you could have bargained your own life on the luck of the cards . . ."

Indira took a long sip of her cocktail and winked, regarding Lucienne with amusement. "The cards? It was never about the cards. People like us can make the cards do whatever we want. I think he just . . . misplaced his attention."

Lucienne looked back, astonished, as the maharani's monocle glinted in the light and everything else—the front of the car, their companions—seemed to fade away. Transfixed, she felt as if it was just the two of them, as if the single lensed eye was penetrating her very essence. Indira's lilting voice spoke directly into her mind.

"As for that little gambit of yours, ma petite—I know you are older than your dewy sheen would suggest; I know you have a few powers beyond the strictly mortal . . .but you have no idea who you were dealing with. Oh, I know it wasn't really you, it was Yu. I am far older even than he is; my incarnations go back to a time before there *were* vampires. But . . . no harm done. And I could not ask for more delightful company." She smiled around at all of them— suddenly nothing more or less than five chic women sipping Negronis on a luxurious drive to Paris.

June, 1929

Rue Cambon

The Fall collection was in progress, and Mlle called her mannequins in almost daily, several times a week at least, to try the preliminary versions of her crisp suits and luxe, fur-trimmed evening dresses.

Natalie, who had been feeding ravenously ever since their return from the casino, was given a warning by La Mèduse: "Your measurements must not increase by a single centimeter for the next six weeks. You are on the verge of being too heavy, ma fille, right on the verge."

This was, naturally, embarrassing, even before Natalie heard Nanou being given the same admonition.

At home

Superficially, life resumed some of the structure and stability that had been interrupted by their recent travels and adventures, but Sally couldn't help feeling that things had fundamentally changed. Lucienne was pensive and withdrawn; Natalie was moody and changeable. They rarely went out together in the evenings; Lucienne claimed she needed solitude and long nocturnal walks to recover her equilibrium, while Natalie took to staying home where she could precisely monitor her nutritional intake. Sally continued to frequent their favorite night-spots, sometimes *en travestie*. She didn't mind it, exactly—she was never on her own for long—but she missed the special aura they used to create as a threesome, the glamour of their grand entrances.

What Sally *did* mind a great deal was being the only one capable of getting them to work on time each day: "Wakey wakey! Rise and shine! Come on, you two—*merde*, are we vampires or zombies in here? Come *on*, Loulou!" Her friend was limp as a rag doll as Sally hauled her physically out of bed and wrangled her rubbery arms into the sleeves of a dressing gown. "To the shower, chérie—maybe that will revive you." She pushed Lucienne out the door.

Sally returned her attention to the pot of coffee heating on their spirit-stove. She poured a hot mugful and brought it to Natalie's alcove; setting the cup on the bedside table, she reached over to arrange the pillows. Eyes still closed, Natalie bared her fangs and grabbed at Sally's arm.

"Easy, chérie, it's me. Here, I'll give you your flask."

Natalie opened her eyes and groaned. "No, no. Not yet. Sorry, ma chère."

"Have some coffee, then, and a bit of breakfast. You know, you really should start coming out with me to the clubs again. I met the sweetest man last night; you'd have loved him—he was Swiss, sweet as milk chocolate. You'd feel so much better in the morning."

"Sally. Darling." Natalie spoke with effort, clutching her coffee cup. "Will you please stop chattering and let me wake up in peace?"

Finally they were all dressed, following a brief rebellion by Lucienne (still groggy despite her shower) who refused to see why stockings were necessary. The finishing touches involved Lucienne doing her mascara with interminable tiny strokes, while Sally combed out Natalie's hair, arranging the front waves and pinning her chignon.

"I don't know why you've decided to grow it long again, darling; you look perfect in a bob. It takes ages to get the tangles out—honestly, you've got to start getting up earlier . . ." She broke off, shocked by the bleakly sorrowful look on Natalie's face.

"Leave it, I'll finish." Natalie stabbed in hairpins savagely, seemingly at random, and in a moment tugged her cloche over a passably tidy coiffure. "Let's go, Loulou—you're not going to become any *more* beautiful—enough!"

"Leave me alone, Baba Yaga—just because *you've* stopped caring . . ." Lucienne snapped, before turning away from the mirror with a gasp. "I'm so sorry, I don't know what's come over me."

"Never mind," Natalie said with a dismissive gesture. "Let's just get going, so that our wardeness doesn't have to march us at double speed."

"I'm just trying to keep La Mèduse off our backs, darlings," Sally protested. "If you like, I'll let you sleep til dusk—though I wouldn't want to face Mlle's wrath if you try to quit with the collection so close."

Rue Cambon

"Natalie." La Mèduse pulled her aside on their arrival. Sally and Lucienne stopped, looking on in concern, but the older woman shot them a stern glance that told them to go on about their business.

"I just wanted to say," Mèduse went on as the others headed for the dressing room, "You've done well— no trace of that extra weight now." She gave Natalie an appraising up and down look and touched her arm gently. "In fact, you're starting to look a bit gaunt— which will show the clothes to good advantage—but be careful not to overdo it. You need to keep up your strength. Go out and have a good *biftek* tonight, *et du vin rouge*." Her mouth twitched, almost into a smile, and she sent Natalie off with a pat on the rump.

Harry's Bar

A young man sitting near the end of the bar caught Sally's eye. He had a milk-fed, wholesome quality, combined with a sort of weatherbeaten look, that she found most appealing. There was something a bit out of the ordinary about his clothes and his way of holding himself—she couldn't immediately identify the difference until she realized what it must be.

"You're English, aren't you?" She slid onto the stool next to him, set her cocktail glass down and put her hand out. "Hello, I'm Sally."

"Well, hello! My name's Derek. Are you . . . English as well?" He gave her a friendly, curious look.

"Ah, no, I am Parisienne."

"But your English is quite good."

"You are kind to say so, monsieur." She flashed a grin of amusement at her own French-girl act.

They chatted for a while, long enough for him to ascertain that, despite her rather forward self-introduction, she was a fun-loving modern girl but not a *cocotte*; long enough for her to learn that he was a pilot who flew a mail plane from London three times a week.

"When do you fly back?"

"Tomorrow, at noon. I'll be here again on Friday."

"And what would you like to do now?"

"Spend time with you."

"Suits me. Do you dance?"

He did, and rather well, in a workmanlike, unflashy way. He was remarkably easy to talk to. Over a round of drinks and a number of foxtrots, he managed to draw out the largely fictionalized life story which Sally kept on hand for just such conversations, but with far more detail that she had ever provided before. She found herself digging into her real memories for whatever harmless amusing anecdotes she could add: the soft gray cat who slept on her childhood pillow, her youthful fondness for geometry and dislike of algebra. His fascinated attention brought her to the present (skipping 200-odd years); she described in detail the workings of the atelier, the schedule and duties of the mannequins, the peculiarities of Mlle and La Mèduse, the seamstresses, the other models—the whole insular world of women working together. When she began to talk about her best friends and flatmates, she had to restrain herself from spilling too much of their recent adventures—though she wished she could tell him the whole story of the Masseys and her time as a cross-dressing fugitive in Berlin, just to see his face and hear his hearty laugh. As it was, she ended up saying that Natalie seemed depressed and moody, and Lucienne troubled and distant, and that she missed their old high spirits.

"Natalie—she's the Russian, yes? What do you suppose she's depressed about? Could she be suicidal?"

"Oh, no!" Sally almost laughed, but turned it into a sort of gasp. "That would be impossible."

"Would it? Is she religious?"

"No, not really, but . . ."

"Well, you never know. You ought to watch her very carefully and try to draw her out. She may need help. And the other one, Lucienne? You say she's troubled —is it a boyfriend? Or family?"

"Both, actually," Sally said carefully. "She has an uncle who wanted her to help him in his business. She eventually told him she couldn't, but I think she feels guilty about it. And then, she also ran into an old flame."

"Ah, double trouble—the pull of family and the heartstrings. And how are *you* feeling these days?"

"Well . . . a bit irritated, to tell you the truth. They're my best friends, I love them dearly but I just want them to get over themselves and go back to being good company. And then I feel guilty for thinking that way. Am I hopelessly shallow?"

"Not at all! I think you're . . .perfect."

"Oh, I'm hardly that," she laughed.

"Maybe not, but you're perfect for me. May I see you home?"

"Certainly not—what kind of girl do you think I am?" Sally winked. "Besides, my annoying best friends will be there. But if you find us a bench by the Seine, I can show you a very good time." She leaned into him with a suggestive smile.

"Heavens, what sort of unprincipled cad do you think *I* am?" Derek touched her cheek with gentle regret. "Actually, I have to be up quite early. How about if I put you into a cab, and we meet again here on Friday?"

At home

Natalie had retired into her alcove, but she called out a fairly cheerful greeting when Sally came in. Settling into her own cozy alcove with her flask, Sally in turn greeted Lucienne, who came in a while later. She thought of getting up to talk to Loulou, but suddenly felt too tired to move.

Sally woke with difficulty the next day, and it was hard for her to summon the extra vigor needed to get both herself and her friends moving; in fact it was Lucienne who made the coffee. After dragging through the day's fittings with little of her usual verve, Sally changed into pyjamas, topped up her flask from the supply in their ice box and retired to her bed.

"Not going out tonight?" Natalie asked, surprised.

"No, I think I need a night off. I'm just going to read." But although her bedside shelves were stocked with everything from Racine to the new Virginia Woolf, Sally closed her eyes long before midnight and slept through to the next noon. She woke feeling much refreshed and aglow with the realization that she would see Derek again that night.

Slumming

Lucienne tried to get out of the flat in the evenings while the others were distracted with their end-of-the-workday rituals. She didn't want any comments on where she was going or how she was dressed: sometimes in a chic evening frock, other times in a drab, shabby coat she had picked up at an open-air paupers' market in an obscure and sad arrondissement. The coat (and the worn-down shoes and battered hat she'd found to go with it) corresponded to a need for self-abasement, but also made her feel pleasantly invisible and free as she explored humble cafes and seedy dance halls, or walked endlessly beside the Seine.

"Don't do it, honey. He's not worth it," a brusque voice with a Marseilleise accent called, as she contemplated the river. Lucienne turned, startled, to see a tremendously fat woman, further enlarged by her many layers of shawls, walking toward her with an uneven gait caused by a broken shoe-heel.

"Oh, I'm not . . ." she began, but changed it to, "Thank you. You're right," as it seemed wrong to reject the woman's kind intention. "Your shoe," she continued, gesturing vaguely; "that must be uncomfortable. Shall we sit down somewhere?"

The woman cocked her head, catching Lucienne's genteel inflections. "Nice of you to mention it. If you could see us clear to a bottle of red, we can sit in the caff just down the way. My pal Pierre the cobbler always drinks there; he'll fix me right up."

"Of course—my treat. After all, you practically saved my life."

They proceeded, slowly, to the small cafe, which was so dim Lucienne couldn't imagine how a cobbler could ply his trade there. She and her new friend, Ynez, settled at a corner table, and as soon as the bottle of wine arrived, so did Pierre. After he'd had a few glasses, he took the injured shoe from its owner and gave it a professional examination. Then with a wink at Ynez, he disappeared with it out the door.

"His shop is just across the way; he'll be back in a bit. Shall we have another, dearie?"

By the time the cobbler returned, Lucienne had ordered a third bottle for him and Ynez to share. "He's your husband, isn't he?" she whispered to Ynez, who sighed and smiled.

"He's a sot, but I love him. Don't worry—you'll find

yourself a good man, like my Pierre, not like that lout who abandoned you. Good thing I came along when I did. We women have to watch out for each other."

Lucienne smiled. "Yes. Thank you again. I'll say goodnight now." She left the dim, stuffy cafe and turned back to the breezy path along the Seine. Streetlights glowed softly and a half-moon had risen, reflected as a spot of silver on the water. As she neared a small bridge, she saw a figure—a slender young woman leaning over the balustrade, her shoulders shaking with sobs.

"Don't do it, honey—he's not worth it," Lucienne called. She came up close and put an arm around the girl's shoulders. "Are you all right? Maybe I can help."

Le Select

The night was warm, and Sally lingered at a sidewalk table outside Le Select slowly sipping a glass of red. Derek had an extra-early departure the next day, and she'd sent him off, forgoing their usual walk. She stared absently toward the street, still feeling the warm glow of Derek's company and the fizzy tingle from a fleeting taste of his throat.

A familiar figure approached her table—Claude, in a cream-colored suit. "Hey there, ma belle!"

"Claude! What brings you to this side of the Seine?"

"Just a one-night gig, filling in at the Jockey. Have

you seen that place—cowboys and Indians on the walls? It's wild!"

"Oh, I think I went there once with Cerise and . . . never mind." She had never told Claude the story of the Masseys and didn't want to get into it now.

Claude sat and eventually flagged a waiter for a cognac. "Sally, honey, what's wrong?" he said, looking at her with concern.

"What do you mean? I've just spent the evening with my new friend; he's an English pilot. It's too bad he had to leave early—he has a dawn flight—but I love being with him. I'm so happy!"

"Really. Cause you don't look happy, not a bit. Pretty much the farthest thing from happy."

"I don't know what you're talking about." She peered at him irritably and then smiled. "And *why* should I listen to anything from someone with a tie like that? I'm taking you shopping tomorrow, mon ami!"

"What are you talking about? This is a beautiful tie; I paid a fortune for it."

"Yes, maybe in 1921! It's not *au courant*, darling. Meet me tomorrow."

Brasserie Bofinger

The man was impeccably dressed in a dinner suit and looked to be about forty, with a small pointed goatee that was not quite fashionable but suited his face. Sitting alone, he was leafing through an art magazine while toying with the remains of a crème caramel, taking occasional sips of his coffee and cognac.

Lucienne took a seat across the table and waited. He turned a page and lifted his glass of *fine*, regarding her with indifference just tinged with displeasure. "Yes?"

"M Morneault. Mutual friends suggested we should meet."

"Did they?" Clearly lacking in curiosity, this barely registered as a question. "And why is that?"

"We have certain . . . interests in common."

"Really." Possibly, one of his eyebrows was fractionally raised, or possibly not.

Lucienne sighed. "You force me to be explicit. I want to be hurt."

M Morneault coughed, dismissively. "Come now, Mlle . . ." He held a hand up as she opened her mouth. "No, I do not ask for your name. You are a beautiful young girl—no doubt, Paris is full of men who will be pleased to hurt you."

Lucienne stood up and then slid into the banquette at the man's right. She picked up his cognac and drained it at a gulp, then leaned in close. "M Morneault. It is not necessary for you to know my name; you will probably never know my *real* name. But you must know this. I am an adult; I am a great deal older than you think I am. You may consider yourself an expert, a master of what you do—and perhaps you are; I hope you are. But, I have hurt people in ways you cannot begin to imagine—and now it is my turn." Taking hold of his goatee, she turned his face toward hers and held his eyes for a long minute.

He nodded, thoughtfully. "I see. In that case . . . you are not entirely uninteresting to me."

"You *see* very little, as yet. But I can guarantee that any time we spend together will be extremely interesting." She turned to signal to a passing waiter. "Another *fine*, please. And some very hot coffee."

Rue St. Honoré

Sally met Claude on the shady side of St. Honoré as planned. "My favorite haberdasher is just down the block. I can't let him know I actually go out *en travestie*—he could get in trouble—but I'm always popping in for cufflinks and ties and golfing socks, *à la garçonne sportive*. We'll get you set up properly."

"Sally, hon, I don't think this is such a good idea. He's probably not used to serving my type."

"Your type?" Sally looked at him critically. "Medium height, slender build, badly in need of a couple of new shirts and ties—I don't see any problem there. Come on."

Claude sighed and allowed her to take his arm. He tried not to tense as they entered the very elegant, conservative-looking establishment. The inevitable bell above the door tinkled, and an immaculate, silver-haired gentleman stepped forward.

"Bonjour, Mlle Lafayette." An unexpectedly wide smile enlivened his narrow face. After a number of pleasantries, she introduced Claude.

"Un pianiste de jazz? Vraiment? C'est un honneur, monsieur! How may we help you?"

After forty minutes of impeccably attentive service, resulting in a purchase of three shirts and four ties on very favorable terms (with Sally's trade discount and a special *consideration d'artiste*) Claude had to concede, "Okay. Sometimes things can be easy."

"You don't know what that meant to me," Claude said, as they sat with cognacs at a nearby cafe. "To be able to go into a fine shop like that and be treated . . ."

"Like an artist? A gentleman? A human being?"

Claude nodded. "That could never happen in the States. A place like that—and even worse, me and you together . . ."

"Do you think you'll ever go back?"

"Not if I can help it," he said fiercely.

"Good." Sally leaned forward and adjusted his new

tie. "Because I don't know what I'd do without you."

Claude smiled, pushing her hand away gently and smoothing his own collar. "Oh come on, now. What would you do without *me*? Same thing you've always done and will always do—go on with your bad self . . . your powerful, solitary, immortal life, with any number of lovers, prey and diversions."

"But not many friends," Sally sighed. "Not like you."

Slumming

"Encore, Loulou!" Her companions laughed good-naturedly, topping up her wine. Lucienne joined in their laughter, toasted the four other women around the table and drained her glass, swaying slightly. It was possible to get so much more drunk, she realized, on large quantities of plonk than she ever did on elegant cocktails in expensive bars. She was enjoying the intoxication, but her hat was suddenly much too tight; she pulled off the crumpled cloche and ran her fingers through her silky bob.

"Ooh, posh haircut," Bijou, at her left said admiringly. "Where'd you get that, then?"

"Um, a friend of mine—she's clever that way. But . . ." she added, anticipating a request for a referral, "she's sick now. I'll probably have to do it myself with nail-scissors next time."

"I used to go the *salon de beauté* every day," Manon,

the tall blonde across the table, said. "When I was kept by the banker, old Brillard you know, I had a standing appointment every morning at eleven—manicure, facial, coiffure. Beautiful establishment, dead classy, everything rose-pink and lovely-smelling . . . But I couldn't keep it up, I was dying of boredom. And then I met Jean-Paul . . . and well, you know how charming he can be, at first . . ." Raucous laughter confirmed the other women knew all too well the occasional allure of their some-time pimp.

"I had a banker once—actually he was a bank president. He worshipped me; I had him wrapped around my little toe." Dark-haired and richly curvaceous, Josette kicked off her shoe to display the little toe in question. "Jewels—my god, you should have seen my ruby parure—furs, gowns . . . What a fool I was!"

"What happened?" Lucienne asked.

"I threw his rubies into the Seine because he was flirting with one of my friends. I was furious . . . but to tell the truth, I thought he'd buy me more. Merde! You'd never catch me now not holding on to my jewelry."

"Mine was a doctor," petite, demure-looking Nina said. "Not as rich as a banker, but a nice man, very generous, and I think he would really have married me. But, can you believe it, I thought he was too old. He was all of thirty-eight!" She paused while her friends howled with laughter. "I know—look at us now! We won't see the right side of thirty-five again, and Jean-Paul must be over fifty. I could be a married lady now, with a car, a fox coat and a distinguished, graying husband."

"Or, even better, you could be a rich and merry widow!" Bijou said with a wink.

"What about you, Loulou?" Josette asked. "Do you have a rich admirer? You should get him wrapped up while you still can; don't be a romantic fool like the rest of us."

"Oh . . . I've had a wealthy lover, it's true. And I've just left him." Interested exclamations around the table encourage her to continue. "He *owns* a casino, he's that rich. He wanted me to work there—not just some hostess position but the number two spot: my own apartment, fabulous clothes, jewels, whatever I wanted . . . I met him when I was just a girl. He's old, but he pretended to be young so he could win my heart. It almost worked, but I ran away, all the way from the Far East to Paris. He wants me so much that he followed me here, set up this casino to lure me back . . ."

"Merde! He wants you badly!" Nina observed.

"Yes, but I can't. I don't love him, I don't want to be part of his world . . ."

"So, you're just like the rest of us—a stupid, hopeless romantic," said Bijou.

"And doomed to stay a tart." Josette put an arm

around Lucienne, and they all leaned together in a warm fellowship of wine and laughter.

"But can't you just . . . you know, vamp him along?" said Manon thoughtfully.

"Yeah," Josette agreed, "if he's as rich as all that, you could drain him for quite a while. He'd never even know—or more likely, he'd love it."

"It's true—I know, you're probably tender-hearted, like me—but really, most men, it makes them happy. You'd be doing him a favor. You could go back, just for a while, get yourself a nest-egg and some good jewels to keep . . ." Nina trailed off wistfully.

"I wish I'd been more of a vampire when I had the chance!" Bijou slurped her red wine.

Lucienne shuddered. "No, I couldn't do that. You don't know what he's like. Actually, *he's* a vampire, and he'd drain *me* if I stayed."

"Ah well, never mind then. But where is this casino, did you say?"

Rue Cambon

Nanou turned sideways to the dressing room mirror and appraised herself approvingly. "The Russian girl, Natalie—have you noticed how skinny she is lately?"

Martine, glumly studying her own figure, nodded. "I know. Everyone but me can lose weight."

Nanou gave her friend a surprised look. "That's not what I meant, cherie. You look fine, really, *très svelte.*" She lowered her voice. "*La russe* is getting far too thin; it's not attractive at all. I wonder if she's ill. I know Mlle wants skeletons to hang her frocks on, but they've got to have pretty faces. Perhaps she'll lose her looks and her job."

Across the large room, Natalie, in a silk brassiere and step-ins, was gazing into her own mirror, dabbing cream makeup on the circles under her eyes and trying to soften her gaunt cheekbones with spots of rouge. Her ribs and vertebrae showed clearly, and her breasts hardly filled the tiny hollows of her lingerie. She frowned, prodding her midsection. "Still too fat."

August, 1929

Rue Cambon

It was five o'clock Friday, end of the work-week, and the three of them were leaving the atelier. Lucienne, who had been out all night, was nonetheless full of vibrant energy and linked arms with her friends.

"Let's go out tonight, the three of us, like we used to." She looked from one to the other, her smile full of roguish promise. "It's time we had a really grand time together again."

Sally hesitated, but only for a moment. "Darlings, let's! We can start at the good old Rotonde. And then, I need to be at Harry's Bar at eleven—I'm meeting a friend—but we should all go, he'd love to meet you. He's an English pilot, very sweet. I may slip off with him for a bit . . ." she winked comically; "but then I'll catch up with you and we can go dancing at the

Olympia. What do you say, Natalie? Natalie!" Sally stopped, and Lucienne whirled around at the alarm in her voice.

Natalie had fallen behind, walking impossibly slowly, barely managing to put one foot in front of the other. Her face was gray, her eyes hollow and unseeing.

They took her arms and helped her to a shady bench in the small park they were passing. They didn't normally bring flasks to work, but Lucienne still had hers in her purse from the night before. She put it to her friend's lips and Natalie, too weak to resist, took a long drink.

"Come on, let's get you home," Sally said, squeezing Natalie's narrow shoulders.

At home

Sally felt closer to Lucienne than she had for a long time, united in strength and purpose as they tended Natalie. They'd felt how light and frail she was, as they half-supported, half-carried her to the flat. They boiled water, undressed her and rubbed her with warm washcloths, helped her into her nightgown and her bed. Natalie protested but was again too weak to resist as Lucienne tipped a flask to her lips.

"This has to stop, Talia. You're not allowed to starve yourself."

"Leave me alone. It's not your concern."

"How can you say that?" Sally sounded truly shocked. "We're a team, a trio."

"No," Natalie said tonelessly. "We're all different, each with our own troubles. You've both been preoccupied—as well you might be—but admit it, you wouldn't even have noticed what I was doing if I hadn't given in to a moment's weakness . . ."

"Hardly a *moment's* weakness, dear one," Sally said gently. "You're half-dead with malnutrition. And I *have* noticed, but I thought you were in control, knew what you were doing."

"I do know what I'm doing. I want to die." Natalie's statement hung in the air between them.

"No," Sally said flatly, after a long silence. "No, that's just not possible."

"Don't tell me. You cannot know what we old ones know. Your own grandmother . . ."

"Grandmère has nothing to do with this. How do you even . . .?"

"Hush." Lucienne put her hand on Sally's wrist. "Natalie, tell us what you're feeling. You know we'll always take your side."

Natalie's eyes were squeezed shut, and slowly a tear began its descent down each cheek. She opened her eyes wide, pale and brimming. "The times are growing dark." She spoke in a low, oracular tone. "Not only for our kind—it will be even worse for mortals. This last decade has been a gift, a treat—dessert! Especially the time we have spent together, my beautiful darlings. But this age is drawing to a close, and I don't want to be around to see it end. I'm tired, beloveds, so tired. I've lived through Ivan the Terrible, the time of the troubles, the Napoleonic wars . . . I don't need to see all that again. Please, just let me go. You're still young and resilient; there's no need for you to concern yourselves."

Lucienne was holding Natalie's hand tightly; she looked utterly stricken. Finally she said softly, "Sally, our supplies are terribly low. Would you go round to the butcher and get us some refills?"

"What, now?"

"Yes—look, we don't even have a full flask in the house, and Natalie needs extra if she's going to make it through the night. Please. I'll stay with her."

Sally nodded and put on her coat and hat. "All right. I'll be fast. Don't leave her for a moment."

Natalie lay quite still as Sally almost soundlessly left the flat. Her eyes were closed, and she seemed to resist opening them as Lucienne said her name. "Little one," she said, finally meeting her friend's eyes. "Why do you concern yourself? Let me be."

"Hush," Lucienne said sternly. "I need to tell you

something before Sally gets back. While I was with my uncle, I learned many secrets. Some he taught me; others I stole from him, working in his office. He is even older than you, you know."

"Yes, the old demon. What did you want with his secrets?"

"Knowledge is power, no matter the source. I've learned things that can help you, help all of us. Have you ever heard of the 'long sleep'?"

"When a vampire sleeps for thirty years or more, as if it were just a nap? I've heard stories, but no vamp I knew ever understood how it was done."

Lucienne smiled. "Yu knows. And now I know."

"The clever bastard!" Natalie looked wonderingly at Lucienne. "And you—who would think you're such a wise and devious soul."

"You're suffering, Natalie, and that hurts me; Sally too. Perhaps it is time for an end, but I can't believe things won't get better. Let me help you rest. We'll take care of you; we'll find a better, safer place. These dark times you speak of—they won't be forever, and they won't be everywhere."

"So, you'll put me to sleep and then cart my coffin off to someplace new in search of vampire happiness? And keep my box safe for a few decades?" Natalie laughed drily and fell silent. Finally she shrugged. "If you must. And if it doesn't work . . . I get what I wanted anyway: oblivion."

"It will work," Lucienne said firmly, "and I promise we will take care of you. But there's one thing you must do."

"Yes?"

"We can't let Mlle down. We have to finish the season and do our part in the show. So you must get your strength and your looks back."

"My looks! Who says I don't look good? La Mèduse told me to lose weight, after all."

"Yes, cherie, your figure is *très elegante*, for a skeleton. You need to feed, darling."

Natalie stared bleakly into the shadows of the dimly lit room and finally released a huge sigh. "You promise me oblivion, after the show?"

Lucienne nodded.

"All right then. I'll eat." The door opened. "Sally! Just in time—I'm so hungry!"

September, 1929

Le Select

Sally sat across from Derek at their favorite table at Le Select. She was grinning so widely she felt as if her fangs would involuntarily emerge. But Derek was frowning, seemingly in response to her news.

"So, she started eating again, just like that?" He sounded utterly perplexed, even slightly disappointed.

"Exactly! Of course, it took an almost fatal collapse for her to come to her senses. But now she truly seems—what's that English saying—right as rain. And the wonderful thing is, the crisis has brought us all closer again; we have marvelous times together, like we used to. I'll bring the girls along next time— I'd love for you to meet them."

"Ah." Derek looked away briefly and then met her eyes again. "The thing is, I'm afraid I have some news too—not so nice as yours. I'm being reassigned; I'll only be doing domestic flights, Scotland and thereabouts, for some time. So I don't know when I'll be back to the continent."

"Starting when?"

"Erm, immediately, I'm afraid."

Even as she was flooded with dismay, in a part of her mind Sally relished his crisp pronunciation ("im-meed-jetly") and filed it away for future use. But her eyes filled with un-analytical and un-vampiric tears. "So this is our last meeting? You won't be able just to buzz your plane over for a weekend now and then?"

"I couldn't justify the fuel use. I don't actually own the thing, you know."

"Well then, this is goodbye."

"I'm so sorry, my dear." He took her hands and held them tenderly. "Tell me, Sally, what else is worrying or upsetting you these days?"

"Nothing, you silly man. Life is good; I'm blissfully happy. Except that this fellow I really like is going away. "

She looked at his kind, handsome face, and her tears spilled over. He leaned across the table and kissed them from her cheeks. They sat hand in hand, not speaking, for a long time, until he raised her hand to his lips, said, "Au revoir, cherie," and left her.

Sally sat unmoving, staring at her stupid glass of plonk, until a young woman approached her table. She was about to gesture to her to take the wine away, but the other girl spoke.

"Can I join you for a moment?"

Sally opened her eyes wider and saw a smart-looking brunette, wearing a fashionable *petit rien* frock of black satin, much like her own.

"Yes, please do," she invited the stranger. "Forgive me, I've had some rather bad news."

"I understand. I'm Simone." Sally introduced herself with a brief gesture. "Please forgive my presumption, but I had to talk to you. That man who was with you, the English pilot . . ."

"Derek?" Sally gave her a look of sharp surprise.

"Yes, Derek Winsor. I know him quite well. We used to meet twice a week, whenever he was in Paris, for almost all of last year."

"Please, Mlle . . . Simone, don't be angry. I only met him about a month ago; if I'd had any idea he was involved with someone else . . ."

"No, no, you misunderstand. It is well over between Derek and me, and for that I am so grateful. You see, he came into my life at a time when I had a lot of troubles. Every time we met, he wanted to know all about what was wrong, and then he would . . .reassure me, I suppose. But I found that I felt more and more weighed down by sadness. I always felt so tired after I'd seen him, but then after a couple of days had passed, I'd be looking forward to his next visit—almost like a *morphiniste*."

"Exactly! That's just what happened to me, the tiredness, everything."

"And then, gradually, my life straightened out, things got better. One day, I realized most of my worries were gone. And when I told him that—I thought he'd be so happy for me—he said he would no longer be able to see me. Oh, he made some excuse about his work, his schedule, but I really felt that . . .that he was no longer getting from me what he needed."

"But—that's astonishing! I've just had the same thing happen. What do you suppose it means?"

"I've had some time to think about it. I think he seeks out girls who are troubled, and somehow these feed something in him. Almost as if he were drinking up our emotions."

"Hmm—fancy that!" Sally stared across at the girl, who was really very striking. "Would you like a drink?"

Simone looked at Sally's unfinished glass with a smile. "No thanks—the wine's rather dreadful here, isn't it?

Would you like to take a walk by the river?"

They walked out together, laughing. "Imagine," Sally said, "they say it's we women who are the vampires!"

8th Arrondissement

The red pagoda was unmistakable, standing boldly on its corner as if to astonish the neighborhood. *Pagoda Paris, C.T. Loo, Art et Antiquités* was engraved on a brass plaque beside the door, which opened almost immediately to her ring. A tall Frenchman in formal morning attire eyed her disapprovingly.

"Mlle Leung to see the collection. I made an appointment by telephone," Lucienne said crisply.

"Of course, the telephone," he said as if annoyed by the existence of the device. "I am M Loo's assistant, Artur Brébant. Come this way, please."

The hall, lined with exquisite lacquer panels, led through an ornate doorway to a suite of splendid, high-ceilinged salons. Lucienne spent a long moment taking in the scene. Frosted glass ceiling fixtures provided a wash of cool light over an array of shelves and cases, arranged with the logical precision of a library or laboratory, filling the center of the rooms. Along the outer walls, however, were a series of low-ceilinged alcoves where dim light, punctuated by sudden gleams of precious materials, and picturesquely heaped clutter suggested an exotic world of the rich and rare: "Oriental profusion,"

"Aladdin's Cave," temples and palaces full of mysterious, forbidden treasures.

Lucienne began to drift slowly forward, staying toward the right-hand side as if to keep her bearings in a labyrinth, wandering between the well-lit shelves and the enticing alcoves. She realized that she had only the vaguest sense of what she was looking for, and no idea where it might be found. The disapproving factotum trailed behind her, keeping a sharp eye on her movements.

An hour, or perhaps more, passed easily, in a dreamlike silence. There appeared to be no one else about. Lucienne viewed careful arrangements of porcelain bowls and vases, with brilliant clear glazes of oxblood, imperial yellow, grass green, heavenly blue, followed by subtle celadons, cloudy grays and peony pinks. Then, the sumptuous painted ceramics: Ming, Sung, Chien Lung. Coromandel screens, embroidered robes, carved rosewood. A dim fragrant alcove held a huge, lacquered bed heaped with rare brocades and surrounded by shelves full of cloisonnée opium sets, filigree bronze lanterns and stone incense burners. Another was furnished for an ascetic, but aesthetic, scholar, with brushes, scrolls and writing materials, a fine tea set, a precious wall-hanging of exquisite simplicity.

Lucienne, her head throbbing, paused before an immense display of carved figures, allowing her eyes to unfocus and roam over the shelves of ivory, coral and jade of all colors. Something had drawn her attention, but she couldn't tell exactly what. Or rather, every piece vied for her notice; each was a miniature masterpiece, but she felt there was one thing here of special significance.

"May I assist mademoiselle?"

She turned to the assistant, who seemed to have shed some of his disapproval. Perhaps her careful scrutiny of the collection had persuaded him of her seriousness. Almost involuntarily, she recalled something from her research in Uncle Yu's office.

"I'm looking for a jade Buddha's hand."

"A jade Buddha's hand?"

"Yes." She spoke with more certainty than she felt.

"Like this, perhaps?" He plucked a small carving from a shelf. The item was easy to overlook and not exactly beautiful. Made from a mottled gray jade, it resembled a gnarled, mummified appendage or a shriveled pod with projecting sepals. Holding it out on his palm, M Brébant appeared to perceive her confusion. "The *main de bouddha citron, n'est-ce pas?* Marvelously rendered." He stroked the piece gently, pointing out its citrus-peel texture and subtle details, all the while studying her with a quizzical frown. "Something appreciated only by the true connoisseur. You had better come this way."

Lucienne was led through the remaining showrooms at double-speed. She glimpsed the accumulation of magnificent treasures around her but she sensed, more and more clearly, that the object she sought (or which, perhaps, had sought *her)* was the small carving in Brébant's left hand.

From the final showroom they continued into a dimly lit, carpeted corridor and then to a broad staircase with steps of gleaming teak, which she ascended carefully, following her guide. Up and up, until the third flight reached an elegant landing facing a large lacquered door, at which her companion knocked gently.

When the door was opened a few inches, M Brébant gestured to her to wait while he slipped into the room, conferring in low, serious tones.

Lucienne did not have to wait long. The door opened wide, and a young Chinese man in a traditional *qi pao* of fine, dark blue damask bowed and invited her in. The room was large and beautifully lit by windows on adjoining walls; they were at the corner of the top floor, Lucienne realized, catching a glimpse of the green tile of the projecting pagoda roof. Across a wide expanse of silky carpet was a large, sleekly designed desk of dark satinwood, inlaid with subtle touches of ivory. A pair of matching chairs were placed in front of the desk and behind it sat a black-silk-clad gentleman who could only be C.T. Loo himself. He gestured to her in a way that was both inviting and imperious, and Lucienne approached. Loo had particularly prominent eyes, suggesting a gaze that missed nothing, and Lucienne was glad that she was, as always, dressed and groomed immaculately.

"Mlle Leung, please sit," the antiquarian said, indicating with an offhand wave that bows or other formalities were unnecessary. "I thought you would be much older," he added, peering at her keenly.

"Appearances can be deceiving."

"True, yet in my field, the surface and what it conveys is of paramount importance. Yours is flawlessly youthful. I would expect more evidence of *mature* understanding in one who seeks the Buddha's hand."

"I believe my understanding is sufficient, even if I do not have the correspondingly deep wrinkles. May I assume that since the item was in your showroom, it is for sale? I would like to purchase it."

"I would like to be assured that you comprehend its qualities," M. Loo said, and Lucienne was again struck by a curious mixture of arrogance and ingratiation in his tone.

She sat up very straight, and though her taillure was impeccably chic, she envisioned herself in one of the tight brocade gowns she'd worn at the casino, summoning the power she'd wielded there. "May I see the *objêt*, please?" She extended a hand.

M Brébant instantly responded to her commanding tone and placed the carving on her palm. C.T. Loo himself seemed to shrink slightly, somehow.

Lucienne turned the small, heavy carving over and over, feeling it grow warm with her handling. "Yes," she said softly, " this is exactly what I require, and yes, I am well aware of its exquisite craftsmanship and its unique properties. Surely you would want to see it in knowledgeable hands, rather than selling it to some mere collector? After all, it is hardly the most decorative piece. And I am prepared to pay a very fair price." Her eyes met M. Loo's, and she held his gaze firmly until he looked down at his desk.

"Yes, of course. Just as you say. However, you should understand—with a piece of this nature, it is not entirely a matter of money. I like to think that what I have here is not exactly a shop or a showroom, but rather a *collection*. Before I let go of something of this degree of rarity and . . . power, I need to obtain something roughly comparable in return."

Lucienne fondled the carving, and M Loo again met her eyes with a strange expression. She felt the jade grow icy cold; for a moment it seemed about to slide from her hands. But she grasped it firmly and willed the warmth back. She toyed for a moment with the idea of using its power to simply freeze the two men in place while she walked out. But she smiled politely and said, "I understand."

With a sigh, she fell silent, the slight crease of a

frown appearing just below her cloche. Behind her closed eyelids, she revisited a moonlit garden. "I have something for you," she murmured. Carefully, she began unbuttoning the top of her blouse; M Loo coughed and looked away in embarrassment.

Lucienne laughed. "I don't know *what* you're thinking, M Loo. Here." She pulled out and unclasped the fine gold chain holding her pendant, and passed the jade oval to the antiquarian.

Loo raised his eyebrows, first at the remarkably deep green of the stone; then, as he took the piece and examined its intricate carving with his loupe, he nodded. "Yes, this will do. And of course, a token amount." He handed her a card, on which he had written a rather large price. "You may settle the details with my assistant."

With a polite smile, Lucienne rose and followed M Brébant.

October, 1929

Autour de la ville

Instead of showing the Winter collection in September, as expected, Mlle had let it be known that there was a be an elaborate, important Winter-Spring show at the end of October. The month was now just beginning. As Natalie regained her strength, becoming sleek and no longer emaciated, the three of them entered into a period of delicious gaiety. Once again they spent virtually all their time together and reveled in each others' company. After their day finished at the atelier, they'd head back to the flat and spend a leisurely interlude—relaxing, perfecting their maquillage and changing into svelte cocktail or evening frocks. And then, out into the night, each time with the sense of freshness and adventure that had marked their first acquaintance.

Aperitifs at a cafe, cocktails at an American bar, tangos at a dancehall, hot jazz and racy entertainment in a late-night boite—wherever they went, crowds parted for them like a warm-blooded Red Sea, appreciative murmurs followed in their wake, and they effortlessly acquired as many elegant and fun-loving companions as they chose.

Sally and Lucienne marveled at the special sparkle surrounding Natalie—of the three of them, she was most apt to find admirers wherever she turned. Sally saw her friend embracing a return to health and optimism; it didn't hurt that her new hairstyle (a giddy mop of red curls à la Clara Bow) made her more attractive than ever. But Lucienne saw something different: a last fling with the pleasures of the world before (if all went well) the Long Sleep. Lucienne had not yet revealed her plan, her pact with Natalie, to Sally. She knew it would have to come out, eventually—she would need Sally's help to transport and care for Natalie's body—but she delayed telling her, day by day. Sally was simply too sanguine to ever really understand the depth of Natalie's despair; her response would doubtless be some form of "Why don't you just bloody well cheer up?"

So, for the moment, Lucienne only smiled and returned Sally's wink as Natalie led a handsome young man from the dancefloor to step outside for a "breath of air."

Enthralled by her beauty, intoxicated by her scent, he

hardly noticed her fingers at his throat as they kissed, undoing a button, loosening his collar. Her delicate butterfly sips at his neck were an easily overlooked detail; by midnight, he remembered only an interlude of delirious passion. At his washstand the next morning, he smiled ruefully at the "love bites" marking his skin. They had never learned each others' names.

Rue Cambon

"Look at her, the redhead . . ." (or perhaps she said, "the Russian;" Nanou's pronunciation was not always as pure as it might be). "What's gotten into her? Last week she was so skinny and tired-looking; suddenly, she's glowing, an absolute beauty. I think Mlle wants her to wear the bridal gown. I heard her talking with La Mèduse about it . . ." (the "bride" being, of course, the much coveted final appearance in any fashion show).

"Well then, we know who the bridesmaids will be," Martine sighed. "They all look terrific lately, I have to say. And meanwhile . . ." she leaned in toward the mirror, "my complexion's completely gone to hell, ever since that sunburn last summer. Damn Mlle and her toasty brown skin!"

"Oh, stop it, Martine, just stop. What do you think maquillage is for? *They* don't stay away from the paint pots."

"Or the perfume bottle. Have you noticed what heavy scents they all wear, especially *la russe*? You'd think she was trying to cover the smell of a rotting corpse."

The weeks of fittings were mostly done, but there was still work to do, hours each day, for the show. Mlle gathered the entire corps of models, all eighteen of them plus the two young men who stood in as escorts. This was unusual—normally, each model met with La Mèduse or one of the seamstresses and received her ensemble, with a card indicating its order in the program. But this time Mlle spoke to them directly, feverish with excitement.

"This will be an exhibition different from all others. We will not merely show some clothes; we will be creating an artistic spectacle. Consider carefully the *mise en scène* of each piece, and do your best to embody the theme when you appear. You will show the clothes, *bien sûr*, but you will also create a mood and play a part in the overall story." She looked at them all keenly, frowning at the obvious incomprehension on most of the models' lovely faces. "For example, scene one: L'Innocence. Marie-Laure, Nicole, Chantal—the beige day dresses. You are innocent, limpid, uncomplicated—show me how you move."

L'Innocence; Cafe au Matin; Rhythm of the Day— three or four girls in each scene, twelve scenes in all;

two or three changes of ensemble for each female mannequin, while the young men came in as required. The basic arrangement was not unlike others shows they'd done, but now each scene was choreographed with specific stage directions and suggested emotions or moods.

The "day" moved on through tailored afternoon frocks and soft, embroidered tea gowns for late afternoons at home, into the gathering excitement and complexity of cocktails and evening: Cinq à Sept; L'Heure Bleue; Les Sophistiquées; on to Un Dîner à L'Infer; Le Bal Masqué; Les Noces à Minuit. The final three scenes, with their sinister titles, were clearly of particular importance to Mlle, yet it was hard to tell exactly what she had in mind, particularly as the gowns for these scenes were still being worked on.

Mlle called Sally over to speak to her privately. "I wish that . . .you and your friends, you three, could be in *all* my final scenes. But, *c'est impossible* . . .I will just have to make do with the others. You are in the grande finale—Natalie is our bride. I'll give you more preparation when the time comes. Be ready."

Sally returned to her place a bit dazed, especially since she had seen La Mèduse showing Nanou, Martine and Violette their gowns for the Dîner à L'Infer scene—deep red velvet with low necklines and voluminous sleeves, almost precisely what the duchess and her friends had worn at the private view over a year ago. Why would Mlle be copying a client's dress? Or had their gowns come from the atelier to begin with? But why include them with the newest looks of the season? Sally shook her head, hopelessly baffled.

Çi et là

After hours, however, the three friends continued to sparkle, in their little black dresses with a dazzle of diamanté and brilliant red-lipped smiles. First, perhaps, to a jazz *thé dansant* in Montparnasse, with a raffish mix of artists, students and bright young things, who then wanted to go on to an American bar for percussively-shaken cocktails. New-found friends piled into taxis together, on to other cafes and bars. Midnight found Sally *et cie* sweeping into the Ritz with a party intent on champagne. The jazz band, while not the Chocolate Dandies, was adequately hot, and while Loulou went to freshen up, Sally and Natalie hit the dancefloor together without waiting for any of the young men in their coterie to ask them.

"Having fun, darling?" Sally led them into a foxtrot.

"It's perfect. I wish it didn't ever have to end."

"Of course it doesn't have to end. Why would it?"

Natalie opened her eyes, which had been half-closed in contentment, and realized that Sally still didn't know about her plan or Lucienne's vow. "Why?" she said lightly. "Things always end. After all, it's almost the end of 1929."

Rue Cambon, 5:00 pm, October 29th

The atelier was full to overflowing—word had gotten out that Mlle's show was going to be something extraordinary, and *le tout Paris* was there.

Peering through the gap in the curtains, Sally spotted (among the usual throng of wealthy clients) a number of familiar faces. "Dolly is here, with Djuna and Natalie Barney. Gaston and Eduouard—oh, and that must be Edouard's wife, how pretty! The Maharani is here, of course. And Louise, Louise is here!"

Meanwhile, la Mèduse was at the door, checking guests' names against her list: "M et Mme Gerald Murphy; M et Mme Harry Crosby; M et Mme Scott Fitzgerald; Miss Gloria Swanson, la Marquise de la Falaise . . ."

"And," Sally murmured, "Mon dieu, it's my Contessa! I wonder if Vladimir is with her."

"Sally!" Lucienne hissed, "Come away from there and finish getting ready."

"One more moment, there's plenty of time—alors, it's Josephine Baker! Oh, she's divine. And, I don't believe it, it's my pilot, Derek, with his new sweetheart—I recognize her from the society pages

—maybe she'll be miserable enough to hold onto him . . ."

"Sally, really, enough!" Lucienne grasped her shoulders to steer her away, and couldn't help looking through the gap herself. "Merde," she gasped; "it's that dusty old Duchesse de Chevreuse and her friends, the ones we had to do the private show for because they never go out in public . . .I wonder why they decided to come."

There was wonderful music, as Claude had been engaged for the occasion. He began to play moody jazz chords and a minor key melody.

"I can't see," complained a tiny ballerina seated between Stravinsky and Serge Lifar; the dancer obligingly lifted her to his shoulder, until there were hisses from the row behind them.

"Mesdemoiselles, mesdames et messieurs, nous présentons les modes d'hiver 1929 et du printemps 1930. La Morte et La Vierge." La Mèduse, narrating, possessed a refined, mellifluous voice—another of her unexpected qualities. "We begin with le Matin . . ."

"Le Matin: the day is new, the mood is youthful. One arises, takes some coffee and dresses simply for the first movement of the day. A brisk walk in Mlle's new cream and coffee jersey dress, with matching jacket. To the greengrocer, the baker, the butcher, the bookseller in a bevy of fresh little frocks. Note the new fit, the half-belt with its suggestion of a trim waist." The models emerged one by one, traversing the stage and sauntering down the aisle with a purposefully casual air, making their turns, opening their short coats, slouching with fists in pockets or hands on hips to display the calculated simplicity of the clothes.

"Yes, yes, no, yes with the jacket, no . . . or, perhaps in beige." The buyer for Bergdorf Goodman watched each model attentively, murmuring softly and making quick decisive notes. She was flanked by journalists who were similarly intent, nodding, peering and jotting notes, though sketches were forbidden.

"Oh, I must have that one," an elegant woman told her companion. "Note the number please; I'll come in and order it tomorrow."

Lucienne, modeling the frock in question and missing nothing, shot her a wink—she knew the woman was one of Mlle's best customers and one who would wear the sleek, sporty knit to excellent advantage.

"Or perhaps," la Mèduse continued, "a short game of golf with one's special friend, in Mlle's cream and grey chevron ensemble, with the new off-the-brow cloche." Francois and Etienne, tall and impeccable in tweed jackets and plus fours, swung golf clubs jauntily as they escorted Sally and Natalie (in two versions of *le golfing*) to approving murmurs.

"Don't forget a long, striped muffler if the day turns chilly," the narrator added. Sally carefully tied a scarf around Francois's throat, smoothing the knot with a solicitous pat, while Etienne looped Natalie's long neck, leaning down to place a small kiss there too. Whispers and laughter were heard, and a woman saying, "Golf would be much less boring if it were more like that."

The models slipped away to change, and Claude took a short break. A gramophone played jazz at a discreet volume and young assistants in aprons delivered teacups or aperitifs to the patrons.

"L'Apres-Midi," la Mèduse announced, after this interlude. "Hours of sophistication and restrained chic for the Parisienne. One pays important calls, consults with one's banker or lawyer, visits *les grands magasins*, lunches at a good restaurant. Gone is the innocence of morning; one must be urban, urbane, guarded, girded, knowing, well-informed and ultra-sophisticated."

A sharp intake of breath came from the more observant members of the audience: *quelque chose de nouvelle*. A simple crepe restaurant dress had a seam at the hipline *and* a narrow belt (with a smart diamanté buckle) almost at the natural waistline. The hem also hit two levels—knee-length in front and dipping gracefully longer at the back. The fit was svelte, the cut impeccable, the color black. The model wore a single strand of pearls, a small furpiece, a velvet chrysanthemum at the shoulder and a cloche that bared a crescent of forehead, showing her exquisitely fine eyebrows. The journalists nodded and noted. Louise, who wore girlish flapper frocks and pulled-down hats better than anyone, instantly understood the allure of this new mode.

More models emerged, gliding with a satiny gait as sleek as their ensembles. "As everyone knows, Paris afternoon dresses are black with few exceptions—Mlle's decree is universally accepted for at least the past five years. These dresses and tailleurs are, however, blacker than black, in lush velvets and fine woolens with an inky depth beyond the visible. Clothes for the blind, for sleepwalkers, revenants, zombies . . ."

The novel and exquisitely cut fashions were engrossing enough so that most of the audience hardly noticed as the narration grew stranger. The models though, if one looked at their faces rather than their well-formed, couture-clad bodies, seemed to be following her script, moving with a dazed, glassy-eyed languor which could be taken for elegance but was also rather frightening. Natalie and Lucienne were the last to come out, Lucienne in a close-fitting velvet suit trimmed in blood-red dyed mink, Natalie in a black dress of complicated, layered tiers, also edged in dark red. Unlike the others, they moved with an air of dangerously directed purpose, their paths cutting sharply through the drift of the other girls and the two young men. Whenever either of them encountered another model, there was a brief exchange: significantly widened eyes, expressions of fierceness or fear. Like a pair of sheepdogs working in tandem, the two of them herded the others toward the wings and exited last, arm in arm, with a wink to the audience.

"Cinq à Sept, l'Heure Bleue," la Mèduse intoned. "The day hastens to its most delicious moment: le cocktail. From all across the city, from their diverse days' occupations, the smart set gathers in salons privés and the chicest of bars to share this precious interlude of . . . intoxication."

At her words, Etienne and Francois burst through the curtain and took up positions at each side of the stage, brandishing enormous cocktail shakers. The syncopated slide of ice cubes accompanied a frenetic yet elegant parade of cocktail frocks. Abandoning, for the moment, her favored black satin, Mlle had produced these in vivid jewel tones and even startling white, which made the close fit and complex seams all the more evident. An unusual hush fell upon the audience—no more murmurs of approval or the reverse, no more exclamations of desire; everyone was simply caught up in the newness on display.

As each mannequin completed her turn down the aisle, she returned to the stage. Grouping and regrouping with restless energy, the girls exchanged showy air-kisses and accepted glasses of bright-colored liquid. As they downed their blue or green drinks, the models swayed and staggered, except for Natalie, Sally and Lucienne, who supported the others to their exits.

An intermission followed, and assistants again circulated, this time with trays of cocktails and champagne. The room buzzed at a high pitch of excitement and journalists slipped out to make hasty phonecalls to their editors: "Startling!" "Daring!" "Ready for a new decade!" "Decadent!" "Too far—the public isn't ready!" "Formidable!"

At last, the pianist returned to his bench, signaling with forceful dark chords the start of a new act. "Mesdames et messieurs," la Mèduse announced, "the hour has advanced. I present to you now, '*Un dîner à l'infer.*'"

Nanou, Martine, Justine and Marguerite sat around a table draped in black linens, with a centerpiece of dead roses and candelabra holding black candles. They wore varied but similar gowns of deep red velvet with softly draped necklines and long loose sleeves. Attending them, four other models wore snug-fitting short maids' uniforms of dark red satin, with starched aprons; they fluttered solicitously around the table, lifting and displaying features of the "ladies'" velvet gowns, while Francois and Etienne poured glasses of burgundy.

"Is it a metaphor?" Djuna asked Dolly as the models left the stage arm in arm, each "lady" with a "maid."

"I'm sure it must be, but damned if I know for what," Dolly nodded.

Abruptly, la Mèduse left her lectern. At the same time, four extremely antique ladies, the duchess and her friends, got up and made their exit, so that people began to whisper and mutter, "Is it over?" "Surely that was a queer note to end on?" "What does it all mean?"

Gliding in from the back, from inconspicuous side doors or from who-knew-where, figures in masks and glorious, extraordinary clothes began to fill the atelier. Cloth of gold, silver lamé, glittering brocades and creamy satins sparkled and mingled among the audience. Surely there were more than the eighteen mannequins now? Surely some of the guests were masked as well? That *had* to be la Baker, n'est-çe pas? And wasn't that the Maharani, in a rose chiffon sari and a charming rose-petal mask, dancing with Stravinsky?

Gorgeously clad women spread out across the room, infiltrating the seated audience and pulling people to their feet. Claude struck up a wildly hot tune, and dancing broke out like fires, so that the extravagant gowns were seen as fully moveable, not mere static display. And if dancing sometimes involved embraces, and if embraces sometimes involved a flicker of teeth against throat, who would notice amid such a baccanal?

Nanou noticed. "I saw you," she hissed at Natalie, as the redhead, hair aflame above a sapphire gown, straightened her panels of trailing silk and put a finger to her lips. Looking up at them with dazed fascination, a crisply-dressed journalist, Janet Flanner, sank back in her seat after an unforgettable foxtrot. Rubbing the side of her neck absently, she opened her notebook and wrote, "Sapphire chiffon: *essentiel du saison.*"

Subtly, gradually, the models began to depart and the audience quieted. The pianist played a meditative etude and the lights dimmed until the room was almost dark.

Suddenly, a delicate piano trill turned into a deeply familiar melody: the bridal march. Two by two, holding white candles, the procession came down the center aisle. A small girl scattered white rose petals; half a dozen 'bridesmaids' were followed by Sally and Lucienne as the maids of honor and finally, here came the bride, in a short gown and a long, diaphanous veil: a radiant Natalie.

Playfully modeled on the *robe de style*, the dresses were

delicate, gauzy, exquisitely detailed and perfect for a wedding—but all in black. Gasps and murmurs were heard, followed by at first a few scattered hand claps and then a thunder of applause.

The procession made its way onto the stage where the 'groom' and the 'priest' waited, their backs to the room. As the women took their places, the priest moved to center stage and Natalie's bridegroom turned to take her hands. Both men had white, death's head faces. The priest made broad, mysterious gestures above the heads of the betrothed couple; the bridegroom took Natalie in his arms, lifted her veil and kissed her. Natalie fell back in an apparent dead faint, the lights went out, and the room exploded with pandemonium.

At home, October 30ˢᵗ

Exhausted, the three friends went straight home after the show and slept deeply into the next day. They awoke to the sound of violent pounding at the door of the flat.

"Come on, open up, you bitches, you monsters! We know you're in there. We won't leave."

"We've come for you, you fiends!"

"Murderers!"

"Open the damned door!"

Sally, bolt upright since the start of the noise, gulped ravenously from her flask, trying to understand what was happening. She recognized some voices—Nanou, Martine and Etienne—though from the scuffle and thumping of feet, she couldn't tell if there were others with them.

Silently, she pulled open her alcove curtain and saw that Lucienne had done likewise, sitting wide-eyed and intent.

"Break it down!" someone cried, with a tremendous blow against the door. There were clearly more than three of them.

"Burn it down!" Nanou crowed, to raucous laughter, though Martine was heard immediately in an anxious whisper:

"Oh, we can't do that . . ."

The voices, however, were now accompanied by the sound of a heavy, slightly uneven tread, deeply familiar to Sally and Lucienne. Mme. Duroc, the concierge, was someone they normally did their best to avoid. Hugely fat and perennially ill-tempered, she was particularly enraged by anything that forced her to leave her snug ground-floor office. (Tenants had been known to live with broken fixtures or dripping faucets for years, rather than face her annoyance.) Now, her formidable scowl could be inferred from the way the belligerent crowd fell silent.

"Quel espèce de merde?" The concierge's voice was

low but implacably menacing. Clearly she was just warming up for a torrent of verbal abuse, which she continued to produce for at least five minutes after the interlopers, with mumbled apologies and scuffling haste, had fled down the stairs.

"We'll be back, with the police!" Etienne called in parting.

Before beginning her laborious descent, Mme. Duroc stepped close to the door and announced clearly, "Mesdemoiselles, quarante-huit heures."

"Did she just evict us?" Sally gasped.

"She did. It doesn't matter; we have to leave anyway. That mob will be back."

"Come on, then—we'd better wake Natalie. Mon dieu, she sleeps like the dead."

Natalie's bed curtains flew open. "No need, cherie. It's time."

Paris - Charroux

Smiling avuncularly at the three exceptionally charming young women, the conductor punched their tickets and left the compartment.

"Start again," Lucienne said quietly.

Sally, sitting across from her friends, reopened *Paris Soir*. Her hands shook as she turned past the dire financial news to an inside page.

"VAMPIRE MURDERS IN RUE CAMBON: 'REVOLUTIONARY' FASHION SHOW TURNS DEADLY

"An evening of, by all accounts, extraordinary new styles and spectacular showmanship ended in a chaotic, candlelit orgy which left four men dead.

"Retired bank president Gaston Lemercier appears to have suffered a heart attack, according to the coroner's report. The other three, however, evidently met death due to massive loss of blood, for which there is no clear explanation—hence the popular sobriquet, 'vampire murders.'

"The victims have been identified as Francois Marchand, age 19, native of Paris"—so young, le pauvre —"Claude St. Clair, 35, an American, native of New Orleans, and Derek Winsor, 38, of London, England . . ."

Sally let the paper fall and stared, eyes glassy. "Derek is *dead?* And Claude, my darling Claude . . . no, *no!*"

Lucienne glared coldly back at her. "What have you done? I know you were angry with the Englishman, but how could you jeopardize our lives by . . ."

"What! You think I killed him? I wasn't anywhere near . . . I would never . .. Anyway, what about little Francois, Natalie? He was holding you when the lights went out. What happened?"

"He—I couldn't believe it—he acted like an animal,

all of a sudden! He tore my dress and tried to . . . ravish me! So I . . . did what I had to do."

Lucienne turned to stare at her. "You clamped on and drained him?"

"Are you mad? Of course not—I gave him a good kick between the legs! I went backstage after that; I never even saw the end. Et toi, Loulou? Are your fangs clean?"

Lucienne shivered slightly. "Sweet Claude—I gave him a little nibble during the Bal Masqué scene. Just like always. I didn't drain him, of course not! But I can say, at least, that the coroner was correct about poor old Gaston. I was dancing with him, along with Rosine and Chantal, and he just . . . went down, quite gracefully. It was instant. And I'm quite sure he died happy. Come here, give me your hands."

She reached across to Sally with her left hand, and took Natalie's with her right. Natalie and Sally joined their other hands, and the three of them stood in the narrow space between the seats, looking into each others' eyes. After a long moment, they sat down again.

"All right then," Lucienne said. "What a crazy night it was; we were all so keyed up anything could have happened. But none of us killed anyone. But who did?"

Natalie suddenly put her hands to her temples, closing her eyes. They waited. Her eyes opened, pale and haunted. "Mlle was standing just behind me, you remember—so she could take her bow at the end. After the lights went out, after Francois grabbed at me and I cold-cocked him, he fell back and she . . . *lunged* to catch him. She . . . I'm almost sure I saw fangs. She went for his neck. I felt sick. That's when I went backstage."

Now Sally's and Lucienne's eyes half-closed, as they too revisited the scene. "Claude! He saw her! She felt she had to silence him," Lucienne gasped.

"And Derek came rushing up to help!" Sally said. "I remember now—I saw him coming toward the stage when most of the crowd was moving away, trying to leave. He must have seen a struggle or a fall and tried to be a good citizen . . .or perhaps soak up someone's distress," she added with a tiny, rueful smile.

Lucienne had picked up the newspaper and read the rest of the article:

"Mme. Mèdoc-Duvallier, Mlle's longtime assistant, has said that Mlle has retired to her country home, having been brought to a state of near-collapse by weeks of overwork on the collection, followed by the horrific events of last Tuesday. The atelier is closed until further notice."

Natalie sighed. "No idea how to pace herself—living on cigarettes and nerves when she's preparing a collection, *especially* this one. No wonder she snapped —she must have been starved out of her mind, la pauvre." She paused, and as the implication of what she'd said sank in, the other two nodded. There were no questions or protests. "And now she has done us —all of us—a great disservice. Times will be even more difficult for our kind now. Are you sure you two are up to it?"

"We *two*? What do you mean?" Sally asked.

Natalie sighed. "Oh. You haven't told her yet."

Charroux

The taxi pulled up to the tidy cottage, undisturbed in its shady garden. Sally produced the key she had received by post with her grandmother's last letter, and they went quietly in. After the cabman had brought in their luggage and gone off with a good tip, Lucienne sniffed the air anxiously.

"Where did she . . .?"

"Upstairs. Her bedroom. She removed the window shutters and curtains, and exposed herself to the bright sunlight, for a long time."

Lucienne shuddered. "We won't go up there."

"No," said Sally. "Come into the sitting room; it's charming."

"I can feel her despair," Natalie said, sitting in the straight-backed chair by the fireplace, "and yet, the beauty, the intelligence, the . . . tranquility of her long life is here too."

"Yes," Sally said. "Grandmère was extraordinary. You are right—she did have a tranquil view of the world, despite all that she knew and saw. I miss her so much. I wonder if . . . if she had known the Long Sleep was possible, if she would have chosen . . ."

"Sally. Focus," Lucienne said quietly.

"Yes, of course. What do we do? Do we have everything we need?"

"This place is perfect. All will be well." Lucienne reached out to squeeze Natalie's hand. "Natalie must fast tonight, and we will too, in sympathy. We'll spend tonight talking together, and in the morning, just when we're starting to get sleepy, we'll do the ritual. All will be well," she said again.

"Don't worry, little one." Natalie smiled. "I know you will do your best, and I will be at peace in my new home." Her eyes strayed toward the large trunk, which the cabman had set down in the front hall.

Sally made an aromatic fire in the cozy sitting room; they changed into silk pyjamas, and they talked all night—sometimes of their early lives, their turning and their histories, but mostly of the time they'd spent together.

"Do you remember . . ." Natalie began, and Sally said at the same time, "I remember the first time I saw you. It was dusk, near the Pont Neuf, and you had stopped by a flower seller. You were staring into a bunch of the darkest red peonies as if you wanted to drink them! And yet, I didn't have a clue; I just thought you were the most beautiful woman I'd seen all year."

"How funny—because as soon as I saw you watching me, I knew. We wore big hats then—I loved those—but still I could see, or perhaps feel, your eyes. I was so glad when you came over to talk to me; I would have been too shy to approach you. My French was still not very good."

"No, of course, you'd only been in Paris, what, 50 or 60 years," Sally teased affectionately. "But then, you didn't have the advantage of learning French *à la mamelle*, like Loulou and me."

"I knew you two were vamps the moment I laid eyes on you," Lucienne said, "but what I couldn't believe was that you were so tall and chic and funny and brilliant! Only the day before, Mlle had said she was desperate for more models, and I was not looking forward to seeing what sort of empty-headed girls she might bring in. I liked the atelier; I adored the clothes, but I was so lonely . . ."

"Oh cherie, what a time it's been." Natalie leaned over to caress Lucienne's cheek. "All the marvelous parties . . ."

"Cabarets, studios, openings. . . ."

"Strolling in our most chic taillures . . ."

"The atelier—what a madhouse!"

"And yet it was sometimes so peaceful and so creative . . ."

"Our travels . . ."

"Dancing . . ."

"The wonderful women we've met—Dolly, Louise, the Maharani . . ."

"And the delicious men—Gaston and Edouard and all the ones whose names we never learned, and of course the most delicious Chocolate Dandies. . .Oh, poor beautiful Claude . . ."

"Darlings, it will be dawn soon. We must begin," Lucienne said quietly. She began to assemble things on the table before her: several flasks, a black crepe scarf, the jade Buddha's hand citron. "Sally, I need a little mirror—can I borrow your compact?"

"But it's Cartier! Gaston gave it to me."

"Don't worry, nothing will happen to it." Lucienne handled the black lacquer, lapis and diamond case admiringly. "So gorgeous."

They each embraced Natalie for a long time, and then at Lucienne's direction, she lay down on a pale silk chaise. Incantations; scented emollients applied to her throat, temples and wrists; more incantations;

drops of a strange-smelling liquid on her tongue. Lucienne raised the jade carving above her head, her lips moving inaudibly, and slowly brought the object gently down to Natalie's chest. The Buddha's hand grew warm, icy, warm again. It seemed, perhaps to move. Natalie gasped, very faintly, and then closed her eyes.

Lucienne closed her eyes as well, and immediately bit her own tongue to stifle a shriek. Flickering across her eyelids like a newsreel, 400 years of horrors sped by: deaths, dismemberments, famines and plagues; men, women, children, infants in mortal pain and terror. She heard unendurable moans, smelled putrescent vapors, felt the visceral depths of disgust and despair. On and on the hideous show unrolled, punctuated by the briefest flickers of light and beauty —a dance, a smile—that made the returning dark all the darker. Until finally, in a sort of luminous bubble like the view in an opera-glass lens, she saw the three of them, laughing and dancing their way through the last decade.

"Oh, Natalie," she breathed, and lay down beside her friend.

Dim blue tendrils of pre-dawn twilight crept in at the edges of the shuttered windows. Sally, her eyes filled with tears, could see Natalie's skin taking on a pale bluish tint, and she knew it was not just a trick of the light. Lucienne, still murmuring, sometimes twitching and moaning, finally fell silent. Finally, Lucienne sat up and wrapped the black scarf firmly around Natalie's eyes.

Later

En route

Paris was now impossible, of course, but they needed a metropolis—smaller towns offered none of the resources or anonymity a modern vamp required. At Sally's urging, they tried London for a time, where Sally—to her chagrin—found that her English was not nearly as good as she'd thought. Lucienne, on the other hand, picked up a workable fluency in no time.

Lucienne learned languages apparently effortlessly wherever they went, a skill she modestly attributed to having had to sort out Chinese, French and Vietnamese as a tiny child. Sally was envious but could hardly be annoyed; Lucienne's facility certainly made their travels easier.

Not that they had too hard a time of it. Because they were always so exquisitely dressed, no one ever found it odd that the two young women traveled with such masses of luggage, including a particularly large trunk. Generous with their tips and smiles, they had no difficulty finding brawny yet considerate men eager to carry the bulky piece, "full of special, fragile things," setting it down where directed with the utmost sensitivity . . .

Manhattan

. . . as these two strapping fellows were doing now, one of them commenting, with a mix of awe and cheek, "Youse goils have soitenly seen da woild!"

Barcelona, Milan, Istanbul, Cairo, Bombay, Shanghai, Buenos Aires, Havana: the colorful stickers embellishing their luggage were the only decoration, as yet, in this empty Manhattan apartment.

"Yes, we have seen the world," Lucienne said with a friendly wink, pressing a roll of dollars into each of the men's hands. "But we're home now."

April, Twenty-First Century

Lucienne heard a key in the lock, and Sally came bustling in. She shed her shoes and flung down her huge shoulder bag.

"Look, Loulou," she exclaimed, slapping several fat fashion magazines down on the coffee table. "It's happening again, in a really good way."

Lucienne had already put down her book and was leafing through *Vogue*. "Mm, not bad. This is awful. That's pretty. *Why* on earth would you put those together . . ." She suddenly gasped and fell silent, turning pages slowly through a long, themed spread.

Shot in black and white, it featured Lagerfeld, Lauren and several other top designers' new 1920s-inspired collections. Although modern touches were evident —top-stitching or zippers here and there, shiny new materials, subtle tweaks of proportion—the homage to Mlle and others of her time was respectful and gracefully executed. Most startling was the choice of three featured models: a small-boned Asian girl with a sleek black bob, an equally sleekly-bobbed fresh-faced blonde and a dreamy-eyed beauty with a mop of red curls.

"I wish Natalie was here to see this," Sally said softly.

"Yes. Oh, look at this one—I wore this *exact* frock in the Fall '27 show . . . or was it '28? Although this hem is about six inches shorter . . ."

"It was long on you because you're so petite," Sally teased. Her eyes strayed to the large trunk (covered in what they now knew were Art Deco stickers) which still stood in the corner of their front room. "Do you think . . .?"

"No," Lucienne said firmly. "Well, perhaps. We'll think about it."

"Oh, check out this clutch bag—so Cartier!" Sally picked up her compact from the table and fondled it. "I'm *so* glad I never had to sell this."

It was quiet, apart from the turning of pages and the gentle gurgle of their flasks, when they both startled at the sound of the door opening. A tall redhead in a dramatic black caped coat rolled her luggage in and held out her arms.

"Nat, darling! We weren't expecting you til Friday!"

"I caught an earlier flight; I just couldn't take the cold. It's wonderful being able to go home again whenever I want, but I find I really can't endure that Russian climate any more."

"How's Vladimir?" Lucienne asked, as they eased out of their three-way embrace.

Natalie grimaced. "Don't ask. Hey, what have you got there, is that the new *Vogue*? I picked one up at the airport. Not bad, eh?"

Sally gave Natalie another squeeze. "I'm *so* glad you're here. Now we can all go tonight—if you're not too jet-lagged, darling?"

Natalie dismissed jet lag with a gesture. "Go where?"

"Claude's opening with his new band at Birdland."

"Fantastic! Dear Claude—he used to dislike me, but I think he's over it now that he's one of us."

"Lucky Claude," Lucienne mused. "We thought he was done for . . . and lucky us, to be able to hear him. I hope the band is good."

"What shall we wear?" Natalie said. "Black satin?" She winked at Sally. "Maybe something from the trunk?"

"All right, but be careful this time, ok?" Lucienne said. She flipped through *Glamour* and pointed out a page whose large type admonished, "DON'T wear head-to-toe vintage!"

"Oh, what do they know? What did Mlle always say: Fashion fades, Style endures. *Non?*" Natalie began to laugh infectiously; Lucienne and Sally joined in, their fangs glinting.

FIN

AUTHOR'S NOTE

Every vampire fiction has its own rules, and I have shaped the genre to suit the needs of my story. My vamps are more-or-less immortal, and they live by ingesting blood, but they are able to survive on a mixture of bottled animal blood and (for the most part) gentle, non-lethal tastes of humans. They avoid exposure to direct, strong sunlight, and they are basically oriented to nightlife, but are able to be more-or-less active during daylight hours. Living in Paris, they cannot be bothered with eschewing garlic or running water, but they will wait to be invited in before entering dwellings; it's only good manners! And as young women of fashion, they absolutely *must* be able to be reflected in mirrors.

Vamps of '29 also reflects the widespread image of the "vamp" in the popular imagination of the 1920s. In particular, the song "The Vamps of '28" by Clifford Hayes clearly shows that being a vamp was all about fashion, explicitly advising the listener: "Buy your wife some clothes just like the vamp that walks the street . . . You'll have a vampire woman at home." And having that vampire woman at home is unmistakably seen as a desirable thing: the jazz-age successor to the Victorian "angel in the home."

ACKNOWLEDGMENTS

My imagination has lived in the 1920s, mostly in Paris, for almost as long as I can remember. I've devoured most of the usual and unusual books, written both during and about *les années folles,* and no doubt all of them have informed my image of this era, which I find endlessly inspiring in its complex embrace of elegance, tragedy, modernity and optimism.

I am indebted to Joan Schenkar's terrific biography, *Truly Wilde,* for my fascination with the elusive Dolly. And I deeply admire Amanda Vaill's *Everybody Was So Young...* about Sara and Gerald Murphy—who are most definitely *not* my characters Cerise and Garry Massey, despite certain superficial resemblances.

I'm lucky to be part of a circle of friends who share some of my obsessions. To name only a few: Sally Norton first articulated the vision of vampires in little black 1920s Chanel dresses. Jacqueline Goudeau truly understands the seriousness of fashion and of Paris. Kristen Caven has been an ever so astute reader and guide to the literary scene. Kimberly Manning Aker: writer, reader, fiercely devoted and stylish friend. Sara Klotz de Aguilar (Miss 1929): reader, musical muse and vintage fashion genius. Lucienne Pavot: divine Deco adventuress.

Lastly, my dearest love, Charles Aitel: constant reader, consultant, taskmaster, mixologist and sine qua non.

ABOUT THE AUTHOR

Alice Jurow has written and lectured on Art Deco architecture, art and fashion. This is her first published novel. She lives in Berkeley, California, with her human and feline family.

Stop by for a visit at vampsof29.com !

www.ingramcontent.com/pod-product-compliance
Lightning Source LLC
Chambersburg PA
CBHW051128120726
47905CB00005B/1462